C000173987

POISON
IN
PARIS

Also by Robert Wilton

The Gentleman Adventurer
Death and the Dreadnought

The Comptrollerate-General novels
Traitor's Field
Treason's Spring
Treason's Tide
Treason's Flood [*projected*]
The Spider of Sarajevo

Shakespeare & Sherlock
Sherlock Holmes and the Adventure of the Distracted Thane
Sherlock Holmes and the Case of the Philosophical Prince

POISON

IN

PARIS

Robert Wilton

Published in 2020 by Elbow Publishing

A catalogue record for this book is available from the British
Library ISBN 978-1-9163661-0-7

Extract from *Le Figaro*, 16th November 1968

DOSSIER DU AVENTURIER GENTILHOMME
A curiosity is reported in Biarritz

M. Tretiot recounts that a charming oriental trunk, sold at auction as 'the property of a lady', was found to have a false bottom. Concealed within this space was a dossier of papers. These proved to be the work of an English Gentleman, Sir Harry Delamere, who in the years before the First World War was a renowned traveller, adventurer and libertine. His later years remain a mystery, and indeed rumour and scandal attached to much of his life, so it is thought that this dossier may be enlightening. The Minister of Interior has directed that the papers shall be first reviewed by his Department before any further steps are taken with them.

1.

The train whistle shrieked. It startled the young man standing in front of me, and he looked hastily over his shoulder and out of the carriage window. Then he was staring at me again.

'You must guard it with your life, Delamere!'

I slipped the envelope into the inside pocket of my coat.

'Your life, you hear?'

The paper, whatever it was, was already as close to my body as I could manage without doing something unseemly in a public place. Short of swallowing it, there wasn't a lot more I could do to demonstrate my commitment. I patted my pocket, in a reassuring guarding-it-with-my-life sort of manner.

He gazed at my chest long enough that I started to feel uncomfortable. At last he looked up again. 'It's simply the most important thing in Europe.'

I attached more importance to the heart against which the letter was resting, myself. But apparently that wasn't the official opinion of His Majesty's Government.

Two shrieks from the whistle, and again he was startled. He was fidgeting to get out of the train compartment, back to whatever passed for routine in the British Embassy in Constantinople. Apparently the power of the mysterious paper wasn't that everyone wanted it, but that no sane man wanted to be anywhere near it.

'You'll hide it, yes?'

I was on the verge of suggesting the one remaining place where it could more intimately be hidden, but you're not supposed to be coarse in government work. Gentleman's business, espionage. The greater the secret, the greater the number of non-gentlemen who are being done over. But they're usually foreign.

I just nodded.

'My Foreign Office colleagues will be waiting as soon as you arrive in Paris,' he said. Again. The very pale complexion was flushed with his urgency, the colour stark against his fair hair. 'All you have to do is guard it until then.'

'You have my word', I said.

That, now, is just the sort of nonsense you're supposed to say in government work. He smiled, rather desperately. 'You're a good fellow, Delamere.'

That's pretty debatable, but I didn't argue. I was more bothered by the tone in which he said it: he sounded surprised, as if he'd just learned something new, or been proved wrong.

I didn't like it. I wondered idly who'd been saying what about me. Less idly, I wondered why, if I was such a doubtful prospect, the British Government were giving me their damn' secrets to carry.

Again the train shrieked, three blasts that blended into one. This time he looked relieved.

'God speed you.' He nodded for one last time, and turned and stepped out of the compartment.

I was putting more faith in the locomotive of the Orient Express to speed me to Paris. But again, that's not what you're supposed to say. And I wouldn't turn down a bit of help from the Almighty or anyone else. I restricted myself to a manly, dependable sort of smile as he glanced back at me over his shoulder.

'Go well,' I said, and he was gone.

At the end of the corridor, he hesitated in the carriage doorway. He glanced left and right along the platform, as if expecting the four horsemen of the apocalypse to be thundering down it at any moment. A pair of uniforms appeared instead, Turkish policemen, and he watched them pass in front of him.

Still glancing warily from side to side, he stepped down onto the platform, walked a few paces away from the train and turned and sat on a bench.

I'm not one of these espionage chappies. If someone's going to stab me I'd rather it's in the front, and reading other people's letters is undignified as well as dull. But I've done enough shady things in my time to know he was even less of an espionage chappy than I. He couldn't have made a worse job of it if he'd tooted a trumpet and yelled out 'Gather round, fellows, Harry Delamere's got a secret in his coat!'

I stepped back into the relative shelter of the compartment. Through its doorway and the corridor window, we gazed at each other a moment longer. I resisted the urge to check that his damn' paper was still in my pocket.

Now he was at the furtive glances again, back and forth. I could see the strain in his face: the clamped jaw, the wide eyes. He was trying to urge the train into movement by sheer force of desperation.

I was starting to feel much the same way. Whatever the opposition were up to, any more of his performance and we'd have groups of passers-by peering in the window and lads flogging them refreshments. I had the uncomfortable sensation of being something in a zoo; something caged.

The point about the opposition had got me wondering, too. Instead of all the desperate urgency and patriotic encouragement he'd have been more use telling me whom, exactly, I was supposed to guard the paper from. But no such thing as straightforward in government work.

People passed to and fro between us. One of the pleasures of Constantinople is the mix of humanity. Every kind of Arab, most of them selling something, all the diverse peoples of the Balkans, plotting against each other or with each other or both at the same time, and a good cross-section of western Europeans with our pallid skins and silly games. All of these -

all the colours, all the shades of skin, all the extraordinary hats - ebbed and flowed around the platform. Thus the most exotic, the most diverse city in Europe, perhaps in the world, at the end of the first decade of the twentieth century.

The whistle shrieked again, and I felt something straining in the train chassis, the beast getting ready to move. My man looked to and fro again. The crowd was thinner now: they'd closed the gate to the platform, no doubt. A pair of priests, a big chap swaying over a walking-cane, a handsome woman with a small leather box slung round her neck, a couple of Indians, a distinguished-looking old chap, one or two more. Each was rushing somehow: checking and rechecking tickets, juggling hand-luggage, staring back to where they hoped their trunks were being stowed on the train rather than ransacked, failing to decide which carriage to make for. As I watched, one of the Indians bent and asked something of my man on his bench. Then the attempt by one of the priests to control a ticket and a book and a small satchel led inevitably to his dropping all three, and he and his mate were scrabbling around on the platform trying to retrieve the ticket before it got blown under the train and pointing and shouting at each other to keep an eye on the satchel.

Another whistle, and they all hurried for the nearest door, trying to maintain the courtesies as they jostled with each other and glanced towards the shouting guard and back towards the unknown fate of their heavy luggage. At last I heard their door slam, and my man was left alone on his bench, his wide eyes staring back at me.

The train strained, and heaved, and at last we started to move clumsily out of Constantinople's Sirkedji station, the first few yards of a million, an epic journey westward across the whole continent, to Paris.

As I watched, the man on the bench slid to his side, and then toppled forwards. The last thing I saw, as we gathered speed and the window took my view away, was the knife protruding from his back.

2.

A figure loomed in front of me in the compartment doorway, a well-built man.

'Caught up with you at last, sir', he said.

I breathed out.

The voice was a low steady rumble, and it fitted the solid face from which it came. My valet's voice and face had the roughness and strength of the Cornish slate that had been their home, and the warmth.

'Ah, Quinn. You're keeping up. Well done.' He had, I realized, known nothing of my meeting with the man from the British Embassy, nothing of the request made to me, nothing of the journey to the station and nothing of my intentions. 'Any of the luggage make it?'

'A surprising amount, sir.' He stepped in, and shut the door.

My valet is dependable and reassuring in every respect, from serving port wine correctly to fighting off gangs of Cairo cut-throats. He's also, when he feels like it, damned opinionated about my habits.

'Had you intended to travel on this train, sir?'

He's far too professional to be openly critical, and far too Cornish to get emotional, but I know when I've stepped out of line.

'I am travelling on it, and that's what counts. Questions?'

'Just hoping I'd guessed right, sir. And was it your intention we pay the bill at the hotel?'

'I was leaving that one open, to be honest. See if the breakfast improved. We can send them the money, no doubt.'

'Just that I noticed you'd mis-spelled your name, sir. And the address. Considerably.'

'Ah, well.'

Quinn knows my instincts. 'Are you... accompanying someone sir?' He smiled. 'Wouldn't want to intrude.'

'Oh shut up, Quinn. Nothing so pleasant.'

The door opened. Quinn stepped aside, and I was looking into the very lovely face of a young woman. She couldn't have been more than twenty, big dark eyes staring up at me with something like alarm, and then curiosity. Her skin was flawless - though she had the tiniest stud on one side of her nose, something I've always found damned charming; might even have been a jewel - and she had the soft coffee colouring of south Asia.

'Oh', she said, and stepped back. The face was all I could see of her. Otherwise she had an old-fashioned long frock on, throat to toe though cut pretty close, and a long silk shawl coming over one shoulder and round her face and away the other side.

'Don't loiter in the corridor, child,' a voice said from farther along; 'if it is Number 9 it is one of ours'. The girl glanced towards the voice, and back at me, then stepped aside from the doorway and just stood there with her eyes lowered.

Now there was a figure to go with the voice; a tall, older chap, also Indian.

'I do beg your pardon, gentlemen', he said suavely. 'I wonder if this might be our compartment.'

'I can't speak to that,' I said, trying to be equally suave. 'But it's certainly not ours. Do excuse me, sir; jumped in the first door I saw. We'll be out of your way now.'

He was a fine-looking man. Fifty at the very least, but age only made him more distinguished. The complexion was weathered, but still tight on the bones of his face. A hawk's face; one of nature's aristocrats.

'You're most kind', he said. 'Pardon my chivvying.' English slang always sounds more elegant from Indians. 'I am Sikander Ali Khan.'

I shook his hand. 'Henry Delamere.'

The slightest something flickered in his eyes: a memory; a concern.

We nodded to each other, and contrived the courtly dance necessary for switching places in the tight confines of the carriage without anyone touching anyone they shouldn't. Quinn led the way in search of my compartment.

'Excuse me.' It was the Indian's voice again, behind me, low but sharp.

I turned. He pulled the door closed behind him, and we faced each other in the corridor, shoulders knocking side to side against the walls.

'It's Sir Henry, I think.'

'Only when I'm trying to get a better price at the hotel.'

He gave this a bigger smile than it deserved. 'Sir Henry, I apologize most sincerely for being blunt; offensive even.' I waited. 'Your reputation is...' - the smile flickered elegant and delicate, but the eyes were hard - 'exotic.'

That made me smile. 'That's the most charming description of it I've ever heard', I said. 'My reputation is tawdry in the extreme.'

'In the drawing rooms you are spoken of with horror; in the barrack rooms with awe.'

'I wouldn't trust either place for accuracy,' I said. 'My sins are much more mundane than they're cracked up to be, and my achievements likewise.'

His eyes considered me closely, dark and hard. 'I wonder at that', he said. Then he shook his head. 'But now I tittle-tattle merely. Sir Henry: from... from one or two sober, prudent men whose judgement I would trust, I know you to be a gentleman. And it is thus that I speak to you.' Again the smile, again the intensity in the eyes. 'Sir Henry, you would honour me by taking a drink with me while we journey together, but...'

'But... that was the last time you expect to find me in your daughter's compartment.'

'Indeed.' It was fast and sharp. He followed up with a courteous nod, but the eyes were narrowed and still studying me close. 'I bring her to England for half a year to complete her education and broaden her mind. But, ah... not too much.'

We nodded to each other, and shook hands again. 'I'm

serious about that drink, Delamere. Always happy to have my own mind broadened.'

'Suspect I'll learn a thing or two from you first, sir. A drink would be my pleasure.'

Quinn had found my compartment, and was stowing a bag when I caught up with him.

'Accompanying someone after all, sir?'

'Behave yourself. When you jumped out the back window of the hotel, did you bring my revolver?'

His face hardened, in understanding. 'Of course, sir.'

'Good man. Sit.' We both sat. 'Here's the business, and pardon me if I summarize. Things are happening rather fast, and I need you in the picture.' The flicker of a nod. 'Chappy from the British Embassy back in Constantinople insisted on meeting. Chappy asks me if I will carry precious Embassy document on Orient Express to Paris, to be picked up by Embassy chappies there. Chappy offers me ghastly patriotic entreaties, but also a fee that will cover our rent for quite a few months and clear one or two outstanding obligations. Chappy has just been stabbed to death on Constantinople station platform. Any questions?'

His eyes widened a little at the last, but that was the extent of the reaction. This is why I employ Quinn: discipline, reliability, broad-mindedness about the essentials on the front line of life, and above all a refusal to flap.

'Poor chappy, sir.'

'Indeed, Quinn. Indeed.'

'A few months of rent, you said.'

'And a ticket home. I hadn't realized people would start getting murdered quite so quickly.'

'Any idea what the document is, sir? Or who's stabbing people to get it?'

'Not a clue.'

'Righto.' He shrugged. 'So we've just to get to Paris with this document, hand it over, and off we go?'

'That's it. Easy enough, eh?' He nodded. 'If we don't get

stabbed.'

'Am I even supposed to be on the train, sir?'

'No chance of oiling out, I'm afraid.' I patted an outside pocket. 'Two tickets. They're gentlemen in the Foreign Office, of course. Wouldn't dream of risking a chap's life without having someone to do the logistics, clear up his body afterwards.'

The door swung open; I hadn't heard a knock. Two Turkish uniforms were standing there. Not the comic opera outfits of the flunkies and jobsworths: these were serious-looking men in plain - perhaps military - uniforms.

'Your pardon, gentlemen.' It was the shorter and apparently more senior one, a thin sharp face. 'I must demand your co-operation, please.' He looked at Quinn, and then at me. 'You were seen talking to another Englishman just before the train departed, yes?'

3.

'No,' I said.

It was instinctive. Couldn't have told you in that moment why I said it, but once I'd thought it through I was sure it was the right answer.

For a moment the four of us just stood there, cramped in compartment and corridor, swaying slightly with the momentum of the train as it weaved out of the slums of suburban Constantinople.

'But surely...' The voice was level, cold; the eyes were hard. He repeated: 'You were seen.'

'I can't imagine who by. They're wrong anyway.' There was no way he could be certain. But certain he was. 'You've had my answer, officer.'

'On the platform, perhaps?'

'Still no. Listen, old chap, what's this about?'

He was staring into my eyes, doubting me, looking for the

flicker. At last he said: 'An Englishman was... taken ill. We wanted merely to inform his acquaintances.'

'Oh, I see. Poor fellow. And very civilized of you.'

He looked again at Quinn. 'Perhaps you...'

Quinn shook his head, regretful. 'My valet,' I said, 'was running late as usual. Barely caught the train. No time for gossiping.'

He was staring into me again. It was a dapper little face, but at the moment it seemed rodent-like in the extreme. It tilted from side to side very slightly, as if trying different perspectives on me. Under the nose, the tiniest most perfect moustache.

On more occasions than I care to remember I've been unfairly accused of some sin or other, and in the moment it's damned hard to make innocence sound convincing. On the present occasion, of course, I was lying through my teeth; and that makes it even harder.

'I shall be staying on the train', he said. This was obvious, unless he planned to jump out of the window while we were picking up speed, but in his quiet clear tones it was a threat. 'Should you remember anything you have forgotten, please to tell me.' Still those dark little eyes. 'I shall continue my enquiries.'

'Quite right', I said. 'Jolly good luck to you.'

I slammed the door after him.

'He knew, sir.'

'Yes, and that makes it bad.'

'It wasn't bad already, sir?'

'If he was on the up-and-up, purely official, just investigating a crime, there's no way he could have been so sure.' I shook my head. 'We're dealing with official killers, or killers exploiting officials.'

The craggy face looked sour. 'Before the Embassy man was killed, sir, I don't suppose you got any of that fee in advance?'

4.

My expression was not, I suspect, all that encouraging.

Quinn returned to his domestic duties, stowing bags and checking the layout of my compartment.

It was worth a look. This was my first trip on what is now a legendary train: I have the appetite for that sort of thing, and an adequate dinner suit, but not the finances. I had to admit they'd done thing in splendid style. Everything that was supposed to be soft was luxuriantly so, velvet cushions and fabric wall coverings. Everything that wasn't was gilded or glass or highly polished wood. My compartment was an Aladdin's cave of excessive comfort. If they'd transplanted the most decadent of Constantinople cat-houses into this railway carriage, they couldn't have made a more sumptuous job of it.

Quinn was exploring the space with a kind of awe. I could tell by how slowly he was moving. My valet was born and raised in some appalling Cornish slum, a tiny fishing village as far removed from the relative benefits of civilization as it's possible to be in Britain. That was his world, until the army offered him a way of escape, and then the dubious attractions of working with me. I'd picked up bits and pieces of his life when we were in the Cape together, whiling away the fretful hours of night and waiting for the Boer snipers to take a pop at us. Funnily enough, his sense of the impermanence of life, the possibility that at any moment a change in the wind might snatch it all away, was very much my own experience of youth. But I'd at least enjoyed periods of affluence, when my old man wasn't pissing it all away at the tables or hiding out on the continent.

More than anything else, it was the neatness and efficiency of the compartment that appealed to Quinn; I could see that. Everything in its place. Every tiniest corner used for storage, everything doubling as something else, everywhere you looked some clever patent gadget for something or other.

Quinn was back on his fishing boat, and everything was ship-shape.

He half-turned to me. 'What's your plan, sir? The next couple of days, I mean.'

What he wanted to say was 'Clear out from under my feet while I stow the doings and investigate this ingenious cigarette lighter'. He also had a deeper point, and he was shrewd as ever. Basically, I had a choice for the next three days. I could disappear, completely out of sight and ken of my fellow passengers. Or I had to blend in, hiding in plain sight, so to speak; nothing to see here.

Tempting as it was to sink back into the luxuriant day-bed and order a 72-hour supply of champagne, I knew that making myself a mystery to my fellow travellers was the surest way to attract attention and a knife in the ribs.

'The plan, Quinn, is for me to have a drink. Inspiration about the next couple of days.'

He glanced at me. 'Life and soul of the party, eh sir.' He didn't make it a question.

This also was shrewd. If I have a fault, it - well, let's say that among my faults - is an ill-concealed aversion to other people, the conviction that if I and the rest of the human race stay out of each other's way we'll get along just fine. I make no apology for this - the rest of the human race are usually tiresome, troublesome, or idiots. But Quinn was right that if I was going to show myself I couldn't be the furtive fugitive. As the grumpiest Cornishman in living memory had so rightly put it: life and soul of the party. Ghastly thought. I patted my breast pocket and set off down the train corridor towards the bar, practising smiles. The things I do for England.

5.

The bar was smaller than any I'd ever seen, but better stocked. The same deftness of design that squeezed a palace of luxury into sleeping compartments no bigger than a billiard table had created a bar the size of a lavatory that still served every possible refreshment. It was all, of course, tricked out in gilt and glass and polish. Two men could have stood at it - provided that neither wanted to move around - and another half dozen could have loitered in the general vicinity, or sat on plush bench seats running along the side of the carriage. Beyond a glass partition, the rest of the carriage was dining tables.

I was the only one standing at it. So I ordered a barley water and moved around to my heart's content. I used this flexibility to get a look at the few others who'd already drifted in. A distinguished-looking older chap with a clerical collar was sitting at one table. There were a couple of women at another: one old, one young, and both rather plain, in a reassuring sort of way; they looked like before and after pictures for An Unfortunate Experience At The Age Of Forty. Their sturdy travelling tweeds would have proclaimed their Englishness, even if the overloud comments of the elder about the bathroom arrangements had not.

I might have seen more of my fellow travellers, but my vision was suddenly filled by the face of a chap with sleek grey hair and a sleek grey three-piece, bow-tie to match. 'How you like a drink, sir?' he boomed.

'Alone', I was about to say. Then I remembered I was supposed to be on good behaviour. 'That's very civil of you, sir', I said instead. 'But I never take a drink until I know a man's name.' I offered my hand. 'I'm Delamere; Harry Delamere.'

He plonked a small brown case, a bit smaller than a shoe box, on the bar and we shook hands.

'Theotokis.' He waved a hand in the approximate direction of the barman to get attention, and picked up the cocktail menu. Another indication that fashion as well as luxury was available on the train, it was a handsome leather affair with a printed card showing the fancy mixes and the more exotic spirits. 'What my friend is drinking?' Theotokis asked the barman.

'Barley water,' the barman replied, in a voice that hinted his feelings about the hand-waving approach.

My new acquaintance stared at me as if I'd just punched his mother. 'Well that's not right', he said indignantly. 'May one ask…?'

The correct answer is that when I want to think straight - when I'm gambling, or shooting, or witness to a murder and being watched by the Turkish police - I don't get carried away on the sauce. But I knew that wouldn't serve. 'Settle my stomach', I said, and added: 'If I'm planning a marathon I don't kick off at a sprint.' I may even have said this roguishly. Ghastly. I glanced to the barman: 'I'll take a whisky and soda, if I may.' I murmured my thanks to my new pal.

'Splendid!' He said. 'The same. We set a good pace for the first mile, eh?'

'Quite right', I said, trying to match his joviality. 'What brings you on the Orient Express?'

'I am Professor of Archaeology and Antiquities at University of Athens', he said suavely. It wasn't really an answer to my question, but he sounded very pleased with it so I didn't interfere. 'Professor Theodoros Theotokis. I have just completed most successful excavation at Anaklia in Black Sea - ancient Colchis, you know?' I nodded as if I knew. He glanced around himself, then tapped the box on the bar confidentially. 'I take my prize piece to display in Munich, at Glyptothek Museum, before it returns to true home in Athens.'

'Pardon me, gentlemen.' We both turned - not without difficulty - and I saw the handsome woman who'd been among those hurrying for the train. 'Mind if I take my turn at the lucky dip?'

We murmured apologies and contrived the clumsy dance necessary to let her get to the bar. Professor Theodoros Theotokis raised the hand again. 'Might I have honour of buying you drink, Madame?'

'It's Mademoiselle, and no. Thank you.' She looked at the barman. 'D'you have bourbon?' He assured her that he did.

Her accent was distinctive, a low drawl. The Professor's hand became a pointing finger. 'You are American, perhaps?' He made it sound like a proposition.

She considered his finger, and then his face. 'Perhaps', she said. A thank you to the barman, and she was away.

We looked after her, with admiration - though perhaps of different kinds.

A bell tinkled, and a steward announced that a light supper would be served for those who fancied a little something before bed and that, because we were taking the less usual southern route to avoid difficulties in Romania, breakfast would be enjoyed before we crossed the frontier into Bulgaria. I managed to avoid sitting with my new best friend the archaeology professor, and instead found myself opposite the old chap with the clerical collar. We introduced ourselves as we sat; his name, he said, was Septimus Wilkinson.

'And, er...' I pointed to my collar while looking at his. 'Unless you'd rather not talk shop.'

He smiled. 'I have the honour,' he said rather wearily, 'to be Bishop of Matabeleland; for my sins.' The last bit was said with heavy humour; it wasn't a bad gag, though he'd clearly been using it for fifty years.

'And how much more would you have to sin to make Archbishop of Canterbury?'

'It is not the quantity of the sinning, my dear sir, but the quality.'

'What quality of sin took you to Matabeleland?' Quinn would have been proud of me, all this pleasant chat. It helped that I had immediately warmed to the old lad.

He was sitting back, and considering the point. It was a fine old head, skin cracked and worn like oak bark and darkened by years of African sun, waves of thick grey hair above.

'When I was younger - not long after the Norman Conquest - I fancied myself a muscular Christian, and went to Africa on missionary work. Then I settled, as one is supposed to: I acquired a political instinct, and a little ambition, and a worthy wife, and started to get on. But I found that I was not hungry enough, and too inclined to my own opinions. In time I lost the instinct, and the ambition, and the wife.' He was staring out of the window in the rattling night. 'Colonial bishoprics are where they send men to die, and men who already have. They had to find something for me; and perhaps I rediscovered a little of the spirit of my youth.'

Wine had appeared in front of us, and I raised my glass to him. 'I salute your spirit, sir. Hope you've found something worth enjoying at last.'

He smiled kindly. 'Sufficient unto the day is the evil thereof.'

A shadow loomed over the table. 'Your pardon, gentlemen.' We looked up. 'May I join you?'

One can't really say no, tempting though it was; I'd been hoping to talk to the Bishop about southern Africa. There was also a question about where the new arrival thought he was going to sit; and indeed a question about how he'd squeezed onto the train at all, unless they'd taken the roof off and lowered him in with a crane. He was a vast person, perched precariously on a walking-cane, and the swaying of the carriage had him in grave danger of toppling over at any moment. He gave as much of a nod as his absence of neck would allow, said 'Karim', and eased himself in next to the Bishop and opposite me.

He was closely - if more delicately - followed down by three bowls of soup.

Where the Bishop was deeply-lined with age, the man now next to him seemed perfectly smooth. A general sense of gravity suggested age, and the fact that he had to have been eating for a good few decades without a break to build up that tonnage. He seemed quite bald, under a red skull cap.

We introduced ourselves, and he said: 'I would not of course push myself onto the ladies' - not without a long lever and a medical team standing by, I thought - 'and the only other man with an empty chair had tried to offer me a drink, without our having been introduced.' Over his shoulder I could see my Greek professor pal, at a table with another chap - and with the American woman, who'd not after all been so successful at avoiding him. There was another table of men, and one with the two tweedy Englishwomen, and the rest of the tables were empty. Apparently the other passengers slept better on an empty stomach. 'I do hope I do not intrude.'

'Hardly', I lied. And the Bishop added something about travellers' pleasantries, and the big chap beamed.

'Most right', he said quietly. 'Such is the charm of this journey. Such a gathering of different peoples. So many new characters.' He looked at me. 'So many new mysteries.'

He glanced to the Bishop. 'You give us too many clues about yourself, your Excellency,' - I'm not sure that's what you're supposed to call Anglican Bishops, and this one certainly seemed surprised by it, but perhaps our new acquaintance had been looking at the passenger list and was bidding high. Now he was looking at me again. 'Whereas you, my dear sir, are a complete mystery.'

He made it sound like an accusation.

I resisted the urge to check that the document was still in my breast pocket.

'We see English gentleman, of course. Dressed appropriately but not showy. Never showy, eh?' He somehow mixed joviality and a sneer. 'But the uniform of a gentleman - the costume, shall we say? - this may hide much. Is it not so, Sir Henry?'

He emphasized the 'sir'. I hadn't mentioned - I don't mention - my rather meaningless title. Either he had the most peculiarly detailed knowledge of the British gentry, or he had indeed studied a passenger list.

'I think we assume you are not in trade. But your affluence, your affairs, your activities, your calling…' A great shrug rippled up his body.

Some ill-mannered sense of mischief made me unhelpful. 'Yes,' I said, 'I do see your problem.'

A heavy smiled crept up over his face. It was a smile of appetite, of predator trapping prey and about to devour. Perhaps that's how he kept his strength up, by eating itinerant Englishmen.

'In the spirit of the fellowship of travellers - of strangers who share soup at midnight, and will never meet again - what brings you on this train tonight Sir Henry?'

'Shortest distance between two points is a straight line', I said. 'I was in Constantinople. I need to be in Paris.'

'And you were in Turkey on the business that sustains your fortune? Or you travel the Eastern Mediterranean for pleasure, on the accumulated wealth of your distinguished forefathers, perhaps?'

'The accumulated poverty of my very undistinguished forefathers - particularly the most recent one, who couldn't see a cross-eyed nag without betting his borrowed shirt on it - obliges me to spend my time in the cheaper parts of the world.'

'Well that is no good, is it?' He turned to the Bishop, as if for endorsement. The Bishop was looking at both of us with alarm; he was probably more comfortable with a village of marauding Ndebele than the present company. 'We need a better story than that. You tell us you are poor, yet here you are on the Orient Express, returning in luxury to the luxuries of the west.' He leaned forwards, threatening to upend the table. 'Are you a better judge of horses than your esteemed father, Sir Henry?'

'I steal from fellow-travellers', I said. 'The pickings are a sight better on the Orient Express than the donkey carts.'

He smiled obligingly. I smiled in return. He eased his bulk away from the table again, and considered me. I considered him right back. We continued to exchange our mutual suspicions - and fortunately the steward intervened with the second half of our supper. Then the Bishop - and I'd have given him sainthood on the spot - decided we'd had enough fun with Delamere and asked our acquaintance what brought him on the train.

Big Karim started off on some nonsense about the affairs of Europe being the affairs of Turkey, and the affairs of Turkey being the affairs of Europe, and finance or something, but I wasn't listening. I knew he was some kind of wrong'un, needling me so deliberately. But what kind? Or was I just getting jumpy?

I had to assume he was a Turkish big-shot. The style, the dominance, the familiarity with the passengers. Which side of the law I couldn't say. If he was suspicious of me, his suspicion pre-dated dinner: I ain't that disreputable; not at first glance.

I had nothing to gain by trying to get back into his good books. I wolfed my food, and excused myself.

As I stood and turned, I found a Turkish uniform blocking the door into the corridor, by the bar. It was the silent, junior one of the pair who'd interrogated me earlier. He was gazing emptily into the dining car, but as I made towards him his gaze focused on me.

I stopped in front of him; biggish lad. 'Good evening', I said.

He considered this. 'Good evening', he replied at last, taking the words slowly and precisely.

'Excuse me', I said.

He frowned, apparently wondering if he was entitled to block my way all night.

He failed to find good cause, and after a moment stepped aside and continued gazing at the dining car.

I walked the few paces to my compartment. I wasn't ready for sleep, but I wanted a few minutes to myself at least. Get my head straight, and take a more considered decision about the mysterious document I was lumbered with.

The compartment was as I'd left it, or as Quinn had left it after he'd finished stowing my light bags. Not much: a bag up on the luggage rack, and a smaller one at the foot of the bed. As before, I was struck by how trim the outfit was. Everything compact, near at hand, fitting together neatly. The bed linen crisp and tucked tight.

I opened the cupboard that concealed a basin, and splashed water on my face, and saw myself in the mirror.

Then I saw something else in the mirror.

From this angle, the light was catching the bed-sheet oddly, where it folded down over the top of the blanket by the pillow: some irregularity, some faint shadow.

I turned and crouched beside the bed. On its edge, there might be a faint impression in the sheet. Just a slight imperfection in the folding, perhaps. Or where Quinn had leaned to straighten something. Except that - indulging my jumpiness further - the impression seemed to have sharper edges; edges like the front half of a boot.

It was exactly where a smaller man might put one foot to lever himself up, if he wanted to check that there was nothing lying flat on the luggage shelf beside my bag.

I pulled down the bag, as such a man might then have done. Everything inside that was supposed to be inside: a few shirts and other linen, roughly folded; down at the bottom of the bag, below everything, my revolver.

I glanced around the compartment, with a searcher's eyes.

There were faint dust-smears on the underside of the pillowcase, as might be left by a man who had swept a hand along the back of a high luggage shelf where it wouldn't get cleaned so carefully, and then checked underneath the pillow, and then done the best he could to disguise the fact by brushing it and upending it.

While I'd been enduring that curious conversation with the large Turkish gentleman, my compartment and bags had been thoroughly searched.

6.

I ambled down the corridor, away from the dining car and forward along the train, into the second-class coach. Here the furnishing was about the same, but each compartment slept two people.

Quinn was supposed to be in 3a/3b. But when I knocked on the door, and it opened, I was looking up over a mighty beard into a dark face, topped with a turban.

'Good evening, sir', it said, in a voice that came from deep.

'Sorry to disturb', I said. 'Mr Quinn receiving visitors?' Quinn announced himself from up on the top bunk. 'Stand to, there's a good chap.' The turban gave a courteous nod to me, and squeezed round to let Quinn out. 'Who's Tiny?' I said, nodding to his room-mate.

'This is Mahan Singh, sir.' Mahan Singh gave a little bow. 'Indian Army. He was in the Cape same time as us.' Now the big man was standing more or less at attention. 'Came out as a groom, rode with an ambulance, bit of this and that. Now he looks after the gent we met earlier.'

I nodded up at him. 'Glad to have you on this trip, Havildar.' He was still staring out over my head, parade ground style. I meant it; as long as he was on the right side. As allies, we knew the Sikhs as the firmest and the bravest. As enemies - yonks ago now, before the Indian Mutiny - they'd been among the most ferocious the British Army had ever faced. Up close you could see why.

Quinn followed me towards the end of the carriage. 'Nice feller', he said.

'If he's not you'll have a rough time of it.'

I found us a shadowed corner by the doorway to the First Class carriage. 'Presumably', I said, 'you packed my linen with your usual indifference, vague pretence at folding, nothing to speak of.' He looked as if I'd accused him of pinching money from an orphanage.

Then he began to see where I was heading. 'Just as usual, sir.'

'Indeed. And my revolver was…'

'Just as usual. Tucked below the top item. To hand but not to eye.'

'Mm.' I nodded. 'That's unfortunate.'

I could see he was, in his quiet way, angry. One does not lightly bugger around with Quinn's domestic arrangements. 'Make much of a mess, did they sir? I can-'

'No, it's not so bad. Can't say I like it.' I thought a moment. 'But there's a slight advantage if they've looked and not found anything. Fractionally improves my reputation.'

He didn't believe it, either. 'Want me to sit in sir? Reception party?'

I shook my head. 'Thanks, but no. Charming company, of course. But I don't want anyone thinking I'm taking precautions; looks guilty. I'll wedge the door, though. Don't want the whole bloody train wandering in and out. Usual knock.' He nodded.

I hesitated. 'Watch yourself too, you hear?'

'They wouldn't think you'd given it to me, sir, surely.'

'They don't all think like gentlemen, alas. More importantly…' - I hesitated - 'they don't all act like gentlemen. They may think they can somehow get to me through you.'

He nodded grimly. Brave as they come, Quinn, but there's no foolish bravado. 'You think there's serious trouble sir?'

I shrugged. 'It seems there's an opposition, and for some reason it seems they've decided I'm suspect number one.'

Quinn eyed me dubiously. 'Perhaps… because it's true, sir?'

7.

I made my way back to the bar, and ordered a barley water. There were fewer people in there now - most of the train would be asleep - and I didn't give them any attention.

The steward gave me my drink and very decently left me alone to prop up the bar.

In his typically blunt and effective fashion, my valet had put his finger on it. The mysterious document obviously had some special status - that much had been clear in Constantinople - and I was the man carrying it. If there was anyone interested in the document, or unhappy about the document - and, again, the business in Constantinople had made that pretty likely - I was a justified target in their eyes.

There was movement near me, and I glanced round to find the woman with the American accent. I called the steward back from laying the tables for tomorrow's breakfast. 'Would you mind getting the lady a… another bourbon, was it?'

'It was,' she said, 'and thank you, but-'

'No strings attached; no conversation required. I came here to drink and to think, not to lure passing strangers into my fatal snare.'

She looked into my eyes. 'Well gosh; that's a relief.'

I looked back into hers. It was a strong kind of beauty: of bones, of eyes, of confidence. 'Of course, if it so offends your principles…'

'Officially I disapprove of your patriarchal and colonial instincts. But I do like bourbon.'

'Life can be trying sometimes.'

The whisky appeared in front of her. 'You must allow me to buy you one in return sometime.'

'Officially I disapprove of your dubious new world egalitarianism and forwardness. But I don't have the funds to buy all the drinks all the time.'

'Like you say, life can be trying. It's a deal then. Cheers.' I raised my glass in my return. 'What is that stuff, anyway?'

'Barley water.' She looked into me again. 'It's basically whisky, but I'm too impatient to wait for the grain to distil.'

Her face opened in an unrestrained smile, revealing very

even and white teeth. 'Cute. But you English are all buttoned-up: you don't strike me as the impatient type.'

'That's what I'm buttoning up.'

'And you're not drinking with your Greek pal?'

'Sometimes life isn't so trying after all. How was dinner?'

'Very educational. He told me a lot about the role of women in the modern world.'

'No wonder you're so determined to buy all these drinks.'

She sipped her whisky, and considered me some more. 'A man who drinks alone, and thinks alone', she said eventually. 'You do everything alone?'

'I make an occasional exception.'

'I'll bear that in mind.' Again the cool smile. 'Well, g'night then.'

She knocked back the rest of her whisky, threw me a little salute, and walked away towards the compartments.

I watched her go. Her outfit was a very simple kind of smart: practical and elegant and modern and I couldn't have told you whether it was very cheap or very expensive.

Then I returned to my barley water.

Apparently - and as the British Embassy in Constantinople had clearly feared - there was someone dangerously interested in the document in my pocket. It would be a spectacular coincidence if the man who'd given it to me had just happened to get murdered moments later. Constantinople has its wild aspects, but I don't think they make a special business of stabbing chaps on railway platforms.

Apparently the opposition were on the train. The ferrety Turkish official who'd questioned me immediately, he was a likely candidate. As I'd said to Quinn, that suggested official opposition, which made this an even more dangerous game: all the power of the state against me - as long as the train was in Turkey, anyway. (Once again I had to ask myself: what the hell had the Embassy landed me with?) Then there'd been the search of my compartment. The other uniform who'd been with the ferret, and had waylaid me leaving the dining car earlier: had that been to give more time for his boss to get clear? And the big man who'd been needling me at supper, was that part of it too?

With an apology, I interrupted the steward again and got another drink.

I couldn't really complain about them suspecting me of being the courier, given that I was.

Except - and perhaps this was tiredness; it was something like two in the morning and it had been a funny old day - I felt that I could complain a bit. Assuming they were onto me, then they'd been onto me immediately. The Orient Express had barely left the station when the ferrety chap was running his magnifying glass over my map. I ain't that shifty looking.

Perhaps they'd been onto the Embassy fellow. But had we really been noticed together? I don't claim any special skills of deception, but if they'd spotted us together - two men in unremarkable costume in the busiest place in the busiest city on earth - then they'd been looking for us together.

And that meant the Embassy's secret plan had been blown open before it had properly started.

Good old government. What a shambles.

'I was observing you earlier', a voice said behind me, and I turned.

He was standing a couple of yards off. Elegantly-dressed chap, with a better complexion than my own pasty excuse - Mediterranean, let's say. Had I noticed him at supper, or not? He could have been forty or fifty, but he was sleek with it, the greying hair oiled back with gleaming precision. He had one of those delicate little moustaches that look like a fellow's misjudged his cup of coffee.

He stabbed towards me with a lit cigarette, held up between finger and thumb. 'And I thought to myself: this is a gentleman who has determined to take the most from life.' The accent reinforced the complexion: Spanish, perhaps. 'And who is it that I find, still enjoying a drink when all the rest have given up for the night?' He produced a smile, and then placed the cigarette in it.

'Life's never given me very much', I said. 'I got into the bad habit of taking.'

He removed the cigarette, but the smile stayed. 'Would you allow me to present myself?' I couldn't think of a good reason to stop him, anyway. 'I am Valfierno.' He said it with a flourish of the rich accent, like he might have said 'I am immortal', or 'I am the most well-groomed man on this train.'

I tried to invest my 'I'm Delamere' with a similar majesty, but I'm afraid it sounded a bit shabby.

'But do please excuse me, sir. You are clearly a gentleman who does not seek the crowd, and I will not interrupt your reflections.' He started to go up in my estimation. 'Perhaps we shall see each other again on the train.' This seemed unavoidable during three days in a living space the size of a cricket pitch, but I was liking his style. I said that would be most pleasant, and wished him good night, and he turned away.

Then he turned back, and again he was considering me. 'A man of reflection… A man who lives life, but is also prudent… A man who meets opportunity half way, and shakes it by the hand. Perhaps…' He shook his head. 'But no. You must please excuse my forwardness.'

And he was gone.

What the hell was that little performance about?

In all, he had said… nothing; nothing of meaning. Except that he had been observing me.

I felt rather weary. Whatever time it was, we were well into tomorrow already.

I'd had more than enough of yesterday. What with the still obscure foolishness that the Government had got me mixed up in, the murder, the searching of my compartment and the various odd conversations, I felt well justified in calling it quits and getting some sleep. Sufficient unto the day is the evil thereof, as the Bish. had put it. I left a couple of coins on the bar and sauntered homeward.

I saw no one. I fancied one of the compartment doors was open a crack as I passed - someone making a last trip to the privy before sleep - perhaps a murmur of voices from somewhere - but otherwise no signs of life.

There are various little tricks you can use to check if you've had an unexpected visitor while you're out. The coin on the door handle, the hair over the crack, the wedged paper. Unless you're dealing with a real expert, who's looking out for the tricks and handy enough to replace them exactly, they're an immediate give-away.

The first time I'd left my compartment, Quinn had still been in there and I'd not been on what you'd call a full wartime footing, and I'd not bothered. The second time - having discovered that someone had been in - it had felt worth it. Bolting the stable door, etcetera.

One of the simplest tricks is just a box of matches, stood on end a certain distance behind the door, ready to be knocked when it opens. Even the experts can't be sure if it's a trick rather than an accident - unlike the wedge of paper or the coin or the hair, which tells them for sure that you're playing serious. And if you've placed it very precisely - a precise distance from something, a precise profile - even the experts will have great difficulty replacing it exactly. My own idea, since you ask.

I eased my compartment door open the minimum necessary to slip through it without disturbing the matchbox where it should have been. Looking down round behind the door, I saw immediately that the box was a foot away from where I'd left it, and lying flat.

Clever Delamere. Once again, someone had come into my compartment uninvited.

Having said that, I had to admit that the fooling around with the matchbox hadn't really been necessary. I could have seen in any case that an uninvited someone had come in, because they'd left a silk dressing gown in a pile on the floor of my compartment, and then got into my bed. And they were still there.

She hadn't been wearing much under the dressing gown, not if the bare shoulders which showed over the top of my sheet were anything to go by.

It was young Miss Khan, and as she stared up towards me, rather defiant, she was looking a damn' sight less reserved than when we'd met in the corridor earlier.

She'd left her nose-stud in, anyway.

8.

How to put this with basic delicacy?

I'm as human as the next man. Especially in the springtime. Everything in more or less full working order; all the usual instincts. I've few of the hang-ups that some of the next men do, about race or creed or class. And, I confess, I've not paid much attention to the conventions attached to the marital state.

What I've never had, however, is that urge to have a go at anything in a skirt simply because it's there. Pardon the expression, but… quality not quantity. And I've never had - always rather despised - that brutish desire which makes a special thing of getting in first with a girl.

I like the joy to be shared out more or less equally, if you know what I mean. And if we both know what we're doing, even better.

All of which is to say: very lovely though Miss Khan might be, even in normal circumstances I'd have found the idea of taking advantage of her pretty sordid. Then there was her father, of course: seemed a good chap, and I had just about given my word to steer clear.

And in any case, these weren't normal circumstances.

She was looking up at me with an uncomfortably mixed expression. Nature had taught her a charming coyness; but she'd obviously heard enough of the realities of men in general, or of Harry Delamere in particular, to be pretty apprehensive about the ordeal ahead.

I had some very serious thinking to do, mainly about how to stay alive for the next 72 hours, and to a lesser extent about how to keep the government happy. Not to seem ungrateful - and no doubt there'll come a time when I'm cursing myself for having wasted such opportunities - but I really, really didn't need beautiful almond-eyed young women slipping into my bed. Really.

'Our poet-king wrote: intoxication stronger than any wine it seemed,' - her voice sounded rather strained - 'transport faster than any steed, a vision more lovely than any I have dreamed: paradise may be ours on earth indeed.'

Dear God... the poor kid had actually prepared the opening line.

I needed to think. And then, soon, I badly needed to sleep.

I tried to go kindly.

'Miss Khan, I thank you - really, very sincerely. But I must decline. Hell of a waste, but there it is. It's a very generous offer, and I'm sure it would be very pleasant; but please believe me that life is going to offer you considerably more marvellous opportunities than a rancid fretful Delamere squeezed into a railway bunk.' She'd look confused, and then stunned, and was now looking rather angry. 'So - thanking you very much for your visit - I'm going to pop into the corridor, and finish my drink and check the coast is clear, and that'll give you space to escape safely and get on with the rest of your life.'

She was trying to speak, and failing. She'd obviously screwed her courage up to the big moment, and I'd let her down badly. I also got the sense that usually life tended to go according to her plans and demands; she wasn't used to being refused. I attempted an apologetic-yet-courteous smile, and turned for the door.

'You beast!' she said to my back.

'Occasionally, yes.'

'I'll - I'll ruin you!'

I turned. In her anger she was sitting upright in my bed now. 'Yes', I said. 'You could, and please feel free to try if it helps. But, without wishing to sound a cad... I'm afraid it's the way of the world that the lady always suffers more than the gentleman in such cases. And, truly, I have no reputation to lose, and you have plenty.' I checked the corridor again. 'I'm sure you'll find a much more splendid and suitable chap soon.'

And the best of luck to him, I thought. There was a moment while she was slipping back into her dressing gown and I stared out of the corridor window into the night. Then the door swung open and she strode out past me and away down the corridor, holding the haughty expression at least until she'd turned her back on me.

Silence, and stillness, and thank the Lord for both. The corridor was still empty. The Bishop's door, which I'd fancied a little earlier might have been open a crack, was closed. Now pretty confident that I'd have the place to myself, I re-entered my compartment.

I took off shoes, tie and jacket, and sat back on my bunk.

My pillow was still luxurious with the scent of Miss Khan. I guessed this wasn't an Indian concoction, but whatever a young lady of romantic disposition had been allowed to buy in Constantinople, by a father who worried about the risks to her purity but would always be looking for them in the wrong direction.

That little unerotic unadventure had been light relief within the increasingly dark atmosphere building up around me.

Bit of fresh air. I tried to open the window, but couldn't get it to budge.

It wasn't just the Embassy chap getting murdered, and my worrying errand with the document, and the Turkish police having a go. Perhaps I was getting windy, but too many people seemed to know me too well, or to be unusually keen on getting to know me. The Indian knew of me. The big Turkish chap, Karim, had been prodding me when we were with the Bishop. And that damned odd exchange with the Spanish or Portuguese bod just now; that was surely unnatural and I'd no idea why. And then there were the women...

And still I was carrying Europe's most precious document in my coat pocket. Deciding that, surely, was step one. I was going to be on the train three days or so, and if the Turkish authorities and God knew who else was going to be taking such an unhealthy interest in me, I couldn't risk pulling out an international secret each time I reached for my handkerchief.

But where, though? I looked down the length of myself, and then around the compartment. Some place of greater concealment on me? Hide it in something that I might be carrying? Or could I risk leaving it in my compartment? I wasn't sure if that was more or less likely. And if in the compartment, where?

The Turks had been relatively restrained so far. They or someone else might get more confident and search me properly.

I got up and had another go at the window. A great heave dragged it down six inches or so before it stuck, having ripped my knuckle.

And could it be even worse? If this paper was so dashed valuable, if the opposition were already in the business of knifing chaps on railway benches, I had to reckon with the possibility that they might just knock me on the head, and search for the paper at their leisure. Was I going to have to spend the next three days watching my back, and never letting myself be alone?

There was a knock at the door.

9.

It startled me, I confess.

I took a moment wondering whether I should pretend to be away or unconscious, but I couldn't see the benefit. I pretended confusion; that was easy enough, anyway. 'What? Sorry - just one moment...' I tucked my revolver into the waist of my trousers, and put on my dressing gown. Carefully positioning one foot near the door to limit its movement, I opened up.

It was Sikander Ali Khan.

I say it was him, because in the *Official Gazette* style he was the senior man in the party. But the man who was really, most impressively and significantly, calling on me was Mahan Singh. He was standing just behind his master's shoulder, like the Himalayas looming over the church at Darjeeling. He was staring with the same impassivity he'd shown earlier, but now it was ominous.

'Evening, Delamere.'

I smiled politely. It wasn't easy. I opened the door all the way. Nothing to hide. No one to hide, more importantly.

He smiled back. He didn't mean it either.

Singh had a sash around his waist. Sticking out the top of it was the haft of what I assumed was a knife. I hadn't seen it earlier.

'Things seemed to have moved on apace, what? I fancied I'd flesh out my earlier remarks. For certainty's sake, yes?' The exaggerated elegances were peculiar enough with his accent. Under the circumstances they seemed insane. Still the giant Sikh glowered over us.

I maintained my polite interest. 'Thing is, Delamere, I was enjoying the hospitality of the dear Bishop, and the door was ajar - help the cigar smoke out, what? - and so of course I saw my daughter leaving your compartment a short while ago.'

'Indeed?' I said. It couldn't have been clear whether I was

disputing the fact or defiant about it. I'd tried to sound calm, anyway; it hadn't worked.

'Indeed. You may imagine my bafflement. Now, I have some idea of your own movements - that gap in the jolly old door - and I know that there was not time for anything untoward to have happened in here.' I relaxed slightly. Then I glanced at Mahan Singh again. Khan smiled. 'Of course, I know that nothing could have happened either, you having given me your word but an hour or two ago.'

I waited.

He gave a single word of command in his own tongue. With a speed surprising in a large man, Singh pulled out what was in his sash, and held it up in front of him. Still his dead eyes gazed down at me.

I'd been right. The haft was the haft of a knife.

Except... You hear 'knife', you think pen-knife, vegetable knife, knife and fork. The weapon that Mahan Singh was holding up for my consideration was something between a cutlass and a shovel. This knife was enormous; it gleamed evilly in the soft yellow light of the train corridor.

'Here, my dear chap, is the rub. It doesn't matter one whit if she invites herself. I care not a jot if you sit here soberly playing gin rummy, not a single impure thought in your heads.' Again the little smile. 'I must care for her reputation. If anyone sees her leaving your compartment, her reputation is ruined, and that I cannot have.' Still the same pleasant voice; he might have been discussing the menu for breakfast. 'Please be advised, dear old chap, that should her reputation appear in the slightest way besmirched by you, Mahan Singh will gut you.'

The last two words, short and ugly after his previous delicacies, were said in the same soft chatter.

'Now, I know what you're thinking. You're thinking that such a deed might throw a spanner into our travel plans, and perhaps you're right; you're thinking that we might incur a little inconvenience, with the authorities for example.'

Actually I was thinking solely and deeply of the knife, but I didn't interrupt his flow. 'But honestly, we wouldn't be so very badly snootered. We'd miss London, of course, but such is life, eh? I'd go back to Punjab and the protection of my brother, and the splendid pensions your Empire so generously grants our family. Mahan Singh would never get to see the white cliffs of Dover or the Royal Opera House, but he'd attain the greatest status in my retinue. And Suraya?' He sighed. 'Well, instead of one of the princes I have in mind for her, she should have to marry one of her retarded cousins. But you, my dear Delamere, you'd be lying on the floor of this railway compartment with your innards all in a pickle.' Again the damned smile. 'I say this with no sense of bully-ragging, no silly melodrama. It is a statement of fact merely. So you are in the picture.'

'I'm much obliged. All perfectly reasonable.'

He gave his little nod of courtesy. He barked a word, and Singh disappeared - in as much as a turbaned six-foot-six Indian carrying a carving knife can disappear in a train corridor. 'Again, please excuse my disturbing your repose, Delamere. Don't forget that drink of ours.'

10.

I don't want to sound like too much of a gibbering hysteric, but I slept uneasily. I've slept in odd places and circumstances in my time - dossed on rough ground knowing that dawn would bring the battle. I don't say one ever gets comfortable with that sort of thing, but it's familiar.

Uncertainty is something else. I didn't know what I was up against; I didn't, frankly, have much of an idea what I was doing. That kept me thinking. There had to be a strong chance that the opposition - whoever and whatever they were - were feeling a sense of unfinished business in my compartment. They'd had a quick rummage in my convenient absence; but given their obvious ruthlessness and the importance of what I was carrying, I had little confidence they'd see my presence as much of an obstacle.

I'd improvised a wedge and stuffed that under the door. If they were desperate, it would do no more than delay them. At least I'd be awake for my death.

There had to be a chance, too, that Miss Suraya would come back in the small hours for, er, another bite at the cherry. And Mahan Singh and his cutlery was a week's worth of nightmares.

At some point I'd woken feeling chilly. A minute's straining proved that the window was now jammed open.

My brittle sleep was broken by a clanking and a lurching somewhere in the train. That got me half awake, and the stillness confused me, and the confusion got me fully awake, and I understood that we'd stopped.

I wandered blearily down the corridor for a piss. At the end of the carriage I found the door open, and stepped down into the chill air of the night.

We'd stopped at a station called - by those who can pronounce Turkish, anyway - Çerkezköy. Whether there was a town called Çerkezköy I couldn't tell you; there was no sign of anything else in the darkness. The world was an eerie monochrome: the sick yellow thrown by one lamp sticking out of the station building, and the rest the empty mystery of Turkey.

A few feet away along the platform, a shadow appeared out of the gloom. Then his features and uniform caught the light, and I saw it was the conductor.

'Another restless spirit', I said. 'How long?'

He pulled a big watch out of his waistcoat pocket, and peered at it under the lamp. 'Six minutes, monsieur - seven. Please don't go far, but I will look out for you.' French accent, a pleasant rumbling murmur.

I thanked him and turned away.

I didn't get far. As soon as I turned my vision was full of a large shadow. A tall man had loomed up in front of me, God only knew from where. With the light behind him, all I could see was his bulk.

For a heart-stopping moment I thought it was Mahan Singh. Sikander Ali Khan must have changed his mind, decided to take no chances, and his brute of a bodyguard was going to finish me off in this one-horse Turkish train-stop and no one would ever know. Then I saw that the shadow included the long barrel of a rifle, held two-handed across the chest. Surely even Singh couldn't have that in his belt too.

It was another of my admirers: the Turkish soldier, assistant to the ferrety officer, the lump who'd held me up at the entrance to the dining car.

'Small world', I said. 'Fancy bumping into you again.' I made to move past him, but he shifted to block me.

Well, for God's sake... I don't pretend any great familiarity with Ottoman law, nor with the platform regulations of the Turkish railways, but I was fairly sure I ought to be allowed to go and discreetly water the plants without fear of the firing squad.

Very deliberately I stepped backwards, and then a yard to the side, and walked away from him. He actually raised a hand, uncertain, thinking about stopping me again but I brushed past it and into the gloom. I wondered where his officer was, what he was up to. Something else I wasn't supposed to see?

It was yet another reason to enjoy the freedom of the night air, and the silence, and the darkness.

A little distance down the platform, well away from the train and facing off into what I assumed was the Turkish landscape, I unbuttoned and eased my conscience. Filthy soldier's habit, but I find it less unpleasant than standing in a cramped railway train thunderbox.

I was back well inside the conductor's six minutes. As I stepped up into the First Class sleeping car, a voice from the shadows murmured: 'All well, sir?'

'You keeping watch, Quinn? Kind of you.'

He scowled. 'Middle of the night: stopping and starting; people to and fro. Best keep an eye.'

'Who've you seen?'

'The two Turkish uniforms got off prompt. Conductor. Yourself, sir. Don't think there's more, but I couldn't promise in this darkness; not to mention the other side of the train, away from the platform.'

'Mm.' We were still lurking between the First and Second Class carriages. 'By the way', I said, 'I need three or four pins - regular sort. Any chance?'

He nodded, of course. There was a whistle. The conductor appeared in the carriage doorway, and got up on to the lowest step. There was an answering whistle from the locomotive.

Then we heard footsteps, from along the Second Class corridor. A burly chap stamped towards us, braces holding up trousers with a lurid check pattern, over a ruffled and stained shirt. I couldn't be sure, in the gloom of the night time corridor lighting, if his expression was aggressive or merely sleepy. But it was surely deliberate when he knocked past Quinn's shoulder, before opening the lavatory door. He glanced back, to see what sort of reaction he'd got.

My valet's face was still and calm, with just the faintest and oddest smile on it. It probably seemed rather mild; passive, even. The lavatory door closed.

'Friend of yours?' I said.

'No, sir.' His lip curled. 'Difference of outlook earlier. Matter of courtesy to a lady.'

'Problem?'

I'd seen that odd look on his face before, very occasionally; it tended to appear when officers were not present. It was the look Sergeant Quinn had reserved for gob-shites in the junior ranks trying it on.

'No sir.'

The conductor blew his whistle, and we heard hurrying footsteps on the platform. The locomotive whistled again, and began to heave. The conductor swung aside on his step with practised skill, and a figure jumped up as the train started to move. Then the conductor was up after him and closing the door and we were gaining speed.

The late arrival was the ferrety Turkish officer. He stopped when he saw me, and his eyes widened.

There was no sign of his soldier.

11.

Breakfast really did feel like a fresh start. New day, new beginning, and all that.

I'd slept, which helped. No one had tried to murder me, rob me, or anything else me.

We were rattling through the Turkish landscape now. Past the windows of the dining car rolled endless miles of hills - bumps, really, nothing to speak of - all the same pale yellow grass. Only occasionally a few huts suggested human habitation, or a herd of something or other milling near their shepherd, invariably a chap squatting on his haunches in the wilderness and contemplating the infinite.

Breakfast was my first chance to see all of my fellow passengers together. The dining car was full, eight tables' worth, with a noisy bustle of polite chat and murmuring waiters and the rattle of knives and forks.

I was feeling more sceptical of my fellow man than ever, but more obliged to be sociable with him. I introduced myself to two men facing each other across a table, and they duly invited me to sit with them. One was a little chap in an old-style business suit, which he seemed to have been sleeping in ever since he'd got it off the body of his late grandfather. He presented himself as 'Jean-Maurice Junot, le petit parisien', which seemed unusually humble from a Frenchman. The other was pale-looking, sickly even, with a suit that was more distinguished than he was: elaborate continental cut, unusual soft fabric, and a most peculiar green colour. He presented himself - at least I assume that's what he was doing - as somethingy-somethingy which I had no chance of working out.

I asked them what brought them on the Orient Express. Jean-Maurice Junot explained he was the editor of the *Petit Parisien* newspaper - that explained that, at least - en route home after visiting Constantinople on business. Mr unpronounceable said he was a musicologist, originally from Budapest, now on his way to take up a university appointment in France. Budapest explained the odd suit and the odder name; once you get into Hungarian, anything goes.

'I may join you, dear gentlemen?' Good news: it was my Greek drinking enthusiast of the night before. He'd made it a question, but he'd clearly decided he was joining us and slipped down into the seat. We offered three token murmurs of welcome for form's sake. As he sat, he put his little case on the table a moment. He caught my eye, tapped the case in the same furtive manner he'd used before, then moved it down beneath his feet.

'Never out of your sight, eh?'

'Never.' He glanced at the other two, then switched on a smile. 'And won't you introduce our friends?'

Probably not, no. I did all right with Jean-Maurice Junot of *Le Petit Parisien*, especially once I'd remembered which way round his first names went. I spun out the description, in the hope that the stewards would bring breakfast or the train would crash or something else would divert us before I had to show off my Hungarian. No diversion. 'And this - Well now, this is very interesting. Our friend here is - you said a musicologist, but I'm sure you can explain that better than I can.' Our Hungarian friend said his name again, or cleared his throat, and then started talking about primitive musical instruments. Apparently a big thing with him. Then I was able to complete the round by presenting the Professor as an archaeologist who'd just been busy in the Black Sea, and that got him started, and we were quite the jolly party.

I said that the dining carriage was full. Actually the complement would be thirty-two people, and for the moment there was still a handful of empty spaces. Thinking about it, a full First Class sleeper of ten and a full second of twenty would still leave room for my substantial Turkish friend to have a couple of chairs to himself, and I didn't know that every compartment was occupied.

At the table across from me, the two tweedy Englishwomen had the aisle seats, and two other women were against the window - Russians, someone had said. I saw the Bishop, and with him the odd chap I'd bumped into in the bar the previous night - Valfierno. Somewhere behind me I heard the heavy voice of my heavy Turkish acquaintance, and the elegant tones of Sikander Ali Khan. Ahead of me, I saw the door to the corridor opening and two women coming in, shepherded by Mahan Singh, with Quinn following. One of the women was a sturdy dark female, also apparently Indian - Miss Suraya's maid, I guessed. The other might also have been a maid, from her clothes - sombre, simple, smart - but was definitely European; a pretty black-haired girl. Singh glanced at the seating options, and stowed the two of them at a table with the two priests I'd seen on the Constantinople platform. Just in case the priests' minds started wandering in too secular a direction, Singh gave them a glare ferocious enough to reinforce their vows of celibacy for life and beyond. Then he and Quinn sat at the table adjacent, with a couple of other men.

I was half aware of the Greek archaeological chat continuing. Then the older of the two Englishwomen leaned across the aisle towards me.

'It's Sir Henry, I think.' I agreed that it was. 'You must pardon me butting in, but I fancied you weren't engaged in the conversation.' Rumbled. 'Battersby', she went on, in a voice they could have heard in the locomotive, and thrust a hand across the aisle. 'Miss Amelia Battersby.'

I half rose, and shook her hand, and reconfirmed that I was Henry Delamere. She was a grand old item, in her fifties at least, a heavy pink face, industrial-strength tweed restraining her bulk, and obviously a formidable personality. She nodded to the younger version of herself opposite. 'This is Miss Winifred Froy.'

I said hallo to Miss Winifred Froy, and she smiled uncertainly at me. It was unfair of me to say she was a younger version of her companion, despite the similar outfits. As well as being a good twenty-five years short of Miss Battersby, and half a hundredweight, Miss Froy seemed a quieter more thoughtful sort of thing. I wouldn't have called her pretty - not with Miss Battersby anywhere within earshot - but it was a gentle, pleasant face.

'Anyway,' Miss Battersby boomed, 'don't want to interrupt the gentlemen's conversation' - be my guest, I was thinking, for the gentlemen were still on archaeology - 'but I gathered you were English.' My expression must have shown the odd logic of this, because she followed up. 'You do much hill-walking, Sir Henry?' She leaned in. 'At every step, one is well advised to assess where the ground enables one to tread with certainty.'

I said that I trusted I wasn't too marshy, and she made a sound like the Orient Express accelerating through a tunnel, and Miss Froy gave a little smile, and then stewards were passing between us.

'Ah, now I remember!' It was Jean-Maurice the journalist, to the Greek; 'I knew I had read of your exploits. This was the Enguri River excavation, no?'

Theotokis's eyes lit up, delighted to have found a more knowledgeable audience than I was ever going to be. 'Indeed!'

'It was said to be the coup of the season.'

Theotokis gave a lavish performance of false modesty, before finally conceding that his discovery had, yes, been the coup of the season. 'But truly, my dear sir, fame of year is nothing. What counts is legacy we leave to all years. I could modestly claim…' - he hesitated, perhaps aware he was incapable of modestly claiming anything - 'that my little discovery sets framework for pre-Christian period that is not likely it will be challenged.'

'And - please excuse my curiosity - a terrible habit of the newspaperman smelling a story:' - he lowered his voice - 'this would be the box that you guard so carefully? Please say not one word if you wish to be discreet.'

Fat chance of that, and sure enough Theotokis was already rummaging under the table and re-emerging with his little box.

It was a simple business, plain leather and opening on top. Theotokis looked around in his usual stage-villain manner, then undid a brass clasp. He pulled out a bundle of blue cloth, and unwrapped it.

To his credit, it was worth the performance. The goblet that gleamed up at us from the cloth was clearly something special. It didn't have the easy sheen of new or cheap metal: it was a dull and battered gold, and that only reinforced its impression of age and power.

Theotokis looked at each of our faces, to check we were reacting appropriately. From his smile I guessed he hadn't been disappointed.

'Is it a single cast?' asked our Hungarian musical companion. It was the kind of intelligent question that I could barely understand, let alone have thought of asking myself.

Theotokis was already re-wrapping his treasure. 'Interesting!' he said happily. 'Interesting. No. Three intricate pieces, individual crafted and then simple fix together. Base and stem and cup. Screw-thread; think of that! But skill makes connections are invisible.' He closed the box around the goblet and replaced it beneath the table.

'There was some controversy, I think', Junot said. 'Some… dispute?' The same quiet polite voice, but I heard a new hardness in it. The serious journalist behind the charm and the ancient coat.

Theotokis had changed too. His face froze for a moment, soured. 'None', he said. 'Superstitious peasants and jealous rivals.'

'Of course,' Junot said, 'of course. I do hope that you will do me the honour of an interview. Your triumph deserves its acclaim.'

As is the way with crowded rooms, at one moment the rhythms of chatter happened to coincide and there was briefly silence, and that was the moment when most of us noticed that the ferrety Turkish officer was standing in the doorway.

It was an odd look, and each of us who saw him stayed silent and watching.

When the last voice had dwindled, when he was sure he had our attention, he took another step forwards, to the head of the aisle between the tables.

He gave a formal bow from the neck, and then began to speak. 'Karim Bey', he said, and gave another nod to the huge Turk who'd joined me at supper the previous night, 'esteemed ladies and gentlemen, I must beg your attention.' His voice was brisk and sharp.

I glanced at big Karim, squeezed at a table diagonally across from me. The Major's deference to him - 'Bey' being a big cheese in the Turkish system - showed just how important he must be.

At the same time, subtly but effectively, it reinforced the Major's authority.

On he went. 'I am Major Hilmi. I travel on this railway train on a most delicate official matter, and I shall require your co-operation.' His eye stopped on me for an instant, and I remembered our strange interview as the train had been pulling out of Constantinople. 'I am charged by my Government to recover an important state document. Investigations suggest that the person who has taken' - he emphasized the word with distaste, the vileness of the action clear - 'the document is travelling on this railway train.'

Well, damn this. I felt an instinctive alarm that the secret paper might be showing.

Just for a moment - determined not to be caught gaping in alarm at the Major - my eyes scanned those around me, the diverse reactions to this performance. No question but he had them spellbound. I looked back at him, putting on my best agog face. 'Now something very terrible has happened. During the night we stopped at Çerkezköy.' I'd got how to pronounce it, anyway. 'I left the train to send some telegrammes regarding the investigation. The soldier with me, Tekdemir, I left to watch the train. When I returned from the telegraph office, I did not at first see Tekdemir. Eventually I found him, in a store-room.' He paused. If Turkish official life ever became a drag, Hilmi'd have a grand future as an actor. Now the eyes widened in the little face. 'He was dead, ladies and gentlemen. He had been shot to death.'

12.

There are times when Quinn really earns the miserable salary I'm intermittently able to pay him. Having seen me in the small hours coming and going from the train, having been there for the earlier uncomfortable conversation with the two Turks, his very natural reaction at this instant would have been to look at me.

Even if he thought he knew me well enough to judge I hadn't shot the chap, he had to be wondering. But no: when I allowed my glance to reach him, he was staring around those at his table, all bewildered innocence and who could have done such a terrible thing?

As it happened, any accusatory glance from him would have been superfluous. Major Hilmi was wearing an accusatory glance enough for two, and he was pointing it straight at me.

'Because the incident did not happen on the train, unfortunately I have no power to stop it.' Genuine bitterness;

he really wanted to stop the train. 'So the station master will ensure the necessary proceedings at the scene and I must continue my investigation as we travel.' He half-turned his head towards the conductor, lurking behind his shoulder. 'You were on the platform at Çerkezköy, conductor?'

'Of course, Major.'

Hilmi spoke in the tone of a man seeking confirmation, or a reminder; he knew where he was going right enough. His gaze came round to his audience again. 'Who left the train during our stop?'

And hey presto, Harry's for the hangman.

'I did', I said.

I couldn't change the facts, but I could try to change the tone of their discussion. 'Don't know if anyone else did,' - I glanced towards the conductor, who was looking pretty uncomfortable - 'must be impossible to be certain in the darkness. But I certainly did. Got off to - pardon me, ladies - relieve myself and get a bit of air.' I looked thoughtful. 'We bumped into your man, there on the platform, right enough. Didn't we?' This last to the conductor again. 'I, ah, wandered a little way off, and I didn't see him after that. You see where he went?' The conductor shook his head. The conductor liked murders and official enquiries in the dining car and fitting up English travellers about as much as I did. 'Minute or so later I was back on the train. Saw a couple of other chaps at that point, though I don't know if they were getting off.'

Major Hilmi made to speak again, but I jumped in. He was going to point out - fairly enough - that the real duration of my minute or so was impossible to verify. My last line of defence had to be that he couldn't actually prove I'd done anything; but I didn't want to go there yet. And I wasn't sure how strong they held to the golden thread of presumed innocence in Turkish military law. 'You must have investigated thoroughly, Major.' I was pretty sure he hadn't, but now the boot was on the other foot and he had to lie or admit the fact. 'How many open entrances were there between the station area and the outside?'

'I doubt-'

'I'm sure you're right. Impossible to be certain. Anyone could have... Grim business. Tough one for the authorities there, I imagine.'

He wasn't being deterred. 'I saw no one else. It is almost certain that the killer is on this train.' He looked around the carriage again, remembering his pose of fairness. 'Now then, I ask you all please to tell me: who has a gun?'

I sat quiet, and then like everyone else looked around to see who might own up.

'I do.'

It was one of the others on Quinn's table, a chap I'd spoken to only briefly: a Scottish engineer who'd been working on a dam in Syria or something. 'A pistol.' He saw the silence around him, and then the uncertainty on Hilmi's face - the Major's frame-up had gone suddenly askew - and felt he needed to say more. 'Sometimes handy out in the desert.'

'And I have a rifle, Major.' It was Khan. 'Though I can assure you I am used to potting bigger game than Turkish policemen.' The arrogance was beautifully done.

Hilmi nodded, as if seriously considering whether this bizarre story had room for an Indian nobleman conceiving a desire to go hunting Turks in the small hours.

Again he looked around, and came back to me.

'I think - do you have a pistol, Sir Delamere?'

'Me?'

'I think you have a pistol, don't you?'

Only because you've tossed my cabin, you toe-rag. 'I do own a pistol, Major, yes.' He smiled faintly. 'I assumed you meant on this train.' He stopped smiling.

'You don't have a pistol on the train?'

I shook my head.

'I thought you had a pistol.'

And why would you think that, Major? Another shake of

the head. Regretful; sorry I couldn't oblige.

If it came to it, I could claim extreme forgetfulness or the Englishman's eternal right to lie to foreigners, and try the consequences. For now I wasn't ready to jump into his noose.

He just stared at me. I stared back.

He surely hadn't proved enough to be able credibly to demand to search my cabin, and he'd provoke a riot trying to search everyone's. And he had to worry that he might not find my Webley a second time, and then he'd be worse off.

I was damned if I was going to give in to him. And I might, actually, be damned. While we were still on Turkish soil he might well feel he could drag me off the train on suspicion, and I'd never see Piccadilly again.

I kept watching his face. He was in control of himself, I give him that.

Another faint smile, and a nod. 'Very well', he said. 'I shall continue my investigations.' He was comfortable again, and that was worrying.

13.

That ended the formal bit of the proceedings, and most of the passengers went back to their breakfasts - or at least to chattering among themselves about the peculiar developments. The stewards snapped back to their rhythms of table service.

I stood, and took advantage of the conductor and one or two others standing nearby, and launched a sub-committee of the main debate. 'Very disturbing business this, Major', I said. My voice was sincere, concerned - and loud enough to be heard by at least two tables. There was some benefit in keeping Major Hilmi off balance, and in maintaining my pose of innocence and co-operation for the other passengers.

I was innocent, of course.

Of some things. Not everything I'd said had been a lie.

I was starting to lose track.

Uneasily, Hilmi stepped forwards into the conversation as I continued. 'And damned odd: I mean to say, no one hearing the shot.'

In the background, the more significant benefit of my conversation stood discreetly from his table and slipped out of the dining car: while I kept the Major's attention away from the exit, Quinn was off to ensure that I really didn't have a pistol in my possession.

'Perhaps people heard a shot but thought it was something else.' Long American vowels.

'Good point', I said. 'Door slamming, or two buffers knocking together. Yes. Still, Major: very odd.'

Odd? The whole business was cock-eyed in the extreme. Either the soldier had been potted long distance, by the mysteriously silent shot, and conveniently fallen into the storeroom, or he'd let his killer get close enough to do the deed without making any sound of alarm; if the gun had been right against him, the noise might have been a bit muffled. Whether or not you believed my story of what I was doing in the time, I was surely right that there hadn't been a lot of it for Hilmi to be sending his messages, hunting his murdered comrade, alerting people then getting back onto the train. Then no argument with the conductor, no delay for investigation or debate, just pull the whistle and off we go? Did Turkey really respect the Orient Express timetable so much?

If poor whatsisname was dead at all. We only had, I now realized, Major Hilmi's word for any of it.

The Major was saying something to the conductor about needing to have a preliminary report ready to telegraph to his superiors by the time the train reached some station farther up the line. A bit more of a crowd had gathered now: the Scottish engineer and the sour lump who'd jostled Quinn outside the privy during the night, and the two tables beside us were listening in.

'And what is this document?' The American woman again.

Hilmi glanced around quickly, another bit of classic stage business. 'It is a document of great political significance in Constantinople.' In his thin sharp voice, he made this sound like a devastating revelation. 'I may say no more.' He could hardly say any less. 'Indeed, the details are obscure even to me.' Which rather begged the question of how he expected to know when he'd found it.

He took a breath through that inquisitor's nose of his, and went on with the performance. 'By some secret dealing, the document came into the hands of the representative of a foreign power. My department observed the individual. One of the individuals, I should say, a crucial link in the chain. This' - again he looked around his audience, and he couldn't have been disappointed by their goggle-eyed attention - 'is how espionage works. He was observed in a garden near the Dolmabahçe. He was tracked entering and leaving the Pera Palace Hotel by different doors, in a failed attempt to throw off pursuit. He then visited the Bristol Hotel in a very secretive way.'

'Fascinating', I said. 'And very impressive to track the chap through one of the most crowded cities on earth.' A bit of flattery, and a bit of doubt; neat, I thought.

Hilmi smiled, just slightly. Behind him, I saw Quinn re-enter the dining compartment, mission accomplished. 'The courier was distinctive, especially in Constantinople. A young western European man: pale hair, pale skin, pale moustache.'

'And you saw him coming to the station?'

There was a rare glimpse of hesitation. 'He was not seen arriving at the station. Some subterfuge, no doubt.' He made it sound very unfair. 'But he was identified later at the station.'

Indeed, I thought; lying dead on a bench. The description was unmistakably my man.

'Extraordinary affair', I said, still trying to play the fascinated - and innocent - tourist. 'And rather challenging for you, I suppose.' The Major looked annoyed. 'He could have met thousands of people on the station, and one would never be sure.'

One would never be sure it was Harry Delamere, anyway, and that was all that concerned me. My point very neatly made, and from Hilmi's expression I could see it irritated him.

At which moment of triumph, the dear old Bishop said: 'Sounds rather like that chap you were with, Delamere, doesn't it?'

14.

I've strayed from good Christian teaching according to most of the menu options outlined in the Ten Commandments, but until that moment I don't think I'd ever had anything actively against the Church. Now I'd gleefully have turned Mohammedan or Satanist and made St Paul's into a nightclub.

The daft old sod was actually looking pleased about it; as if he'd said something helpful, or amusing. 'Funny coincidence, what?' Not as funny as me beating you to death with a large print version of the Old Testament, I was thinking. 'Even if it wasn't actually the man in question.'

Hilmi was triumphant. Up until that point, he'd not had anything clear on me. He was agin' me for some reason, had been from the off, but he'd had nothing definite to counter my pose of ignorance and innocence. Now he had all he could hope for: apparent corroboration for his suspicions, from a most trustworthy source.

The sharp little face screwed up into a smile, took in a satisfied breath, and let it out with equal relish. 'Now that', he said with heavy irony, 'is most curious. Surely, Sir Delamere, you told me you were not talking to a man at the station.'

'Quite right', I said. 'Because I wasn't.' I glanced at the Bishop. 'Fraid you're mistaken, sir. Easy enough in that scrum.'

He looked a little flustered. 'Well, I'm sure you're right of course. Could have sworn I...' I still had enough self-control not to look directly at the faces gathered round, but I could see they were all gazing at me. 'Where, though? Perhaps on the station, rather than in the train?'

I shook my head. 'Can't think where or how.' I couldn't, either. My pale companion had been as furtive as possible, and in the Constantinople crowds you'd have had to have been right on top of us and paying close attention to see anything you'd remember.

The Bishop settled back into silence. He'd probably spotted that I was wearing an expression last worn by Henry II when he put the mockers on Thomas à Becket, and he'd nothing to add. It didn't matter. Hilmi had all he needed, and he looked like the cat who'd got the cream as well as the spare key to the dairy. He was most comfortable. Now he had the crowd on his side, too. As long as we were on Turkish soil, he could come at me when he wanted.

I had to defuse this. Suspicion was fine, but I had to get back to being just another one of the passengers. 'It's certainly most confusing, Major', I said, sounding as confused as I could. 'And I don't see where it leaves us. Even though you didn't see your mysterious man meeting anyone, I presume it's possible the package or document or whatever is on the train. Presumably you have the authority to search us all - our compartments - you can search me, by all means - have us all up against the wall, search all of us' - I sensed the unease around me, as I'd intended; they didn't like that idea so much. In particular I saw the Greek archaeologist looking uncomfortable at the thought of Turkish hands rummaging around his precious artefact - 'and you're welcome. I'm sure we're all happy to co-operate. Not the ladies, of course, I trust.' A couple of murmurs sharing my concern. 'That's your right, no doubt. Bit old-fashioned, presumably; bit heavy-handed.'

For a moment, I saw he was thinking about it. The

complacency was replaced with calculation. I had him in the same bind as with the pistol. If he called my bluff he might not find anything, and that would weaken his credibility with the rest of the passengers.

Still he just smiled.

15.

Into the uneasy silence that followed, the conductor eventually murmured: 'Major, may the stewards finish serving breakfast now?'

And mercifully, Karim Bey, the big cheese in every sense, added: 'That seems most desirable.' He looked politely to the Major, and the Major pretended to think about it, but he wasn't going to disagree.

I made sure I wasn't the first to turn away. Just gave the Major a courteous nod, nothing to antagonize, and then went back to my table.

'Rum old place', I said to the Theotokis as I sat. 'Picturesque, of course, but…' He nodded anxiously. Trust a Greek to mistrust a Turk, especially when the Greek's carrying a rare archaeological artefact out of Turkey.

There was movement in the aisle as those who hadn't yet developed indigestion took their seats, and I was aware of a female form moving past. I'm no expert on ladies' costume - nor on wine labels - but this was very simple, conservative even, and very stylish; money as well as taste. I'd only glimpsed the woman's face - a relatively older, more distinguished kind of handsome - when I realized that my French neighbour had half-risen from his chair, and produced a little bow in her direction.

As he came back up he opened his mouth to speak, but she cut him off. 'No scandal, *chiot*, not before breakfast. Back in your kennel.' Deep, elegant French.

Junot's reaction was equally surprising. He made an even

more elaborate bow - not easy when half-trapped under a dining car table. And because he had attracted her attention, the rest of us at the table felt obliged to sort of stand and sort of bow too; we looked like a bunch of geriatrics who'd dropped a shilling. When she'd gone, Junot sat again, and smiled. But he glanced after her.

'Marvellous', he said. 'What a woman.' He leaned closer in beside me. 'Is it so strange, to fear what you admire?' Again the glance. 'Officially I must hate her, challenge her. But…'

'Excuse my ignorance, but..?'

'Of course; your pardon. That is *La Toute-Puissante* herself, Madame Marguerite Dewoitine.' I failed to give the impression I knew what he was talking about. 'The Queen - the Empress - of industry and of power.' He glanced at me. 'You understand the concept - politically I mean, not in the football - of the right wing? Well, if you go as far as you can go - yes? - in the right wing, and then you go out the window, down the path and over the fence, there perhaps you will find Madame; if she is feeling restrained that day.' Now I fancied I'd read the name. I don't follow politics and business in England, let alone France, but I must have tripped over a reference to her at some point. 'Should she have been a man, she would have been Premier most certainly, or a second Charlemagne. As it is, she has outlasted her husband - she may indeed have poisoned him, or, like the insects, devoured him whole after the act of love - and she rules his empire of commerce with… with subtle brilliance and extravagant success.' He was getting quite carried away, poor chap. 'She is richer than two Croesuses, and she has all of French politics in her hand.'

I managed not to turn and stare, but it was impressive. And I was struck by the diverse kinds of power that seemed to have gathered to share this train journey with me. Power, and of course threat.

'Good morning, my dear sir!' Talk of the devil; it was big Karim, the Turkish grandee, who'd been grilling me over supper. The walking stick strained as he leaned on it. 'Do you find clearer motives for your journey now? Or should we ask Major Hilmi, perhaps?' I smiled politely at this hilarity, and he was gone. When his bulk had passed down the aisle, like a freighter down the Suez Canal, he was followed by Sikander Ali Khan; Khan likewise looked at me as he passed, amusement and curiosity. And when he had passed it revealed the American woman, sitting a short distance away, just gazing at me in apparent fascination.

It was damn' tempting to jump from the train when no one was looking and make a run for it across country. But in the meantime, while I tried to come up with a good reason why not, I couldn't afford to look like I was hiding. I ordered a second helping of whatever the steward was offering - I didn't hear a word of what he was saying - and tried to seem relaxed.

It was another two hours before we reached the Turkish frontier, and they were among the more anxious I've ever spent. I forced myself to spend most of them in company, perched in the dining car talking nonsense to anyone who was bored enough to listen. In every face I fancied I saw curiosity, or suspicion. I'd concealed it, but the blasted document was still right in front of them: surely everyone could tell.

And all the time - every minute of those two hours - I was waiting, and wondering. When would Major Hilmi take it into his head to jump at me? Why hadn't he yet?

Was he waiting for some further evidence? Did he think I might incriminate myself more? Was he waiting for reinforcements at-

I caught myself. Realized I'd stopped paying attention to the chap opposite me - Swedish, I think, something to do with plants - and that my face alone was as incriminating as any Turkish officer could hope.

'Do beg your pardon', I said hastily. 'Miles away for a second. Thought I saw a giraffe. Barley, you say?'

'Delamere, my dear chap, I'm most frightfully sorry.' I

looked up into the Bishop's earnest face. 'Spoke without thinking - bit of an ass like that - and rather landed you in it.'

There were many things I could have said, none of them very Christian. Instead I forced out a laugh. 'Not at all! Funniest thing. Make a good story for me: time I almost got shot as a spy by the Turks! Perfectly natural mistake to make, and no skin off my nose at all. Please don't mention it.' Please, please, don't mention it.

The morning rumbled on like the train, through the empty spaces of European Turkey. Most of the passengers had drifted out after breakfast. I held out in the dining car. Most drifted back in again at some point; a morning cup of something, a bit of company.

At one point, Theotokis insisted on us having a whisky and soda. At eleven in the morning, for God's sake. I accepted jovially, and left mine untouched.

I felt the train slowing: felt it in the unnatural restraint in the wheels, saw the landscape passing more reluctantly. A few scattered buildings began to appear through the window, then more, and we slowed to a crawl.

I felt my stomach stiffening.

A threadbare little town rose around us. This was it. The last stop in Turkey.

Now, surely, Hilmi would make his move.

The train was creeping forwards with painful reluctance now, mirroring my own apprehension. A sudden break in the buildings around us and then, looking down through the window, I saw the end of a low-level platform. It oozed past the window, and the brakes screeched as a station building appeared.

KAPIKULE, the sign read. We came to a complete stop.

Major Hilmi, I realized, had disappeared.

16.

The platform was empty. No uniforms. No shouts.

Still no Major Hilmi.

Two tables away, I caught Quinn's eye. He looked worried.

Quinn almost never looks worried. I realized he was reflecting my expression. He stood, and wandered out of the dining car, no doubt for a recce.

I badly wanted to move too. I was right on the point of saying to my companions that I'd take a stroll on the platform, when I realized they would immediately wonder who I was going to murder this time. I stayed put, teeth gritted, pretending to listen to Sweden.

We waited. Still no uniforms, no shouts, no Hilmi.

Somewhere, a door slammed.

We waited. An age passed. Some sensible part of my mind recognized that there were probably formalities for the train staff to complete, at this last stop.

We waited.

And then - strangely, for I hadn't been arrested - the train whistled, and whistled again, and the locomotive began to thump into life again and we were moving.

We didn't get far. Several hundred yards, at the same agonising crawl. This took us five minutes.

We stopped again.

The town had fallen away behind us. To our left, through the window nearest me, I could see a river. This might form part of the border. Through the opposite windows I could see bare ground, and a couple of huts fifty yards off.

The conductor came in from the corridor. 'Ladies and gentlemen,' he said, 'we are approaching the border with Bulgaria. For those of you who are not familiar, I should explain that we must change locomotives here, to a Bulgarian engine which will take us onwards for the next part of our journey. The train doors remain locked while we are in transit through the border zone.'

It seemed pretty unlikely. In that moment I caught a movement in the doorway behind the conductor, and I fancied it was Hilmi. Then he was gone again. Did they really change locomotives at the border? I glanced at my companions, and they seemed untroubled.

'Always a little tedious, this arrangement', my French friend said. 'Not so much of the romance, yes?'

'I might advise you to remain seated', the conductor said. 'The uncoupling and coupling of the wagons may perhaps derange you slightly.' I was feeling like I'd been deranged already about as much as I could stick.

A pause. Then from somewhere ahead there was a clanking, and we heard the train whistle and then the thumping of the engine, but we weren't moving.

Our locomotive appeared in the opposite window, lumbering slowly backwards on a parallel track.

It disappeared as it had appeared, away back into Turkey.

Now our train had no power. It was only a few carriages, alone on this isolated stretch of Turkish railway line.

In the lull between derangements, the stewards hurried along the aisle refilling coffee cups. They only filled them halfway, and even in my distraction I noted this practised good sense: no spillages on the Orient Express.

I heard a shot.

17.

Perhaps only I heard the shot. I can't think anyone else was so high-strung as I was in that moment, so alert to trouble.

Everyone heard the second shot, and even if they didn't hear the shot they heard the instantaneous shattering of glass.

Lots of things started to happen at once.

Someone screamed, perhaps more than one; shock as

much as fear.

Another shot. 'Heads down!' I called out.

'Bandits!' That was Hilmi. More shots. Again glass smashing somewhere along the train.

I started to rise from my chair, looking for the vantage point, and dropped back immediately at the sight of an enormous Sikh bearing down on me. Mahan Singh was racing along the aisle and no one was going to stop him. A couple of indecisive bodies were simply barged aside, and then he had Sikander Ali by the shoulders and was pushing him back down and into a corner. I saw Hilmi faffing near the door, and the conductor crouching nearby. Khan snapped an instruction, and Singh was hesitating, obedience versus bodyguard's instinct. I saw the young English woman lifting her head and peering towards the window. I rose again, and this time the big Sikh did knock me as he thundered past.

I lunged across the aisle and wrapped an arm around the English girl and pulled her away from the window and round and down. She gasped and stared at me. 'Glass in the face is almost as bad as a bullet', I said. 'Safety today, adventure tomorrow, eh?' She nodded uncertainly, and stayed down.

I immediately ignored my own advice and stuck my head over the level of the window sills. A stone's throw away I could see half a dozen figures. They were moving towards us, some with rifles up. The shots were coming irregularly, but they were coming.

'Conductor!' I seemed to be doing all the shouting; unhealthy busybody instinct of the junior officer.

'Monsieur?'

'This end of the carriage - the kitchen, yes? Does it have a door to the outside?'

'A loading door, and the carriage end, but they should be locked.'

'Go and make sure. Locked and blocked, please.' He nodded and was gone.

'Bandits!' Hilmi said again. Assuming it wasn't a Bulgarian

invasion or the local branch of the anti-railway league, this was damn' obvious. 'Often they attack travellers in this region, but I have never-'

I didn't have to listen to what he had never, because the conductor had shuffled back to report. 'So this end of the dining car is secure?' I said. 'No other ways in or out, dead end?' He nodded. 'Then this is our redoubt. Ask the stewards to bring out any boxes of supplies; we may need a barricade.' And off he went. He was looking a little unhappy at the idea of his beloved train being treated as a battlefield, but he was calm and disciplined and sensible and in that mad moment I was very glad of it. I guess he hadn't been picked out entirely by accident to run the most valuable train in Europe across its most dangerous terrain.

In a moment he was back again. 'Now look around the compartment', I said. 'How many passengers are missing?' He started to glance around rather wildly, and I caught his arm. 'Do it slowly, monsieur, and do it once only.'

One passenger was no longer missing. The door from the corridor smashed inwards, and I doubt Mahan Singh even noticed the obstruction. He had Miss Suraya wrapped tight against him, half hurrying and half carried. We were used to his single-mindedness now and the aisle cleared and the girl was packed down safe with her father in the corner.

I risked another look out of the window. I could see perhaps a dozen figures now, moving slowly but definitely towards the train. They didn't seem to have uniforms: a mixture of rough costumes. Several had rifles, and I thought I saw I couple of pistols.

Through the opposite windows, towards the river, I couldn't see anyone.

Two stewards were scurrying along the aisle with boxes and large tins of food. A couple of passengers got the point and joined the effort. I took a box off one of them and showed him to put it on a table, against the window, as extra protection.

'Nine are missing, Monsieur', the conducted murmured. That's why you pay top dollar for the Orient Express; all the courtesies, even in a gunfight. 'Two of the First Class, and seven of the Second Class.'

'The passengers must all return to their compartments!' Hilmi, crouching nearby. 'Lock themselves in.'

'No', I said. 'They shouldn't. Quinn!'

'On my way, sir.'

'Scottish chap, where are you?'

A figure turned from where he'd been helping a steward stow boxes by the bar. 'You rang, English chap? It's Craig, by the way.'

'Delighted. Your pistol easy to get, Mr Craig?'

'Easy it is. I'll go along with your lad; lend a hand.' He scrambled away after Quinn.

Sikander Ali Khan had asked the conductor, and the conductor was saying that the baggage wagon was locked and couldn't be reached from inside the train. So that was his hunting rifle out. On the upside, I turned round to find Madame Dewoitine pulling a small pistol out from her handbag.

Hilmi saw it too. 'Madame, you did not mention that you have a pistol!'

'Why should I have mentioned it?'

'But-'

'The sordid violence of Turkey is no concern of mine.' She was still looking at her pistol, not him. Now she glanced up, and saw his anger. 'I knew that you would accuse me of nothing, because if you did accuse me, of anything, I would send a single telegramme and your whole country would be bankrupt within an hour.'

For the first time, I saw Hilmi properly baffled. He didn't like it, but he knew he was far out of his depth. Then my attention was caught by the Bishop and the mysterious Valfierno hurrying in, rooted out and sent back by Quinn and Craig. And then beyond them, through the window:

movement. Some of the bandits were skirmishing closer to the First Class sleeping car, and I saw that they'd get to it before Quinn was back from the front end of the train, and he'd be cut off.

More shots. Some sounded different, closer. Craig was doing the sensible thing and keeping heads down as he and Quinn brought the stragglers in. I felt a hand on my arm. 'Sir Henry,' - even in these circumstances, Madame Marguerite Dewoitine felt no need to adjust her haughty murmur - 'should I give you my pistol?'

'I think you know how to use it, Madame, and are not afraid to.' She smiled coldly. The pistol was tiny. 'Do so, but only at very close range.' I hurried towards the corridor, ducking low. I'd the impression of a couple of blurred and anxious faces under the tables, and bodies crouching by the bar, and then I was wriggling through the door.

Again I risked looking above the window sill. A few of the bandits were hanging back, but one more lively sportsman was creeping towards the door at the far end of this carriage. I scrambled forwards, a clumsy lurch. The conductor had said the doors would all be locked, of course, but that couldn't slow them for long if they really - The chap outside turned the handle and it opened easily. I grabbed at the inside handle and wrenched it back and my anger gave me the advantage. In his surprise he lost hold and fell away. Another shot and the window shattered above me and a shower of glass fell around my head as I ducked.

'Here sir.' Quinn, close by.

'Hurry along, damnit!' I kept a desperate grip on the handle, but I knew it was pointless: they could get a stronger hold from outside, or they could come through the window or any of the other doors or just shoot me. 'Last omnibus leaving now.'

I heard shuffling and gasping behind me, Quinn shoving his charges along the corridor towards the dining car.

Then something pushed into my jacket pocket: my pistol,

back where it needed to be, and Quinn was saying 'Now sir, let-'

'Get them clear, man!' The door jerked outwards, and I clung on and swung it shut again.

We had a couple more seconds of tug-of-war and I was about to call it a day when a shadow loomed over and grabbed my shoulder. The bandit had opted for the window, and was using me to pull himself in. I tried to wriggle free, which didn't quite work, but as he fell on top of where I'd been his other hand brought down a knife.

We both came up at the same moment, and before I could pull my pistol he was jumping for me, knife high. I leaned into him. Stupid thing to do perhaps, but one doesn't always get these things right and I'd punched him in the face and grabbed his knife wrist with one hand and was scrabbling for his throat with the other.

We were frozen like that for a moment, staring at one another. I saw a little fellow, moustache, rough clothes. It helped that he was relatively small, because he had the only free hand between us and with it he was trying to punch and grab at me but he didn't have the reach to get much purchase. More shots from the dining car.

My man tried a kick. It didn't get home, but sent me off balance, and I almost lost his knife hand and he was lunging forward and then I had him by the throat again and drove him back against the wall. 'Delamere!' - a woman's voice in my ear, strong and clear - 'I'm here.'

An American accent. Insanely, it was actually reassuring. 'The pistol I told Hilmi I don't have:' I hissed; 'it's in my right hand pocket.' I felt her reaching under my arm and still my assailant was wriggling and struggling and kicking out at me.

I don't know what I thought she was going to do with the pistol. Threaten him with it, or perhaps- Instead she pushed it against his chest and shot him dead.

18.

The bandit went limp in my hands, and I dropped him. Then I was pushing the American along the corridor to the dining car.

We burst in a bit breathless, and a crowd of people was staring at us in alarm. Suppose they'd no idea who was coming. All the passengers and stewards were there now, huddling at the far end of the dining area or squeezed low in chairs and under tables.

Hilmi was crouching nearest, and half-rose when he saw us. In fact, what he first saw was the pistol in the American woman's hand.

She looked down at it, and then at him. 'This pistol I got off that bandit, Sir Harry:' she said; 'maybe you'd be better off with it.'

I took it. 'Mr Craig!' The Scotsman had been crouching at the window, and now he turned. 'How many rounds d'you have for your pistol?'

'Dozen or two. Grabbed what I could.'

Already our problem was clear. 'Excellent', I said, and he knew I was lying. 'As you are. A shot at the nearest man, no more than once in thirty seconds.'

He nodded. The problem was clear enough to him too. 'And if the bad man's climbing in the window?'

'You can punch him in the face and save a bullet.' He smiled, nodded, and turned back to his window. 'Major Hilmi-' I looked around for him.

He rose from his crouch by a table. 'I do not take orders from-'

'I very politely ask you then, to do the same as Mr Craig. Try to conserve-'

'I am in charge here!' He was properly angry, and I could understand why, but it really wasn't the time for diplomatic protocol. 'This is not your shooting party! What can you know of such a situation? Have you ever fought such a battle?'

'No more than half a dozen.'

'That is no proof of-'

'I'm alive, ain't I?' He stared at me. 'Do as you damn' well please, Major. Just stay out of my way. Quinn!'

'Sir.'

'Trenching party. This end, the exit into the corridor, block it completely. These boxes, anything else from the kitchen.'

I got the murmured 'aye' which was all he normally wasted on the formalities, and he'd already turned to his Sikh pal and beckoned to a couple of stewards.

A handful of shots from outside. 'Delamere!' Craig. 'They're having a go.' I could make out two or three figures scurrying towards the train. More shots and smashing and I ducked. Hoping that their reloading and volley-firing drills weren't too sophisticated, I popped up and found a pair of bandits a dozen yards off and fired. Craig was doing the same and I fancied I heard a cry. Then another fusillade and we were under cover again.

Silence. Slowly, I stuck one eye and then both above the parapet. Two men were dragging a third away. I could see a couple of rifle barrels beyond them, and then they saw me and let off another shot.

'Back to the occasional shots, please, Craig. No sense wasting rounds till they're closer.' He grunted understanding.

'Sir Harry. Do forgive my interrupting the sport.' Sikander Ali, of course. 'Might those of us without pistols do anything? I feel I've turned up to the dance and forgotten my trousers.'

'Kind of you, sir. Worst case, if Craig and I get overrun, you'll need to have Quinn and Mr Singh raid the cutlery drawer and lead a bayonet defence.'

'Jolly good.' He clapped me on the shoulder. 'Carry on then.'

'Where's Major Hilmi?'

'Not the foggiest. I think I saw him heading into the

kitchen area - checking the defences.'

'Quinn, how's Hadrian's Wall?'

'He'll do, sir.' The far end of the dining car leading to the First Class compartments was now a pile of boxes and food cans. 'Got a stool wedging some boxes against the door, so he'll not open easily.'

I lurched to Craig's side by the window. 'How's the scenery?'

'Suspiciously quiet.'

He was right. I could still make out at least one barrel from the line of cover forty yards away, but nothing more. I peered around towards the front of the train, and then tapped Craig on the arm and pointed. 'There.'

He saw. 'Oh yes. Little so-and-sos.' With our heads dangerously exposed, and peering back along the length of the train, we could see a handful of figures moving nearer along the trackside, approaching the back of the Second Class coach. I stretched my arm out and let off a blind shot, and I was still dragging it in when there was a reply from one of the rifles.

'Very occasional shots', I said. 'So they know we haven't gone to sleep. Otherwise no point wasting the brass.' I looked around, and saw a dishevelled French journalist huddled under a table. 'Junot, without exposing yourself too much, please keep a look out of the window on that side. Don't want too many surprises.' He nodded.

Crouching between two tables, I turned to the rest of the carriage. 'Ladies and gentlemen, here's the latest from the front. I've not seen more than a dozen of them, and I can't tell what exactly they are. Major Hilmi says bandits, and that's good enough for me.' I saw Hilmi now, crouched at a table halfway along, watchful. 'They're making for the other end of the train now, and we can't shoot at them without exposing ourselves dangerously, so I'm afraid they'll be able to have a go at our compartments.' I tried to produce a smile. 'But they don't seem to have the firepower or the tactics to get at us in here. Long as we don't waste our ammunition, we can keep them out.' I turned to the window. 'Safe enough, eh Mr Craig?'

From behind me, there was a scream.

19.

It wasn't the first time I'd been proved totally wrong that morning, but it was perhaps the most spectacular.

From the doorway to the kitchen area a bandit emerged, his pistol levelled at us.

The people crowded at that end of the compartment shrank away from him, lower to the ground, further into corners, back under tables. He stood still, slowly turning to and fro, pistol covering everyone in turn.

He looked just like the one I'd fought in the corridor: youngish, smallish, same rough mixture of clothes, same little moustache.

'Your guns:' he said, the English words slow and heavy; 'down!'

'Yes', I said, clear and firm. It was a message to the others as well as to him. Very slowly, I lifted my pistol, sideways, away from me, a very unthreatening slow arc. 'Very careful, Mr Craig. No trouble now.' I had to hope he was as smart as he seemed, that he wouldn't try anything fancy. The bandit looked nervy enough for anything, and a single shot in any direction could easily hit two or three people.

I kept my pistol on its slow journey, down towards the table. It was the centre of attention while I glanced quickly around the compartment.

As my pistol reached the table, my eyes met those of Madame Marguerite Dewoitine. Even hiding under a dining table from a gunman she seemed poised, at ease. Brilliantly, she was looking at me and not the bandit. As I let go my pistol on the table with a little thump, my eyes moved to her bag. Faintly, she nodded.

I took a slow step forwards. The bandit's pistol came up, and fixed on me. I raised my arms more obviously, to my shoulders. Nothing to see here. Shielded by her body, Madame Dewoitine had her hand inside her bag and was retrieving her pistol.

I hoped I wouldn't have to use it. No moral scruples, but that kind of jumpy close-quarters gunplay is a mug's game; people were bound to get hurt.

I needed him relaxed, unthreatened. I needed to know what he wanted.

Hilmi was staring at me in alarm, and at the gunman likewise. In that moment I knew he would try something stupid, that his pride would force him to defend his national honour. 'All right, Major?' I asked quietly. 'No trouble, eh?'

The bandit was still watching me. I smiled. 'How can we help?' I said, pleasant as I could. It wasn't a fatuous question. I needed him to feel that everything was going his way. And I really needed to know what he was after.

I glanced around my companions, the same big empty smile on my face. Everyone easy. It was vital that no one did anything sudden, anything reckless.

At which moment Miss Battersby lunged for his gun-hand.

20.

By rights, someone should have died in that moment.

Even if the bandit didn't shoot her, me, and everyone else in his anger, her action was guaranteed to produce an accidental shot. And an accidental shot in a dining car stuffed with better than thirty people couldn't miss.

She went for his gun-hand, and I didn't see what she hit it with. By some instinct or chance she hit upwards, and she hit hard. She was a sturdy unit, Miss Battersby, and not one to be held up by bandits lightly. The pistol fired and we all flinched and by a miracle the shot went into the roof.

All the calculations had changed and I had no time to scrabble for Madame Dewoitine's pistol and I could only leap forwards and hope to get at him while he was reacting. But I was far too far away, and his pistol was level again - and then the Bishop hit him over the head with a bottle. Yet again someone should have died - the trigger finger of a man who's been hit over the head is just as effective as normal and twice as unpredictable - but yet again we were lucky. He went staggering back and he was scrabbling for balance and his hand jarred against the doorway and he dropped the gun.

Well that was better. But when I rose again with Madame Dewoitine's pistol, the bandit had pulled out a knife and grabbed at the person nearest him and I had no clear shot. It was one of the Russian girls. He'd grabbed her by her jacket and was pulling her in and the knife was sweeping round to her throat.

Then she wasn't there. On some mad instinct of chivalry Sikander Ali had grabbed her by the shoulders and spun her away out of danger. In doing so, momentum meant that he was moving himself into it. The bandit clutched at his shirt-front and pushed him down against a table and the knife was high and about to plunge.

Everything froze: I was transfixed like everyone else, waiting for the death; Sikander Ali was trapped against the table and the bandit was poised above him.

He stayed poised, except that now he let out a ghastly noise. Half choke, half scream.

In the doorway last night, and intermittently through the restless hours that followed, I had speculated on what it would be like should Mahan Singh ever find cause to use that great cleaver of a knife. Now I knew. I may only be imagining that the tip of the blade actually appeared through the bandit's chest - the mind plays tricks on these occasions - but it was certain that the big Sikh was suddenly behind him and a hand had grabbed his shoulder and the knife was driven through his back. He made that ghastly noise, and perched there in that final ludicrous posture, and then he dropped dead to the floor.

Singh was immediately checking his chief, and Sikander Ali was brushing himself down, and I gave the Russian girl to Miss Battersby to look after and ordered Quinn to go and do a better job of blocking the door in the kitchen area.

Then there was silence. We were all a little stunned.

From behind us, we heard banging, from the First Class sleeping coach.

21.

And that was how it was for the next twenty minutes.

Quinn was back promptly from the kitchen to report that the door to the outside was well and truly blocked. If Quinn blocked a door it tended to stay blocked. And though we were all more on edge, what with the bandit's appearance and then ghastly death, we were secure enough in the barricaded dining car.

Our compartments were not. Even with occasional shots from Craig the bandits had been able to get to the front of the train, and then in. We were in no position to stop them having free run of the two sleeping wagons. Judging by the noise, they were making full use of it. They must have been going through our bags with great speed and violence, and apparently having a go at the fixtures and fittings as well.

Most of the time we huddled in silence. At first we were all apprehensive about another attack on our redoubt. Then we were all wondering what was happening to our kit.

Theotokis had his precious box cradled in his arms on his lap

At one point I said: 'Major, does this sort of thing happen often?'

He shrugged. Embarrassed, apparently. National honour, and all that. 'It is not unknown', he said. 'Especially here near the border, there is lawlessness.'

The poor conductor looked ghastly. He'd be offended if someone so much as scratched the paintwork of his beloved train, and now quite a few someones were shooting damn great holes in it and tearing up the compartments.

My own thoughts were a little different to those of my fellow-passengers. As well as wondering whether I'd be able to bill the British Government for shirts stolen by bandits while on His Majesty's service, I was speculating about the attack. Not unprecedented, said Hilmi. But the way I saw it, behind the gunplay and melodrama, what was actually happening was yet another ransacking of my compartment while I was in possession of the mysterious document.

Come to think of it, was I a fool for taking Miss Suraya's visit at face value? How much time had she had to go through my things before slipping off her dressing gown and climbing into my bunk?

The banging continued from along the train. Again I looked into the anxious faces of my comrades. How could the bandits know which was my compartment? Were they even targeting me, or were they taking the opportunity to look at all the passengers?

'I have a question', Junot said. 'The Turkish locomotive has left us. But where is the Bulgarian locomotive that should take us onwards?'

This was a very good question, and a couple of dozen faces were immediately interested. Humans being humans, several showed not only interest at the absence of the Bulgarian locomotive, but indignation.

'It should be one hundred metres ahead of us on this track.' The conductor. 'Usually, as soon as the Turkish locomotive has retired the new one comes to couple up with us and lead us out of the border zone and into Bulgaria.'

Then Craig's voice cut in, the Scottish accent sharp and

calm as usual. 'They're clearing out.' Now I noticed that there was no noise from the compartments. I moved to the window beside him. Sure enough, figures were dropping down from the carriage doorways and hurrying off, first along the track away from us and then scurrying into cover in the grass and uneven ground.

They didn't seem to be carrying much. A few small bags, and perhaps what could be stuffed into pockets. Lot of effort for a limited haul.

I turned back to face the Conductor. 'Where are the men who drive the locomotive? Waiting on it?'

'Perhaps, but it is not usual. There should be a controller, directing the movements, and these are quite precise, because of the border protocol. Usually the engine has been stopped ahead of us, with steam up, and the engine-driver and fireman wait until the controller allows them to return to it and come and collect our coaches.'

'So where are they then?'

The Conductor pointed at the rough grassland outside. 'There is a 'ut, over there.' I looked out of the window, and he scuttled over beside me. 'You see? To the left.'

I saw the two huts I'd seen earlier, fifty yards away across the empty ground. The left-hand one was a simple brick business: a closed door, and a blank window. 'That's literally a battlefield. And you're saying that the men we're relying on to get us out of here are stuck in the middle of it?'

He nodded.

'You really think they're in there?'

'Perhaps they were on the locomotive already, but that would not be according to protocol. Or perhaps they have been taken. Otherwise they should be there.'

'Assuming the new locomotive is just ahead of us, can you or anyone else on the train drive it?'

He shook his head.

I scowled into the Turkish morning. Or perhaps it was a halfway Bulgarian morning now. I drew my pistol, and let off a shot towards the concealed ground. Immediately there were a couple of shots in reply.

The bandits were still there, armed and watching and not finished with us. If they'd put on that show to try to get the document, they wouldn't give up just because they hadn't found it or its bearer in the compartments. If no one got the train moving, they could wait there until the biscuits ran out and we had to go and parley.

I looked across the ground to the little hut. It seemed an awfully long way away.

22.

Quinn and I crouched on the railway track, in the shadows between the First and Second Class carriages, contemplating the little hut.

It still seemed an awfully long way away.

I found myself gripping the rail in front of me. I felt the chill of the metal, perhaps trying to absorb some of its sharpness and strength.

Nice to be out in the fresh air, anyway.

The previous five minutes had been active but untroubled, certainly compared to what had preceded them and what seemed likely to follow. Against the objections of the Conductor, we'd smashed through one of the dining car windows facing away from the bandits, towards the river. The drop to the trackside had been a moment of alarm - would the bandits see us from the other side? were there any of them on this side after all? But we'd sat there against the wheels for a count of ten, peering intently along the river, left and right towards the back and front of the train, a count of twenty, and we hadn't got shot so that was a good start.

Then Mahan Singh had joined us. If I'd had to pick two men to have beside me in the pinch, the Cornishman and the Sikh would come high on the list. The two of them had beetled off to the luggage wagon, and I'd scrambled down to the river's edge. The slope meant I couldn't be seen from the other side of the train, and I'd worked my way forwards past the First and Second Class carriages, and then the open track beyond, and so to the new locomotive.

It was where the Conductor had said it would be, standing alone a hundred yards up the track, a trace of steam escaping the funnel. Also as the Conductor had said, the driver and fireman weren't there. He'd said it, and I could hardly complain when he turned out to know what he was talking about on his own railway. But a bit of luck would have made a nice change.

I'd scrambled back using the cover of the river bank until I came level with the dining car again, and rendezvous'd with Quinn and Singh. Then the former had given the latter a bunk up to the window, and that left the two of us out enjoying the scenery, and now here we were lurking under the train and gazing at the hut.

Unless we decided to take up permanent residence in a Balkan railway siding we needed a locomotive to pull us out. For that we needed the men to drive it. They were understandably reluctant to wander up of their own accord, what with the small battle that had developed around the train.

'All right, Sergeant', I said. 'Describe the ground.'

This was an old habit. Two sets of eyes discussing the terrain identify far more than one, and saying it out loud makes you pay closer attention.

'Aye sir. To our left, the track continues into Bulgaria. Working round from there, in the first quarter the ground's dropping away. Good cover there.' Quinn was in action, and following a good habit of action. In other words he was as calm as you could want, and about as happy as he ever gets.

'That's also the direction they approached the train from', I said. 'Suggests they know the ground there, and it gives good access to the rest of the field.'

'Aye. Nearer in, that quarter's pretty flat. Still a possibility

74

of a hole here and there; firing position.' His voice was slow. That was his nature, and the discipline of considering the ground bit by bit. 'Swinging round towards the hut. Looks flat enough, but I don't like this long grass.'

'Nor that crate.'

'Nor that crate, sir. Good firing position, but he might be a bit isolated.'

'He might. But from what I've seen these chaps aren't experts. Smart, but not trained.'

'No wonder we're doing so well, sir.'

'In your own time, sergeant.'

'Two huts. Opposition inside, or behind, or both?'

'Indeed.' I nodded. 'We'll want to come at our hut on the angle, so they haven't got too easy a pop from the window, and so the first hut blocks fire from the second. But that's taking us a bit close to the hidden ground to the left.'

He grunted. 'Round to the right the ground's rougher. Plenty of possibilities there. Another crate thirty yards away - and another beyond him.'

'I've definitely seen them firing from cover there. There's a ditch, I think.'

'Then round towards the back of the train - the dining car - and the track again. Building there, but he's too far off to worry about.'

I was considering the building. 'Horses there?' I glanced at Quinn. 'I'm wondering how they got here. Funny business, this lot.' He grunted agreement. 'Don't suppose you noticed if they were talking Bulgarian or Turkish.'

The Quinn smile. 'All Greek to me sir.'

'Might have helped to know which way they came, and so which way they're planning on leaving. Ah well.' Once more I scanned the ground in front of us, and once more I turned to the man beside me. 'I'm bored. Ready?'

Quinn nodded.

The Conductor had been right that the driver and the fireman weren't on their locomotive. Surely that made it likely he'd be right when he said they were in the hut.

Quinn whistled, once and shrill. Using the rail I launched myself forwards and up into a run.

23.

The whistle had put Craig on alert, and as soon as he saw me he started firing towards the bandits. Immediately there was rifle fire in response, crackling from the long grass ahead.

I knew Quinn was running close at my heels. I'd like to pretend this was my heroism or his deference, but actually it just made us a smaller target to the bad men ahead or the bad shots behind.

I angled left at first, running even farther away from the dining car. The brilliant theory was that Craig's pistol would both keep the bandits pinned down and distract them away from Quinn and me. It had seemed brilliant while I was discussing it with him, anyway, sitting safely back in the train. I still hadn't got shot; so far so good.

After ten yards I pulled out my pistol and held it ready, pointing wherever I was looking as I ran. Hopeless way of firing if you actually intend hitting something. But it looks impressive and makes the other chap think twice. We were looping round from the left towards the hut. My mind was still on the hiding places, and on the blur of the hut, and on trying to keep my balance on the rough ground.

Anyone who talks about their icy calculation on the battlefield, about time slowing down in the moment of crisis, all that stuff - they're lying. It's a madness of noise and movement and your brain can't process one tenth of what it's seeing and you have to hope that you've training enough to load your weapon and not shoot yourself in the foot, and otherwise you shoot at any shape you see and if that doesn't work you use the gun as a club or you punch and you keep on running. I don't pretend to be any kind of battlefield expert but, as I mentioned to Major Hilmi, I've survived a few.

A shape appeared to my left and I fired and still the ground was jolting and bumping beneath my boots. The shape disappeared, and there was another and I fired again and then he was gone too and now I was coming up on the crate we'd spotted. The grass was clutching at my feet as I ran, but I wasn't feeling the effort yet. I was watching the crate - it was so obvious a hide - but I knew I shouldn't get too focused and as I ran I glanced- A shape appeared over the crate and the Webley veered towards it and fired, and somehow the shape had gone and- 'Left!' Quinn's yell and I turned and I saw the rifle up and pointing and there was no way I'd aim and hit him in time but I had a go.

Then he was gone, punched sideways by a single shot and I was alive and still kicking over the rough ground. Amid the chaos, there was after all one expert shot on the field. Craig couldn't guarantee to hit anything with a pistol at that range; I might as well have been making funny faces at the bad men as shooting; and the opposition had had trouble enough hitting a four-carriage train. But to a man used to tracking and shooting a moving tiger from a moving elephant and a range of three hundred yards, killing a stationary bandit at less than fifty was no challenge at all. We'd recovered Sikander Ali Khan's very handsome hunting rifle from the luggage car and, with the implacable Singh helping him reload, he was having a gentle afternoon's sport as my guardian angel.

Quinn and I raced up to the hut on the line I'd planned. I let off one shot into the lock just in case and then launched myself bodily at the door.

I crashed through and I felt Quinn's arm on my shoulder adding his weight. Immediately there was a shot. But it was a shot aiming at a normal man, not at two men collapsed on the floor. 'Don't shoot!' I shouted. I put my hands up very obviously, pistol held unthreatening. 'I surrender, don't shoot.' We stood. Quinn's hands were also up.

These bandits all seemed cut along similar lines: slender
little chaps they were, natty moustaches and rag-bag clothing.
This one's face barely registered behind the barrel of the
pistol he was pointing at my head. I kept on looking harmless,
Webley held high and safe, and I edged away from the door.

The cannon of a pistol barrel followed me round, which
was what it was supposed to do though I can't say it felt so
clever in the moment. Very slowly, I moved the Webley
forwards and downwards, barrel still pointing the wrong way,
ready to hand it over. Then a noise from the side and the man
spun to it and started to react to the stool Quinn had kicked
at him and then my barrel was pointing the right way and the
man was dead.

Two men were sitting on a bench, behind a table with
some playing cards and the remains of a meal. Next to the
table a stove, with a pan of water beside it. By the door a line
of hooks, with coats and a couple of oil lamps. In one corner
a few tools stacked.

I looked back at the men.

I put on a big smile. They didn't go for it.

'You…' - I pointed to each of them - 'drive train?' With
my arms I made piston motions.

Uncertainly - I grant it hadn't been brilliant miming - they
nodded.

Trying the smile again, I raised a finger and beckoned
them, and pointed out towards the train.

They were more certain this time. They shook their heads.

As if to prove their point, there was a new flurry of shots
from outside.

I dropped the smile, and nodded grimly.

They shook their heads with new energy. This time I
raised the Webley, and beckoned again. They weren't to know
the pistol was out of bullets; and my finger was pretty
ominous. 'Every rifle in the place is going to be pointing at
this doorway', I said over my shoulder. 'Not sure what we can
do about that.' But when I turned, Quinn had the two oil

lamps down and was lighting them.

There were a couple of shots in our direction when Quinn's arm appeared through the window and threw the lamps, one after another, onto the nearby grass. Yet the lamps smashed satisfactorily and the grass was dry enough to catch fire quickly. The shooting increased, but the bandits were even less sure what they were looking at now and any of them who stuck his head out too far was likely to get it shot off by Sikander Ali. We gave it half a minute. Then, with flames and smoke billowing around us, and each dragging a Bulgarian railway worker by the scruff of the neck, we launched ourselves out into that arena of noise.

24.

I don't know how you feel about Bulgaria. Personally, until that day I'd not given it much thought. Take it or leave it.

But on that mad morning, I'd never been as glad to cross a border into a place; and you can tell Tsar Ferdinand I said so. No Israelite set foot in the Promised Land with as much relief as I felt when the train inched out of Turkey and gave a little whistle to mark the achievement. The Israelites had been on the road longer, as I recall, and had had their difficulties; but they had more help than I did.

The last leg was the easiest. I think the bandits had more or less given up by that point. Sikander Ali had bagged a handful with his hunting rifle, and the rest were keeping their heads down or wondering how briskly Quinn's little bush fire was going to reach them. Once we were out in the open the Bulgarian driver and engineer had discovered their running feet pretty smartly, and we made the safety of the train in one short dash. I don't say they were exactly grateful, but when we'd got them to their locomotive they needed no persuading to get it moving. They needed a bit of persuading to edge backwards the hundred yards necessary to couple the rest of the train on, instead of escaping forwards immediately. But it was done efficiently enough. The shooting had died away now, and we covered the last few yards out of Turkey in relative serenity, and it almost felt normal. Except for the shattered glass and splintered wood, and the utter chaos of our compartments.

I was also calculating that Major Hilmi would be less of a problem, now we were off his turf; less able to throw his weight around on foreign soil. He looked rather forlorn, poor chap, as we left the homeland behind.

As we crossed - a couple of stone posts with flags painted on them marked the spot - everyone glanced at each other and then the conductor for confirmation, and he nodded, and there were a few muted cheers. Then we all hurried to our compartments. Fortunately I'd only had the two bags, and nothing in them worth pinching. Both had been emptied over the bed and floor. The bed linen had been ripped off and the mattress slashed. The little cupboard doors were open, and various scuffs and dents showed where they tested the solidity of something with a kick.

They weren't just looking for valuables: they were looking for something in particular. Instinctively I patted my lapel, ran my thumb under it. Originally the document had been inside an envelope, marked 'MOST SECRET' in the typically fatuous government way. Reckoning by feel that the paper itself had a wax seal on it, I'd taken it out of the envelope and tossed that from the window at the earliest opportunity. The paper was no more than regulation letter-writing size, folded to a third and sealed. Now it had been folded again and pinned firmly under my lapel, and that had been unobtrusively pinned against the coat. It could easily be transferred between jackets.

It took me ten seconds to register the damage to the compartment and I didn't waste any more. A moment later I was crouching by the body of the dead bandit, my wrestling partner - until my charming American acquaintance had shot him. He was still wearing the surprised look.

Contrary to what you get in the music halls and the novels, the average bandit is never dapper: the waxed and twirly moustache, the tasselled boots, the elegant swordplay and the witty quips, forget all that guff. I've bumped into a few in my time - generally not by choice, but there have been a couple of more social occasions and I once got a good dinner off a gang of Albanian cut-throats - and bandits tend to be the roughest, poorest, most broken and stinking men you can find.

Which made this chap a bit of a surprise. The moustache wasn't waxed and twirly, but it had been trimmed in the last couple of days, and he'd had a shave too. The boots were without tassels, but they were of adequate quality and in good nick. The clothes were an odd mix, but clean enough at first glance. I had a rummage through his pockets - sordid business, but I was curious, and apparently we'd given up on the Queensberry rules a while back. A fair bit of Turkish money, which I left - I wasn't planning on going back any time soon, not after the recent nonsense - and an identity paper in the name of Yıldırım Akbulut. That I pocketed, in case I was ever on speaking terms with Major Hilmi and it was worth pursuing.

We pulled into the first Bulgarian station like survivors from a shipwreck. As the train slowed to a stop, I saw the officials waiting on the platform, their faces passing one after another. Each pair of eyes widened, in confusion and then surprise and then shock, as they took in the smashed windows and the bullet holes and the general devastation.

The conductor had to explain it all while we waited on the train. I gathered from the expressions of the Bulgarian policemen that he gave it the full dramatic effect. Then there was much sombre shaking of heads. Clearly, this was what one had to expect, if one was rash enough to visit Turkey. A bit rich, given that our attackers could as easily have been

Bulgarian, but I guess they were entitled. I think Hilmi got a pretty robust interrogation, and quite right too.

The conductor hurried off to telegraph ahead, and the police came on and checked all our papers. Most of us passed the time trying to restore order in our battered compartments. And then, thank God, we were moving again and it was time for lunch.

I found myself sitting alone, which I was glad of. The other tables filled. Then someone stopped in front of me. I looked up.

Sikander Ali: he sat opposite me.

'Delamere…', he said. It was the voice doctors use when they're giving bad news. His eyes locked on mine. 'I like to think that we respect each other too much for me to ask you a question that would force either an uncomfortable truth or a lie.' He glanced around briefly. 'And I'm not really here on behalf of your fellow passengers, but I suspect that I'm speaking what's in all their minds.'

He hesitated, struggling for the right way to phrase it. I stayed silent. I owed him that, at least.

'I suspect the nub of the thing is this', he said. 'I rather fancy we're all wondering if there's going to be any more of that sort of tomfoolery. I mean to say, one travels to see the world and see life and so on, but I'm not sure one likes to be shot up before luncheon. Not to mention all the interrogations.' He leaned forwards. 'The thing is, my dear chap, that it's hard to escape the impression that you're at the root of all the trouble.'

25.

'I thank you for your delicacy', I said, and I meant it. 'Very truthfully: I have no idea what's going on.'

I meant that too.

'Obviously there's something badly wrong,' I went on,

'and yes: somehow I seem to have been caught up in it. But God knows what or how.'

He was a good chap, and I didn't really want to lie, not too much.

'Well, there we are', he said, and smiled and sat back and called to the steward. And with that, the atmosphere of the whole dining car seemed to lighten. Despite the fact that a couple of the windows were still smashed, and so we were all wearing coats and feeling pretty chilly.

I ought to have been a bit offended. I mean to say, a thank you or two wouldn't have been out of place, given that I was the one who'd been wrestling bandits and rooting out Bulgarian locomotive drivers to whisk us to safety. But he did have a point: I had the strong suspicion that all of the madness was for my benefit. Everything suggested that the melodrama was focused on the document I was carrying, and that meant I'd put all of their lives in danger.

This line of thought was broken by the awareness of two frocks pausing beside our table. I looked up to see the Russian pair. 'Your pardon, Excellency', one of them said to Sikander Ali; a blonde girl. 'I thank you for your brave action. You rescue my life.' He had risen immediately - that's a gentleman for you; his ancestors had been demi-gods when hers were barely human, and still his courtesy was instinctive - and gave a little bow of the head.

'Neither title nor thanks are necessary', he said. 'I do hope all that kerfuffle doesn't give you the jitters.' She didn't know what these were, but smiled anyway. Then - sportsman as well as gentleman - he suggested they joined us for lunch. 'A man of my great age is surely not dangerous company for a young lady, and Sir Henry has eyes only for the Turkish police.'

They didn't look like they believed any of it, but accepted politely, and Sikander Ali shuffled round to my side as they settled opposite us.

I've not been in Russia much. From the papers, you get the impression of an over-elaborate aristocracy - desperately complicated pecking-order for who sits where at the theatre and whom one doesn't speak to before teatime - bedevilled by bands of bearded bomb-throwing anarchists. These two didn't seem to fit either mould. Just a regular couple of girls, out to see the world. Oksana - and don't ask me her surname; if that train journey taught me one thing, it's to appreciate a world of Smiths and Joneses and Browns - was the one the Prince had wrestled away from the bandit, the blonde one, and a real traffic-stopper. She had very blue eyes, and the sharp high cheek bones that you seem to find more often among the Slavs; and she was relatively the chattier of the two. Her companion - Mariam - was darker in all respects: black hair and brown eyes and more guarded. I had the uncomfortable sense that she was studying me as much as I her.

They looked to be in their late twenties. They were off to Paris for a year. There was an aunt with money, somewhere, and that was paying for the adventure. Some suggestion of studying - music, perhaps, or art - but the plans were vague. Most of this from the lovely Oksana, her words and voice measured and matter-of-fact. Their plans might have seemed a bit flighty, but they themselves were not: the outfits were plain, sensible, even dowdy; and they spoke with a briskness to match.

'You, Mr Sir Henry,' dark Mariam said suddenly; 'why do Turks chase you?'

I tried to keep up the jovial ignorance; half of it wasn't too much of a stretch. 'No idea', I said. 'Strange business. I've really nothing to do with politics.'

She gave this more consideration than I was comfortable with. 'I think there must be more.' She glanced at my clothes. 'You are not only English person. You are not so different in class from most others on train. Are you very rich?' I shook my head sadly. 'Have you very bad reputation?'

'Well...' She was watching me closely. 'I still don't see why they have to fix on me.'

'They are empire without elite. Luxury without beauty. Like old man who walks only on stick, or building held up with scaffolds, they only have structures and procedures of bureaucracy to hold them. The material - the flesh' - she prodded herself in the chest - 'it has rotted.'

Her friend murmured something to her, not in English, and for the first time there was the suggestion of a smile on Mariam's face. 'Excuse please. Too much honesty from me, this is my sin.'

'It's the rarest of the sins', I said. 'Especially on this train.' I liked her, for that private smile as much as for the honesty. I wondered how honest it really was. 'Did you spend much time in Constantinople? You've obviously thought about it.'

She shrugged. 'Not so much. We did what good tourist should do. Character of empire you see in policeman, in waiter, in landlady, as much as in national strategy.'

And then she pretty much shut up shop again. The other one, Oksana, started to talk soberly about new constitutions and new governments.

Lunch passed in that fashion: a bit of bright chat from Sikander Ali, a bit of politics from Oksana, and me watching Mariam watching everyone. I'd just knocked back the miniature coffee with undiplomatic speed, when I heard a little cough.

It was the younger Englishwoman, Miss... Froy. First name Winifred; I wondered at the grandmother or similarly ancient ancestor who'd cursed her with it.

'I wanted to thank you, Sir Henry', she said. 'I think you saved my life when you pulled me away from the window.'

Pleasant, like I said. I was about to insist she should drop the Sir-ing and call me Harry, but I could see that Miss Battersby wouldn't like that. 'Please don't mention it', I said. 'Really. Always a bit of a flap, skirmish like that. Forget it. I just hope the rest of your journey is less eventful.'

She nodded, but I could see she was doubtful.

26.

I'd had God knew how many hours of being polite to people, only relieved by a brief gunfight, and I'd surely earned a few minutes to myself. I found a nice spot by one of the smashed windows, where it was too blowy for anyone to want to stand. I stood there and enjoyed the wind on my face, and a thoughtful cigarette.

I say thoughtful. I was happy enough in the silence and the fresh air, but I can't say I produced any new ideas. I'd survived a night and a morning, which on this train seemed an achievement. But I was still hunted, and still pretty rattled by the lurking sense that half the train was scrutinizing me.

This bit of Bulgaria was endless forest, with occasional glimpses of low mountains blue in the distance. The monotony of trees rushing past the window was happily mindless, but reinforced the sense of confinement.

When I turned away from the window at last, I found the American woman sitting two yards away on one of the luxuriant bench-seats, just watching me.

We gazed at each other a moment.

'I didn't want to intrude', she said. 'You were doing the solitary thinking again.'

'Not a charming habit.'

'Get anywhere?'

'I never do. But failing to think is more socially acceptable than failing to make small talk.'

I still felt I was being considered, evaluated. 'The journey's hardly begun. You can't jump off until you've won or you've lost.'

'And if - may I?' - she accepted me at the other end of her bench seat - 'if I don't know what game I'm playing, how will I know when I've won or lost?'

Her head tilted slightly, and then she shook it. 'You're not a man who quits. If you're not dead, you've not lost. And if you don't mind breaking a rule or two…'

'Never. I make up my own rules, instead.' She nodded. 'Speaking of which, is it time for that drink you offered?' Miraculously - for normally these moments are ruined by the waiter's absence, unless I'm telling a joke in which case I can't keep him away - the steward was immediately with us, and almost as immediately he was opening a bottle of the Gosset '98.

I offered my glass in salute, and my hand. 'Harry Delamere.'

Hers was a brief handshake, but firm. 'Peg Madison.'

'Peg? Short for..?'

'Choice.'

I nodded. 'And tell me, Miss Madison, what game are you playing?'

She took a sip of the champagne. 'My own.'

'Is it difficult?'

'Fiendish. But I cheat.'

'Thank you for saving my life earlier. Shooting that chap was... decisive, and bold, and I'm grateful.'

She shrugged. 'This kind of thing isn't so rare on American trains. Like you told your Turkish friend, I don't say I'm an expert, but I've survived.'

We sipped our wine companionably, and I watched her. She was handsome enough that this was no hardship - she had the resolute jaw that seems more common across the Atlantic, and lovely green eyes. Her hair, whatever it was like, was tucked out of the way somewhere, which was unconventional. And again I was struck by her outfit, a kind of practical elegance; European women are supposed to seem, not do.

And I own I was interested. The greater liberty and licence of American women is a cliché, and in that sense she was as clichéd as a chap could wish; but there was also a rare reserve, a self-control. She was one of the very few people I'd met on the train who kept themself to themself.

She raised an eyebrow at my obvious scrutiny. 'I was just

thinking,' I said, 'that you're about the only person here who hasn't started telling me things about me.'

'Well you tell, then.' She took another sip of wine, and then leant sideways a fraction, so her face appeared as if from hiding behind the glass. 'Are you carrying this mysterious secret document of theirs?'

It stopped me dead. For the first time someone had asked me the direct simple question, and it was so direct and simple that I very nearly said yes.

I managed to convert my surprise into mild affront at the outrageous suggestion, and added a laugh for dramatic effect. 'Yes', I said. 'I have it sewn into the lining of my hat.'

Another sip. She shook her head. 'No. Not in your hat.'

'You've checked?'

'Not your style. Too obviously the discreet English gentleman.' The last words were heavy with irony.

'And apparently I'm not that?'

'Oh, you're English all right. But not in any of the obvious ways. All that stuff you're doing, "terribly sorry old chaps" and poking people with your umbrella, that's all for show. And that means you're much more discreet.'

'And much less a gentleman?'

She smiled, and considered me. 'We'll see.'

I hesitated as someone walked past us and into the corridor. 'I'm beginning to wish', I said, 'that I did have their damn' paper. I think it would make everyone much happier.'

'Better to keep up the mystery: it's a long train ride.'

'What do you think it really is, anyway? The document.' I don't say I was comfortable with her conversation, however charming she was; but I didn't want to be too obvious about steering it onto neutral ground.

She shrugged slightly. 'Important letter between Emperors? New map of somewhere? Some big scandal - international intrigue - blackmail - the secret that could bring down the Sultan, that kind of thing?' It was flippant, but her voice had lost its playfulness.

'Now I definitely wish I had it.'

'I interviewed half a dozen people in Constantinople. I got the impression each one was in a different faction, and no one was saying which.'

'Interviewed?'

'I write some. A couple of journals back in the States. Mainly it gives focus to a place. Better than looking at paintings and fountains and what-not.'

I remembered something. 'And the case you were carrying: a portable camera.'

'You noticed it, huh?'

'Eventually.'

She nodded. Curious: serious things she discussed flirtatiously; flirtation made her serious. 'Hobby', she said.

Her eyes shifted over my shoulder. 'Pardon me sir', she said, a little louder, to whoever was there. 'Mr Karim, is it?'

I looked round. It was indeed. He was wedged a few tables away, waiting for the staff to come and refloat him. He beamed at her. 'Dear lady?'

'A couple of ignorant foreigners are curious about this paper that the Major is looking for. What do you think it is?'

He glanced to and fro between us a couple of times. Bland charm to Miss Madison; open scepticism to me. 'Usually,' he said, opening two heavy hands, 'it is the ignorant foreigners who know more than the poor Turks.'

We weren't buying that. We waited.

'For decades now,' he said eventually, 'my poor country has been the pawn of all of the European powers. If they say "jump", we jump.' It conjured an unlikely picture. 'If they say "buy", we buy. If they say "sign", we sign.' Still we waited. 'The powers are fighting their battles of empire, over the carcass of my empire. At any moment, one of them may have fractionally greater influence, just one dirhem in the scale, and we must pledge ourselves, in blood and in ink.' He shrugged, a great ripple across the body. A picture of innocence, he gazed at Madison. 'I honestly could not say, dear lady.'

I bet you couldn't, I thought. Especially if you knew, you could not say.

27.

Mid-afternoon we pulled into Plovdiv. One of those names it's fun to say. In what I assume was a regular habit, Miss Battersby nodded at their guidebook, and Miss Froy read out a couple of details.

We usually got at least a few minutes at each station, and I went to get a bit of air and stretch my legs on the platform. As I came out of the dining compartment and reached the carriage door, a figure was climbing up into it.

So her face was suddenly very close to mine: very dark eyes, very dark hair, very beautiful. I thought yet again of the attractions of Bulgaria over Turkey. She looked at me longer than she was supposed to, and I stood in her way longer than I was supposed to, and then I was stepping courteously aside and the moment had gone, and that's how life passes and dreams are kindled. I watched her walk away down the corridor a few paces, then turned away.

Again I was blocked by someone climbing up into the carriage. A man. Again I stepped aside, this time without the preliminaries.

In fairness, I suppose I should comment on his attractions too. Pleasant enough I'm sure, though not quite my type. Youngish chap, smart but not showy, wire-rim spectacles and a 'tache.

He came up level with me, blinking hard as he adjusted to the gloom of the corridor after the sun. He glanced at me blankly, then down the corridor to where the woman was just disappearing towards the Second Class carriage, and he called something after her. Then to me again. 'Your pardon, sir.'

'Not at all.'

'You're very kind.'

'Don't mention it.'

He nodded enthusiastically, smiled, and disappeared after what I assumed was his wife. Lucky fellow. Unhindered at last, I stepped down onto the platform.

I wasn't surprised to find Quinn there, and ambled over to him. He grew up by and then on the sea; any space more confined than his North Atlantic makes him ratty. He was standing out of the way, solid and still, watching the sky while being able to watch the platform, and taking in deep breaths of Bulgarian fresh air in exchange for unfresh air from his cigarette.

'Nice-looking woman there, sir.' He said it in the same tone he'd used in the morning to point out the various places bandits might be shooting at us from.

'Really? Didn't notice.'

'Probably best. Sure you wouldn't want a distraction.'

'Quite right.' I glanced along the train: the multiple signs of damage from the bandit attack, bursts of steam, the mysterious shouts of railwaymen. 'Too damn many people along on this trip, Quinn.'

He said nothing; he waited.

'Someone's got it in for me; someone's after the paper. I assume Major Hilmi. I suppose that means Karim, too, the big Turk; he seems official. But what about the bandit attack? Surely that wasn't coincidence. And that means someone else is after it too. But who's got Turkish bandits handy? And what happened to Hilmi's man, the soldier he says was murdered in the night? Did that even happen? If so, was that the bandits' friend clearing the way for them a bit?'

Steam gusted around us.

'Whole business is cock-eyed', I went on. 'And why do I get the impression that everyone on the train is watching me, or needling me, or trying to trap me in something?' I glanced at him. He said nothing. I shook my head, irritated - by him, by the world, by myself. 'Night patrol, sergeant. Seeing Boers behind every bush. Need to get a grip.'

He said nothing. He gave a single heavy nod.

I made a brisk march down to the end of the platform and back, largely ignoring the back windows and shacks and rubbish heaps of downtown Plovdiv.

Legs stretched and lungs refilled, I stepped onto the train as it started to move. At the end of the corridor there was a kerfuffle of some sort: the Conductor snapping in French at one of the stewards; a couple of passengers waiting nearby.

Quinn was lurking at my shoulder, no doubt checking I'd not been left behind or tried to run off.

'What's the ruckus?' I said.

'Odd business, sir. Apparently someone's pinched the Conductor's passenger list.'

I looked at him, and then along the corridor again. 'But why on earth..?' Another mystery was hardly a surprise, not on this trip; but what benefit could a bad man possibly get from the passenger list?

I turned away, still pondering, then stopped. 'Having said that, the list might have been handy. Help put this shambles in order. Wouldn't have minded pinching it myself.'

Quinn's voice was even quieter than normal. 'If you look under your pillow, sir, I think you'll find that you did.'

28.

FIRST CLASS CAR

1. M. le M. de Valfierno
2. Sir H. Delamere
3. Bishop S. Wilkinson
4. Karim Bey
5. Mlle P. Madison
6. M. Theodoros Theotokis
7. M. Győriványi Andrenyi-Cserháti

'Dear God,' I said. 'Must be the Hungarian. Beloved of

reception clerks everywhere. You can't blame me for struggling with that.'

8. Mme Marguerite Dewoitine
9. H.E. Suraya Khan
10. H.E. Sikander Ali Khan

SECOND CLASS CAR

1a. Mlle Amelia Battersby
1b. Mlle Winifred Froy
2a. Père G. Meazza
2b. Père L. Piontek
3a. M. Singh
3b. M. Quinn
4a. Mlle Goswami
4b. Mlle Lemarchant
5a. M. Charles Chehab
5b. Dr Zia'eddin Jam

'Chap on here called Dr Jam, Quinn.'
'Aye, sir. Pretty sure I've seen him. Darker; tidy beard.'
'Seriously? Dr Jam?'

6a. M. Alexander Craig
6b. M. Tomas Svensson
7a. M. Jean-Maurice Junot
7b. M. Jozef Munk
8a. Mlle Oksana Vorontsova
8b. Mlle Mariam Chichinadze
9a. Major Hilmi
9b. Tekdemir

'Hilmi and his man added in pencil. Late to the party.'

10a. -

10b. -

'And 10. is vacant.'

'Don't think I've seen anyone down there. That couple that just got on - the pretty woman you didn't notice, sir - guess they'll go in there.'

I nodded.

The list itself told me nothing, of course. But I knew the outlines of the problem, at least. A clearer view of the battlefield.

About to open the door, I heard steps and voices outside and hesitated.

A touch nervy, perhaps. But after a moment I realized that what had actually caught my attention was one of these unknown people, passing in the corridor, saying 'Delamere'.

29.

I didn't want to leap out right behind whoever it was, and by the time I opened the door they'd gone.

Wondering as usual just why I was so damn' interesting to everyone, I made my way to the dining car for tea.

I don't say I'd memorized the passenger list. But having the names laid out like that gave everything a bit of structure. A few more faces were fitting into place.

Ahead of me, my shooting companion Craig was with the Swedish agriculture chap. And he would be Svensson, who Craig was bunking with. Easy. The couple who'd got on at Plovdiv were chatting with the Spanish-looking chap who'd been asking me odd questions the night before. I remembered his elaborate production of his name, Valfierno. Now I knew he was Monsieur the something de Valfierno.

Not sure what difference that made to anything, but still.

I found myself opposite Bishop S. Wilkinson, who asked how I was enjoying the journey. It took us each a couple of moments to realize how ridiculous this sounded, and we both smiled. 'Sorry', he said. 'Platitude. Parish meeting stuff.'

'Not at all. It's been - what? - several hours since anyone tried to shoot me, so the day's working out well.'

'I suppose I meant how you manage being cooped up like this. Outdoor sort of chap. Myself, I enjoy the comforts, but when the horizon's less than twenty miles off I feel somewhat squeezed.'

I smiled at this; agreed.

'And that odd business with the Turks', he said. 'You ever get to the bottom of that?'

I shook my head. 'Not sure what this paper is he's banging on about, and not sure why he was so sure I had it. Hopefully it's blown over now.'

He smiled, trying to look reassuring. 'You asked him about it? Straight out, I mean. These, ah… these more simple peoples, they don't wriggle away so easily when you confront them.' It wasn't a bad point. I remembered how I'd been thrown by Miss Madison asking me bluntly if I was carrying the document. 'Or who else could you talk to? Pin the thing down a bit.'

I was still thinking this over when someone said, 'May I join you, gentlemen?' We did the polite thing, and he sat down opposite me.

Young chap, darker skin - Arab, almost Indian - and a very trim very black beard. I remembered the description. 'It's Dr… Jam, I think.' I said the name uncertainly; surely that couldn't be how you pronounced it.

'Dr Zia'eddin Jam, at your service.' Apparently it was. Little smile, little bow. We introduced ourselves. Dr Jam, we learned, was from Teheran, travelling to Paris for a year at the University working on tropical diseases. Preliminaries done, he said: 'I trust I find you well, gentlemen?'

'You mean health-wise,' the Bishop said, 'or more generally?'

'I always ask the question seriously, of a man's health. It is surprising how often one may identify some small dis-content, and sometimes from this a more serious affliction. I ought to ask you to extend your tongue, Sir Henry.'

'Not at tea, I hope.'

He grinned, lots of good white teeth. 'Perhaps we take a chance with you, Sir Henry. Active man. Healthy life, I surmise. I have seen you at every station, always stretching the legs and taking the air.'

'Quite', I said emptily. I hadn't noticed him watching me.

'And we are all in your debt for your valiant deeds against the bandits.' Perhaps, Dr Jam, but no need to bang on about it. I tried to look manly and humble, and hoped he'd move on. 'Apparently you were a soldier, though, so we should expect it. In South Africa, so I was given to understand.' He turned to the Bishop for confirmation. The Bishop nodded his confirmation. Both beamed at me.

Now I really was uncomfortable. I looked away. By chance, instead I caught the expression of the chap sitting across the aisle and one along. The chap who'd literally bumped into Quinn, when we'd been chatting in the corridor in the small hours. When, indeed, the Turkish soldier was apparently getting murdered. Very fair hair, very pink complexion, and again a charmless expression. It was more or less a sneer.

I smiled at him, and turned back to Dr Jam.

'You got a bloody nose there.'

I unturned back, and looked at fair hair. 'I beg your pardon?'

'In Southern Africa. Your British Empire got a bloody nose.'

I gazed at him. 'Yes,' I said eventually. 'Well put.' And this time I turned back to the doctor more successfully, and concentrated on his discussion of fevers more than I cared to.

It wasn't the time or place - and nor is this - for a more balanced discussion of the ideals and idiocies and heroism and humiliation of the British war against the Boers at the turn of the century. Going through it once was miserable enough, so I tend to avoid repetitions.

Nor was it the time to remember all the dead faces, Boer and British, and kick this chap through the window on their behalf.

The faces flickered at me anyway, and I tried to focus on the Persian doctor.

'So tell me, Sir Henry, how do you occupy yourself now? You interest yourself in diplomacy, or more muscular adventures?' His eyes dropped a moment, as if he was checking whether I was up to it, muscle-wise. Then he smiled at me, wide-eyed interest. 'What brings you on the train?'

And so the afternoon dragged on. I kept up the conversation, because it was marginally more appropriate than punching someone or throwing myself under the wheels out of sheer weariness. The Persian doctor and the Bishop kept talking - I saw their mouths moving, and I even felt mine do so once or twice - but I don't remember what was said.

Other voices rolled around me. Valfierno - M. le M. de Valfierno, indeed - was talking to the Bulgarian couple. He was going at it full steam, and I couldn't blame him: sober murmurs for Mr and elegant nods and subtle touches of the arm for Mrs. At one point her attention wandered - she'd already lasted longer than I had - and her eyes met mine; and then dropped. I wondered if they were getting the same odd performance from him I'd had. I heard Miss Battersby talking at the Hungarian, who was looking a little alarmed, while Miss Froy seemed to be considering his fingers. Craig, the Scot, was talking to the two Russian girls with his Swedish bunk-mate.

Voices, and faces, rolling around me with the train-wheels, as we pushed through the late Bulgarian afternoon.

At one point I went out in the corridor to open a window and get some air. I found myself standing close to the conductor, who was considering something in a piece of paper. I checked I wasn't in his way.

'Getting back on top of things?' I added.

He smiled sadly. 'In Sofia, perhaps… But…' He looked at his paper again, shook his head.

'Hell of a business. Anything like this happen before?'

He considered the question gravely, as if struggling to recall exactly how many times his train had been invaded by bandits. 'Always there is something on this journey', he said, English heavy with French consonants. 'Deaths. Births.' A little smile: 'Everything in between. A little drama, a little scandal. This' - he gestured with his thumb over his shoulder, as if Turkish bandit attack was the name of a station we'd just passed through - 'in detail is new, but in danger not unknown.'

I'd always assumed train journeys were rather a routine business. 'What an extraordinary life you must have.'

He shrugged. 'For three days, Monsieur Sir 'Enry, we squeeze all of the world into a few railway carriages. Also we squeeze all of the world's dramas.' Another shrug. 'My ancestors, Monsieur, my school-friends, none has travelled more than five kilometres from our village. Me? I try to arrange my son may have the same fortune I have had.'

'I hope he has a quieter time of it', I said. 'Monsieur..?'

'Michel, Sir 'Enry. Paul Michel.'

Back in the dining compartment, I was almost immediately confronted by the Bulgarian couple coming the other way. A nod of courtesy from him; a delayed lowering of the eyes from her. 'We have been hearing about you, sir', he said. That had me uneasy right away. 'The Argentinian gentleman says that you spent some time in Trieste. I should be fascinated to hear of it.'

Which was very curious. As it happens, I had once been in Trieste for a spell, long before. A decaying and unsettling place; but I'd been young, and with reassuringly beautiful company. I had certainly not, however, mentioned my stay to M. le M. de Valfierno or anyone else on the train.

30.

As afternoon flirted with evening we pulled into Sofia, the capital of Bulgaria. Great enthusiast though I was, by this point, for the many virtues of Bulgaria and the Bulgarians, especially compared to Turkey and the Turks, I'm afraid I can't tell you much about it. I'm pretty sure they're Christians, but don't take that as a recommendation from me. I've fought in one all-out war and any number of scuffles and skirmishes, and pretty much everyone who's ever tried to kill me - and everyone I've ever tried to kill - has been a Christian. Mohammedans and the rest, they've generally left me alone, and I'm most grateful.

As the train was slowing, Miss Battersby pointed to a large dome looming out of the greying sky and informed all of us within reach of her hefty voice that it was the mosque of the many baths, so-named because it was built on top of the thermal springs, and centuries old, a legacy of the prolonged rule of the Ottomans over what was now Bulgaria. Then Miss Froy, with occasional glances at the guidebook, pointed out a collection of little domes and suggested that they were the restored church of the Eastern Christians. And someone else said there was supposed to be a synagogue that was making great strides too. God knows. Or, at least, I hope he makes his mind up.

The various domes came and went in the gloom, and then a new set of buildings rose around us and the conductor declared that we were in Sofia station. That was clearer. I've spent more time in railway stations than in churches; know where I am with railway stations.

As soon as we stopped there commenced a great faffing. The Orient Express had arranged for a replacement dining car, and so we were hustled out of the old one and it was uncoupled and taken away. Hope they touched the Association of Turkish Bandits for the repairs. The train people began to bustle away at the uncoupling and recoupling, and the conductor was fussing around his stewards and the local rail authorities and, by the looks of him, grateful to have a sympathetic audience to hear his troubles.

At the same time, the Bulgarian police weighed in. They weren't going to import a battle-scarred train without asking a few questions, and it was quickly clear that the investigation at the station where we'd crossed into the country a few hours earlier had only been for starters.

First the conductor disappeared for a couple of minutes, escorted into an office on the station. Then Hilmi, who must have been having a miserable day; last thing the up-and-coming Turkish official wants is to have Bulgarian officials lording it over him. He was there for five or ten minutes. Then they started on the passengers. Karim Bey was early - they were noticeably polite with him, which suggested they knew what they were doing and weren't just trying to cause trouble. The Bulgarian couple were in there early too. I couldn't see any logic to the order; perhaps they were suffering from the lost passenger list too.

I lurked on the platform, waiting my turn. I strode about a bit. I paused in front of a noticeboard displaying several fading generations of pinned-up timetables, timetable amendments, police orders, hotel adverts and play-bills. For about the hundredth time in my life I tried to give a damn about architecture.

Some of those who'd been interviewed took advantage of the stop to pop out of the station for a spell. I saw the Misses Battersby and Froy marching out and marching back again after some healthy sight-seeing; no doubt the guide-book publisher would be receiving a list of corrections shortly. The two Russian women came back with a parcel each, and I think I saw Miss Madison and the Swedish chap back from the shops too.

Can't say I've ever really longed to see Sofia - despite the mosque of the many baths and the church of the Eastern

Christians, not to mention the great progress of the new synagogue - but I felt somehow excluded from the lightness of life, burdened by the paper hanging heavy under my lapel.

What I eventually realized - as I trudged up and down the platform, pretending that I was keeping fit and active, stopping occasionally in front of the noticeboard to see if the show at the Imperial had changed since I'd passed five minutes previously - was that I was being kept until late in the list.

Last, it turned out. Coincidence, perhaps.

I was standing in front of the notices again - gazing at some kind of official order in angry Cyrillic, which for all I knew could have been warning me against carrying firearms, smoking in the ladies' lavatory or loitering in front of the noticeboard - when I felt a tap on my shoulder.

A couple of chaps with rifles and ferociously heavy uniform greatcoats escorted me into a waiting room. We were all pretending this was a courteous and civilized bureaucratic procedure, but in practice I was a prisoner under armed guard.

The chap in charge had read all the best adventure books about villainous policemen; or perhaps it's the training they get. His back was to me when I came in, and it stayed that way an unnecessary moment longer. Eventually he turned round, glanced distastefully at me, then continued looking at what I guessed was my passport.

He had the same hefty uniform, an even bigger and shinier peaked cap, and one of the most monstrous moustaches I think I've ever seen. A great bushy, sagging business. Like a pair of squirrels had died under his nose, and were now hanging there symmetrically forever. I'd heard - never happily - of people growing moustaches, as though they were some sort of terribly challenging artistic endeavour. This was the first time I'd met someone who'd gone shooting them.

He started talking to me, without looking up. Bored bureaucrat plus sneering tormentor in one easy gesture.

Classic stuff. Some preamble about routine questions for all passengers, which neither of us believed.

At last he looked up at me, holding my passport as though he'd just found it down the back of the latrine. 'Name?' he said grimly.

'Yes, that's right', I said. 'On the first line there.'

The eyebrows were little cub versions of the 'tache. They frowned. 'You have name?'

'Yes indeed.'

The eyebrows jumped, like baby squirrels in the springtime, and crashed to earth again. 'What is your name?'

'Henry Delamere.'

He puffed out a great breath, commiserating with my bad luck. The strands of his moustache wavered sadly in the gust. 'What is your business on the train?'

'I'm a passenger.' All the various rodents on his face came to life, and I relented. 'I'm travelling all the way to Paris, and then on to London. I have no business.'

He started murmuring bleakly about the attack on the train, the unstable political situation in the region, the obligations of a prudent police force, and various other things that I ignored because they were only waffle to justify picking on me. 'It is our duty', he said at last, 'to search you.'

I had feared exactly this, but I didn't want to seem to give in too easily.

'Don't you need some sort of justification for that?' I said, trying not to sound as unco-operative as I felt. 'Most countries I've been in, the authorities can't search a private individual just on a whim.'

The chap took an enormous breath up his nose, as if trying to suck up the moustache. Then he breathed it out thoughtfully, and the moustache fluttered and re-settled.

'Train has been scene of crime. Investigation is justified. And-or train is not in right condition, is not correct train; could be someone smuggles railway train. Investigation is justified. And-or in centre of mystery and political unrest, foreign man enters Bulgaria without good reason. All investigations are justified.'

'Righto', I said. 'Try not to get shit on my shirt.'

Two more policemen approached me, and reached for my jacket.

31.

Out on the platform, I sucked in a deep breath of freedom and locomotive soot. I paid a last sentimental visit to the noticeboard. While my body blocked anyone's view, I unpinned Europe's most secret document from its temporary place beside the police warning notice, and sauntered back on to the train. I hoped the pin-hole hadn't blotted out anything important.

Eventually the bustle and hassle were done, and with a great sigh of relief the Orient Express started to pull out of Sofia station. Quite a few of us made our way along to try the new dining car. It looked much like the old one, so much so that part of one's brain was tempted to forget that anything much had happened since we'd left Constantinople. Once again, I had to admire the organizational power of the Orient Express company: carving a corridor through the wildest corners of Europe, then filling it with luxury, and making that luxury part of a machine of logistics that - on top of all the regular demands for fuel and fresh food and so on - could rustle up a spare carriage when one got shot to pieces.

I found myself beside the Bulgarian couple. Mr and Mrs Petrov, apparently. After the irritations of the station, they were pleasant company for trying to pretend that nothing unusual was happening around me. He seemed a nice enough chap: unlike a surprising number of men on the train he was quiet and discreet, with intelligent conversation to pass the time. Mrs Petrov made intelligent conversation too, and if an intelligent conversationalist happens to be very beautiful I'm not one to complain.

'The police in Sofia were very excited, very mysterious', she said. 'And of course we saw the condition of the train. What has been happening please?'

'Major Hilmi - little chap with a moustache - says they're hunting some very important official document that was sneaked out of Constantinople. I think your police were interested in that as much as the bullet holes.' I sat.

'The affairs' - Mrs Petrov drew the word out, and it sounded very charming on her lips - 'of Turkey are the affairs of Bulgaria.'

The nearest table was free, and I pulled out a chair for her.

'We have been a great kingdom,' Mr added, 'but we have lived in the shadow of Turkey for a millennium.'

His wife asked: 'What was the document?'

I was moving to the other side of the table so they could sit beside each other. 'There's an important Turkish chap on the train - Karim Bey; he hinted it might be some kind of treaty.'

There was a snort at my shoulder, and I turned to find Theotokis standing there, listening. It wasn't clear whether his scorn was about Karim Bey, Karim Bey's hint, or the whole Ottoman Empire. 'Byzantium is dead', he said with elaborate mournfulness. 'Great polis of Constantine is dead. These corrupt and hungry vultures feed on body.' There wasn't much we could say to this. Petrov nodded, and Theotokis continued. 'Ottoman Empire is obsolete. It must be dismantled now, and true nations freed from its dead hands.' Petrov nodded again.

'That's already happening, surely.' I said. 'For the best part of a century now. The European Great Powers managing the collapse of the empire.'

Another snort from my Greek friend. 'Greece liberated herself in 1827,' he said proudly. 'And at last the wrong of a thousand years is reversed. The other, little peoples of the Balkans...' - he waved his hand, the little peoples of the

Balkans just a few dots at the end of a Greek sentence. 'So-called Great Powers trying to create so-called countries. Really playing own games. Russia against Austria. Austria against Italy.' He glanced at me. 'England against all. This will be secret treaty.' That was that, apparently. 'Now, beautiful lady has no drink!' He bowed to Mrs Petrov, his eyes looking at everything except hers as he went down and up.

Mr Petrov hadn't managed to sit yet. 'There is a significant misunderstanding about the peoples of the Balkans', he said earnestly. Theotokis had turned towards the bar, but stopped and glared at the possibility of someone disagreeing with him. 'Really there are not so many. Mostly they are sub-groups, speaking dialects of greater nations.'

Theotokis considered this, nodded and slapped Petrov on the back. 'Most right!' The two of them set off towards drinks again. 'Greeks of course most ancient people, and then of course... Where you said you are from?'

Which left just me and the lovely Mrs Petrov looking at each other over the table. 'Looks like the Great Powers have left the little peoples alone for a moment', I said.

She smiled, hungry and sure. 'You must please excuse enthusiasm. My husband is amateur scholar of history.'

'Jolly good. Seems a splendid chap.'

She nodded. 'He has excellent post in the regional administration in Plovdiv.' The name sounded even better when she said it. The Slavic accent is always lovely - the thick 'l's and 'r's - and her voice was a deep murmur.

'Most impressive.'

'I'm a lucky woman.'

'Blessed in many ways.'

'But...' - languid regret - 'it is not exciting existence.'

The discussion at the bar was suddenly louder. Petrov and Theotokis had dragged someone else into the conversation. Presumably that made three great peoples of the region now, and they were all arguing over the cocktail menu.

Mrs Petrov saw where my glance had gone, and smiled

fondly. 'As a girl, I dreamed of adventure. No girl dreams of accompanying her husband on professional visit. I dreamed of railway trains like this, of elegant conversation with... mysterious foreign men.'

She lowered her eyes, very coy; then she raised them again, not so much.

'I don't pretend to know the constraints of any woman's life', I said. 'But life is as mysterious and elegant as you make it.' I make no great claim to wisdom, but now and then I can make something sound wise. It went down all right, anyway.

She seemed to breathe it in. 'And you, Mr Harry,' - she made maximum advantage of the double 'r', turning a name that normally sounds like a hiccough into the opening line of a folk song - 'have you dreams?'

'Right now,' I said, 'reality seems magical enough.' Bullseye to Delamere, England for the win.

She smiled, lowered her eyes a moment, a polite suggestion of shyness and an impolite suggestion of pretty much everything else.

But now the scholarly conversation at the bar was making its way back towards us, Theotokis juggling his box and his drink and his energetic gestures, everyone talking at once, and the lady and I broke our glance and sat back and contemplated the table decoration, a fresh flower in a spindly golden vase. The ships had passed in the night, all most pleasant but now the dreams must be packed up where they belonged.

Except that Petrov was gesturing beyond our table, and they weren't stopping. He and Theotokis had picked up not one but two fellow enthusiasts - the Hungarian musicologist and someone else were bunched close behind and they were all gesticulating with full glasses of drink - and they needed an empty table to continue the debate.

They passed without even acknowledging us.

Our eyes came up from the table decoration. 'For now the little peoples have been liberated', Mrs Petrov said.

'How shall we celebrate our independence?'

'Take me somewhere else', she said. 'Just for one moment. Take me to one of the places you have been. Take me to England.' On her lips, it sounded a much more romantic place.

'On your lips,' I said, 'it sounds a much more romantic place.'

'You do not think England is romantic?'

'It's all right. Plumbing's adequate, and I like getting lost in the countryside. England's a wife, not a mistress.' She smiled at this. Nice to do business with an expert.

'You are very English, I think.'

'Not particularly. English by accident. The stork was flying around for days trying to drop me off somewhere, and no one else would have me. The English were the only people too polite or too absent-minded to refuse. It was probably tea-time.'

She laughed prettily at this, head back and showing her teeth. She looked into my eyes again. 'And you were brave soldier in Africa, this I know.' I scowled gracelessly. 'You won medal for heroic actions in battle. That is so… fascinating.'

It was fascinating indeed, mainly because my war record - and Modder River of ill memory - was something else I hadn't mentioned to anyone on the train.

'And even now,' she went on, 'even on simple train journey, there is excitement around you. Adventure.' She made it sound like the name of a long-lost love. 'Most men manage to have a life without any of adventure.'

'Perhaps I have a different definition of life to most men.'

She smiled. It was most effective, the mouth open to add a calculated hint of pleasure. 'And you find adventures even on railway train, Mr Harry?'

'Especially on a railway train.'

She glanced over my shoulder, to where her husband was still in loud debate with Theotokis and Co. 'There doesn't seem so much room for adventure, in this little train.' She gazed at me. 'Everyone crushed together, I mean.' Again the heavy rolled r, the open vowel...

'Crushed together?' I said; I can follow a script all right. 'That's when the greatest adventures start.'

32.

As we squeezed along the corridor of the Second Class coach - she'd not hesitated in the First Class car, and a glance had suggested she thought it too close to Mr - I murmured something about making sure we weren't disturbed. I knocked at Quinn's compartment.

He stuck his head out of his door just as Mrs Petrov was disappearing into hers with a long glance at me.

Quinn hadn't missed it either. 'You seem to be in danger, sir.'

'Worst kind.'

'Er...' He waited until I was looking at him. 'Our decision-making up to scratch is it, sir?'

'I'm being distracted from something. Find out what.' I handed him my pistol.

'Of course, sir.' He hesitated. 'The finding out sounds important. If you preferred to do that, and leave me to be distracted...'

'I'll struggle on, thank you. Perils of command; first out of the trench.'

'And first in, sir? You are sure it's a deliberate distraction? She hasn't just fallen for your great charm?'

'She laughed at my joke about the stork.'

'Dear God.' He looked startled. 'The poor woman.'

'Go away, Quinn.'

He did. I think I heard the faintest chuckle as he went. Damned odd sense of humour, the Cornish.

The next ten minutes or so were very pleasant. Without further preamble we indulged ourselves agreeably in what you might call standard long-form travellers' dalliance, boiler running hot but no risk of an explosion. As well as being very lovely, Mrs Petrov had obviously travelled on this track before. If I called her a professional you'd get an unseemly impression, but she certainly knew what she was doing. Mr Petrov was either hopeless, or a very lucky boy.

I have to say my heart wasn't really in it. It was enjoyable enough, of course, and I trust I was courteously attentive: a chap likes to do the decent thing. But my mind wasn't on the job. I still had the impression that this was a performance for my benefit - and thanks very much for it; most kind - and my thoughts were elsewhere in the train.

So when I heard the softest knocking at the compartment door, in a rhythm I knew, it wasn't unwelcome. We'd come to a halt just a moment before - we the train, not we the lady and I - and I was more alert. 'My goodness!' I said, disentangling myself. 'I'd quite forgotten: meant to write to my mother before dinner. Do excuse me.'

She looked a bit surprised, but not unhappy. Perhaps her mind had been wandering too.

I straightened myself out, and found Quinn in the corridor where the First and Second Class wagons joined, keeping an eye on both. He glanced critically at my tie. 'Not too badly wounded, sir?'

'Only my heart, Quinn. What's up?'

'Chummy slipped into your compartment - the husband - little after you set to with Madame.'

'Cheeky sod. He's hardly the first, and on this trip he probably won't be the last. Nothing to find in there anyway.'

'He's still in there. I was only away for a moment to knock, and he didn't come this way and I've checked he's not in the dining car. And it's gone a bit quiet.'

We started along the First Class corridor. 'Dropped off, you think?'

As I reached for the door handle of my compartment, Quinn held up a warning finger.

'I don't need to be furtive going in my own billet', I said.

'How's he going to react, sir?'

It was a point. Perhaps Mr Petrov hadn't got as blasé as I had about all this breaking and entering. 'I want to avoid a fight,' I said; 'but I suppose you'd better have the piece handy.'

Quinn reached into his jacket pocket, and - more keyed up than before - I opened the door to my compartment.

I stood aside to let Quinn see what I'd seen.

The compartment was empty, and undisturbed.

'You seeing imaginary Bulgarians again, Quinn?'

He grunted. 'And not even the pretty ones.' He pushed at the door, checking that it opened without obstruction.

Through the open window, the station platform was deserted. A fence, some buildings, and the name of the place on an elegantly-lettered sign: KOSTINBROD.

As I watched, the locomotive gave a whistle and the carriage jolted and the elegantly-lettered sign began to slide out of my vision.

'So:' I said, 'comes in, gets what he wants - or rather, doesn't get what he wants - and hooks it out the window so no embarrassing questions in the corridor.' I glanced around the compartment again. 'Nice tidy job of it. Your kind of burglar.'

Quinn was peering past my shoulder out of the window. 'Quieter side of the train; dark now. Might reckon on not being noticed.'

'Mm. And leaving - I wonder… Back in a sec.'

I walked back to the Second Class wagon, and knocked at the Petrovs' compartment. As I waited, the Swedish chap - Svensson - emerged from a few doors along.

He looked surprised. Misplaced morality I could do without, especially at this stage in the game. I gave a charming smile. 'Lent Mrs Petrov my pen', I said.

Svensson shook his head. 'She has gone. She got off, at the station there.'

33.

And not even a rose left on the pillow.

You had to admire their efficiency, the Bulgarians. Among other things. I was assuming this had been an official Bulgarian delegation, having their go at the magic document. Aware of it and after it because apparently every last inhabitant of the Balkans was aware of it and after it. The details about me they'd got from their own resources, not from conversations on the train. Border police had grilled Hilmi and he'd no doubt named me as guilty of whatever they fancied; if he couldn't get me, someone else would do the job for him. Mr and Mrs waiting ready, and on at Plovdiv. The interrogations at Sofia confirmed Dela-mere as everyone's favourite suspect, but they'd not found the document on me. And we'd hardly left the station before Mrs was open for business so that Mr could take his turn tossing my compartment. Timed perfectly to be able to do the milkman's flit at Kostinbrod, no one's honour touched except mine. Nice dealing with professionals.

If I have to get played by foreign spies, let them be beautiful Bulgarian women loose with their morals and their lacewear. But I was feeling oddly sour. I suppose the layers of unreality of it all, chaps getting knifed and bandit attacks and everyone having a go at my bags, were starting to get to me.

I wrestled my window closed; young Petrov hadn't had any difficulty with it, apparently. Then I fretted in the compartment for a minute or so, straightening bags that were already straight and tidying bedlinen that was already tidy and staring out into the Bulgarian evening. Beneath me, the train wheels rattled and clicked rhythmically on the track.

There were only ten minutes or so before dinner, so I'd let Quinn go and smarten himself up while I changed. This was the unshakeable routine of the Orient Express, and it seemed both ridiculous and reassuring. All of the wildness of the day - and still, like clockwork, all along the train we were back in our own compartments and putting on our smartest and combing our hair.

My seductress and her mate had thought of that, hadn't they? It would have taken a bit of nerve to toss my compartment and then make small talk over the dining table. And we were due to cross the border into Serbia fairly soon after dinner; they wouldn't want to sit through the faddle at the border and end up in the next country.

So the timing had been deliberate. They'd been aiming at Kostinbrod all along, and the interval before dinner. Mrs Petrov had known when to flutter her eyes at me, leaving the right gap for the other half to run a professional search and for them both to get away during the five minutes or so that we usually stopped at the smaller stations. I glanced around the little space again, as the wheels chattered beneath; he'd made a tidy job of searching in such a short time.

I remembered again her expression as I'd left. She'd been about to call it a day herself. Train arrives into station. Give Mr a minute to get out the window. Then the sudden attack of remorse, I-hear-my-husband's-footsteps-in-the-corridor, that sort of thing. She'd have shoved me out - last snatched kiss, thank-you-for-this-brief-taste-of-paradise - and as soon as my back was turned she'd have been on the platform and away. All very neat.

Quite elaborate, all that business - poor Madame's appalling sacrifice for her country - just on the off-chance that I might have left the document lying around my compartment.

Or had -? A sudden chill of blood stabbing through me, and I was frantically checking my lapel. Had she somehow found it and lifted it while I was having a quick nibble of the forbidden fruit? She'd have had to-

Thank God. No. Still there.

I heard once again the relentless chatter of the wheels on the tracks, heard it echoing in my chest.

So. Funny business. Not without its compensations,

espionage, but a bit bewildering.

I think it was that sense of unease, an unfamiliar kind of funk, that prompted me once I'd got my tie adequate to lie down for a moment. There were still several minutes before I needed to step along to the dining car, and I knew that my physical restlessness and my mental confusion were reinforcing each other.

Lie down. Limit the body's movement. Stare at the ceiling. Simplify the view, simplify the thinking.

It worked.

Lying back on my bunk, staring up sightlessly, I could hear the clicking of the wheels on the tracks beneath me much more distinctly.

Except it wasn't really a rattling, or chattering, or clicking. It was a ticking.

A ticking, coming from right underneath my head.

34.

'Quinn!' I yelled it up into the night, though he'd obviously not hear it a whole carriage away.

All the nice things I've said about the Bulgarians were taken back. I was off the bunk like it was on fire, rolling on the floor and scrabbling at the little doors to the cupboard which ran the length of the bunk. I stuck my head in.

The ticking was loud and clear now. I squeezed an arm in beside my head and stretched far under the pillow end of the cupboard. A box, and I was clutching at it and pulling it towards me and back out into the light. Plain, thin wood, the size and shape of the box for a bottle of brandy and about as heavy. The ticking hammered at my head. I was scrambling up off the side of the bunk, one-handed, and turning to the window.

The window wouldn't budge. Not one-handed, not this window, not tonight. I pulled at it, hung my whole body-weight from it, and it slipped half an inch aslant and stuck.

No time. Still struggling to hold my fatal parcel under one arm, I swung the other elbow at the glass. I swung it ferocious with fear, with desperation, and it should have smashed through like a steam-hammer. What actually happened was that at precisely the wrong moment the train lurched with some curve or irregularity in the track, and my balance was thrown. My elbow smacked hard against the window but not enough to smash it. Instead I jarred the nerve and my arms were a juggling mess and I dropped the bomb. It hit my knee - that stung like hell too - and bounced away into the cupboard under the bed again.

It's a bloody ridiculous contortion, bending yourself double in that narrow space and then squeezing your shoulders through the two little doors. I guarantee that I hold the world record for it. Practice makes perfect. Once again I had my head thrust into the darkness like the chap in the joke about the doctor and the opera singer, once again I'd wriggled an arm in there too, once again I was scrabbling for the bomb and failing to get a hold. The ticking was louder, faster, the last mad seconds of my life.

'Are we... are we hiding, sir?'

'Open the damn window! Open it!' It sounded muffled and incoherent even to me. I was wriggling backwards out of the cupboard and lurching and sprawling and trying to find my feet with the bomb still ticking in my hands. I staggered upright, one hand clutching at Quinn's shoulder for balance, and miraculously he'd opened the window - apparently it was quite easy - and I was barging him aside and swinging for it.

A roar, and the vague shadows of night were replaced with a rushing wall of bricks inches from my face. A tunnel, dear God not a tunnel. And apparently He heard and it was only a bridge and the night opened vast in front of me and I flung the ticking horror far out into the darkness.

I turned back to Quinn, who'd regained his balance. I own I must have looked insane. Wild-eyed, no doubt, and pretty ragged what with all the in-and-out of cupboards. Quinn considered me, a mild and rather snooty concern on his face.

From the darkness, there came an explosion, and a brief burst of flame flaring in the distance. Now Quinn's eyes showed the alarm, and I got to look superior for once.

'I've revised my opinion of Bulgarian women', I said, breathing a bit heavy. 'Lovely no doubt, but they play too rough and charge too high.'

35.

Quinn nodded. Then he considered me again, and reached forwards and straightened my tie, and brushed at my shirt-front with his hand. His eyes met mine. 'Stiff drink before dinner, I think sir. Earned this one.'

'Yes,' I said, 'I have. Close the window, would you? I can't work the damn' thing.'

He did, easily, and I started to put on my jacket.

I stopped. A couple of minutes before - and it's strange, isn't it? the madness probably had been only a minute or two - I'd been feeling confused by the whole business. Now I was feeling angry. The game was too much. I was in over my head. I was paying over the odds. I'd expected a bit of risk, a contest of nerves, couriering the government's secret paper across Europe. I'd not expected bandits and beautiful Bulgarian murderesses and bombs in my bed.

One last deep breath, and I felt I'd regained some control. I pulled up my lapel, and unpinned the document. I looked at it for a moment: its apparent thinness, its innocence.

I glanced at Quinn, saw the question in his eyes.

'I think', I said, 'that if I'm going to continue doing this damn' silly business, I'd like to know what it's about.'

As gently as I could, I broke the seal, and opened the single page. I considered it for a moment. Then I showed it to Quinn. I guess the surprise in his eyes was a mirror of my own.

The mysterious paper, which had cost the life of its previous bearer, and nearly cost my life three or four times, and which had in passing wrecked the train once and now almost a second time, gave up its secret at last.

It was blank.

36.

'Those miserable, treacherous bastards.'

Oddly enough, my words were calm.

Quinn wasn't taking any chances, and kept silent.

I understood the sense of what the British Government had done, and to that extent I couldn't fault it.

'A decoy!' That came out angrier. 'Wound up to all this nonsense, and I'm the bloody decoy.'

Quinn was looking uncertain.

Ostensibly I was talking to him, and that probably kept my language and volume within polite limits, but really I was talking to myself, and not very respectfully. 'I thought that boy at Constantinople was playing the clown... All that furtive looking to and fro, the extended interview when anyone passing in the corridor might have seen us, then plonking down on that bench and staring at me.' Unconsciously, my fist was thumping gently against the wall with each phrase. 'I thought he was a clumsy amateur. Instead he was a sneaky professional, deliberately drawing attention to me in every way he could think of. I hope he felt smug, just before they stabbed him for it.'

My valet was still looking at me with faint concern. 'Sir, if you could just-'

I waved the blank paper at him. 'Harry Delamere is not the Government's courier, Quinn. Harry Delamere is just Harry Delamere, well-known magnet for trouble, the single most obvious person to be a British spy from the perspective of a Turkish policeman, a troupe of bandits or a Bulgarian assassin. The Government couldn't have made it more obvious I was their courier if they'd taken out front page advertisements in all the European dailies. And I'm not their courier.'

'And the business about rushing it to Paris?'

'That still seems right. All the fuss from the Embassy, and all the chaos since then, confirms that this document is deadly serious, whatever and wherever it is. Everyone's in a rush; that's why they're going to such extremes.'

I paused. 'And it only makes sense to have me drawing the attention so obviously, so desperately, if the document really is on this train.' I was looking at Quinn yet not seeing him.

'But if it's not me, who is it?'

37.

I looked around the dining car with new interest.

Previously I'd been curious, about whether one or more of them might be part of the threat against me. Plus a faint sense of superiority towards all the others, the innocent sheep, who were ignorant of the remarkable business in which I was central.

Now it turned out that I was the most innocent and ignorant of them all. And somewhere among them was the British government's real courier: part of the scheme to gull me and make me the target. The sod had probably spent most of the last twenty-four hours smirking to themselves at my troubles. Oh, good-oh, Delamere's getting another grilling from the Turkish peelers. Ha-ha, Bulgarian bint's near as dammit just blown up his bunk! What a lark.

One conversation I was definitely looking forward to.

But with whom?

Ever since I'd got on the train, I'd felt what it was like to be the one people naturally suspected of being a British spy.

But now I definitely wasn't, and it was my turn: who did I think was the most likely courier?

I focused, to find Sikander Ali Khan smiling pleasantly at me over the table.

Wrong, of course. Who did I think was the least likely?

I'd have preferred to choose my dinner companions, to help my investigation. But they rather invited themselves. Khan, and then Junot the journo, and the Hungarian. Pleasant enough company, but I wasn't sure what I could get out of them. The polite chat and the dinner formalities began, with the stewards' usual deft glides and swoops.

It was probably too obvious for the Embassy men in Constantinople to have chosen someone English. Besides, I couldn't really see the Bishop or Miss Battersby wrestling Turkish policemen or dealing with Bulgarian bombs. My mind briefly wandered on how - back in the day - the Bishop would have fared with Mrs Petrov.

Focus. No. For whom was I the most effective decoy? Who was the opposite of Harry Delamere?

'A votre santé', the Hungarian said to me, polite smile; 'cheers'. We all toasted each other. I was trying to think of a line relevant to Hungary or music, but of all the topics on earth, Hungary and music are probably my weakest. I was about to mumble something when I realized he wasn't interested.

He was trying to stand and bow. 'Mademoiselle Froy,' he began, and she paused beside our table. He put a whole lot more gurgle and vowel into the name than I'd have managed. He tapped a little box on the table beside his place, a polished wooden thing about a foot long. 'I have here the aerophone, the ancient flute which we were discussing, should you be interested to inspect it after the meal.' Miss Froy looked a bit pink and nodded and thanked him, and he sat again.

You sly dog, I was thinking. Ancient flutes, indeed. And I could easily see little Miss Froy inclining towards a touch of the earnest intellectual; speaking myself as whatever the opposite of an earnest intellectual is. Sikander Ali was politely inspecting the box of the ancient flute, and I turned to Junot beside me.

'Sorry if I'm talking shop at dinner', I said; 'but it's just for the sake of conversation, really. As a journalist, looking around our compartment, who seems to you most interesting? Which interviews would you dream of for your newspaper?'

He was immediately into the spirit, and began looking around eagerly, while soups were placed in front of us.

'There are some I am obliged to seek, because my journal cannot be seen to miss the *grande affaire*, the important politics, the scandal of the day. For this I asked our archaeologist friend, and I would beg a quotation from Madame Dewoitine though I know she would spit on me.' He took a long slurp of soup, which I guess the whole carriage heard. 'But no, these are not my dreams. I dream of the secret insight, the unusual perspective. Officially I should ask Madame about the condition of the French economy, but I should prefer to ask her about the condition of the French marriage. I should ask His Excellency here about life in India, but I should prefer to ask him about life in your British Empire. I should like to discover that the large Turkish gentleman is secretly an anarchist, that your so-terrifying English aunt there is a passionate communist, or that one of the Russian girls is the daughter of the Tsar.'

'Very well. So who is not what they seem to be?'

Big smile at this, and he thought and spoke busily between slurps. 'Good! Good. First we must rule out those who are too well known as who they are to be who they are not. Madame Dewoitine, of course, and one or two others.' He nodded discreetly across the table towards Sikander Ali. 'Then there are those who for some reason, perhaps of physicality or character, could not be other than they are. Karim Bey. The English ladies.'

I made noises of agreement; he was nicely on the scent.

'That, if I may say, is the difficulty with you, dear sir.' He was considering me like a disapproving uncle. 'You don't appear to be something specific, and so you might be anything, and that is most interesting.' It might be to him, but it wasn't a path I wanted to follow. 'If by chance you are… something other than what you are supposed to be, may I suggest that you find something more distinctive to be supposed to be?' He giggled.

'I'll bear it in mind.'

He nodded as if I was serious. 'So, we are starting to make progress. The priests, the Bishop, who knows? It is not a mentality I understand, you comprehend?' He tapped his head. 'If I was bon catholique, perhaps, but alas… Now, here is a good example: the man who is an engineer - and also his companion who works with agriculture - myself I cannot tell if they are what they are supposed to be. And there is the brewer from Prague.' These would be Craig, and Svensson who shared a compartment with him - I wondered if that was accident or if they knew each other - and the chap who'd offered his wisdom about the Boer War at lunch. 'If I knew how to build a bridge myself, or what type of wheat is most appropriate to the Asian winter, or how to use that wheat to make a beer, I could test them. I do not. You?'

I shook my head.

'Then, our Greek friend.' Junot continued, and sniffed in distaste. 'He seems to favour red wine with fish.'

Clearly a scandalized headline was imminent. 'Perhaps he likes it', I said. Of all society's fetishes, it's one of the sillier.

He didn't seem convinced. 'In any case, I don't know enough about archaeology to challenge him.'

'I don't know much about Persia or medicine, either.' I nodded to where the dapper Dr Jam was sitting, next to a podgy chap with a complexion I couldn't place. 'And I don't know the man next to him at all.'

'I would be interested to hear a Persian opinion about the Ottoman Empire. The distinctive perspective, yes? With the other man I may be a little more confident. A gentleman from Beirut, excellent French. We have discussed French politics a full hour earlier. And yet...' - he smiled - 'I still do not know his business, and his vagueness is most thorough.'

We were into the main course now. 'Bit unsettling', I said. 'How much do we know about anyone? And yet... One of those same people you're interviewing, with some unfamiliar profession: if they're not what they're supposed to be, they're running a risk.'

'Ah yes!' Junot prodded the air with his fish-knife. 'They must hope that the stupid French journalist is ignorant of their trade. If you pretend to be a specialist of the agriculture from Stockholm, and then you bump into someone who knows that the cathedral is really on the other side of the square or that it would be madness to plant cabbages in Arabia...!' He sucked his teeth, and waved his fingers in that peculiarly French gesture for bad consequences. Then he ploughed into his fish again.

'Better to be vague, perhaps.'

'Indeed!' he said. 'So much harder to disprove. So easy for the charming American lady to call herself a writer. And myself I do not know what the Marquis de Valfierno is even supposed to be.'

At least I now knew what the M. stood for. 'I was wondering that. You had much chance to talk to him?'

'A little. He is something in art. But I had the feeling...' - he shrugged - 'he was not wanting to talk to me. And that perhaps is the most interesting thing of all.'

'Not so good for your interview.'

'Well, I would make up some melodramatic foolishness if I needed to. Master criminal, absconding bankrupt, lost prince... My pages do not fill themselves, you understand? His flexibility works for me as well as for him.' He glanced around the compartment. 'More difficult to disprove. But perhaps so much more suspicious. The writer. The art enthusiast. Or...' - he looked sadly at me - 'the English traveller.'

38.

Not long after the last of the food, we crossed from Bulgaria into Serbia. Again there was the palaver of switching locomotives, as we all sat in the dining compartment trying to time our sips of liqueur between jolts.

Again I felt the sense of relief, of escape, as we clanked slowly out of a place which had been so nearly fatal. Then I remembered how that had turned out for me last time.

Once, walking along the aisle, I caught the glance of little Major Hilmi, sitting quietly at a table with the two priests. Not exactly the Folies Bergère, as tables go. I gave him a courteous nod. He did not reciprocate.

I had thought our business was finished. Apparently not.

He surely couldn't be thinking of coming for me again. He was now a whole country away from his legal authority. Except, of course, while we were still in the Balkans he might feel he had room to manoeuvre. I've spent a bit of time among the tough, independent spirits in that part of the world: up front they're careful of their dignity and love a bureaucratic obstacle or three, but behind the scenes it's Liberty Hall - or, rather, less liberty than you might hope Hall. And they change alliances once a fortnight.

For one ridiculous moment I wondered about trying to explain to him that I, too, had thought I'd had his damn' document but - what a mix-up! - apparently not and could we be friends? Otherwise I drifted in and out of the conversation, and watched the tables around me, and tried to decide whom I would pick me as decoy for.

A few people had wandered away after the meal, but things were still pretty jovial. At the next table the Bishop was saying something about Mesopotamia to Craig across the aisle, and offering cigars to him and to Peg Madison.

Quite possibly a first on the Orient Express, a woman smoking at table, and she wouldn't have got the option anywhere in London. Another example of how Americans can move the world forwards, and of how this particular American dealt with the world. A purely personal preference, but I find few things more handsome than a woman smoking a cigar: the assurance of it, the unrestraint. Grand. Credit to the old Bish., too: no wonder he'd not made Archbishop of Canterbury.

Elsewhere my Hungarian chum was discussing ancient flutes with Miss Froy, carefully watched by Miss Battersby - who, whatever her familiarity with musicology, clearly knew the old tunes when she heard them. I noticed a similar performance at another table, where Svensson the agriculturalist was talking one of the Russian girls through the contents of a box of little somethings, each in its own much tinier box: I took a wild guess at seeds.

And I tried to guess about Svensson. He obviously had enough subject knowledge to talk to the ladies; did that mean he passed Junot's test of credibility? He was another of the fit and independent young men on the train: like the Persian doctor, like the Hungarian, like a handful of others. And there was no reason why one of them couldn't do a bit of diplomatic couriering on top of his regular trade. A box of plant mould, or a limp manner and a peculiar suit, might seem ideal disguise for someone ruthless enough to do the job.

Lord, it was a tedious game. This is precisely why I've always shied away from diplomatic and intelligencing work, on the rare occasions when they've come anywhere near me. It's all so damn' vague and shifty.

Craig had been saying something about the Ottoman administration wherever he'd been building his bridge or dam or whatever it was, and the Bishop said: 'But surely that's nonsense, my dear fellow. The way Turkish governors operate-'

I caught Sikander Ali's eye, and we exchanged empty smiles. He, surely, was too exotic a bird to be involved in this sort of foolishness. But then again, you wouldn't get Turks tossing his compartment or Bulgarian spies blowing it up;

they wouldn't dare. So perhaps-

'Oh you -!'

Mercifully the next word had been swallowed. Among all the languages on the Orient Express one doesn't hear much Anglo-Saxon, especially not in the dining car with ladies present. And especially not from a Bishop.

Apparently distracted in their disagreement about near eastern politics, Craig had knocked the Bishop's cigar box onto the floor. Now he was trying to apologize and rather uselessly to help the Bishop regather the contents, and a couple of stewards were racing in to help, and there was half a minute of general flap before the old man sorted himself out. I saw Craig sitting back in his seat, watching the proceedings, a bit guarded.

It's a traditional arrogance to say 'English' when you mean 'British', and t'other way round. Now I was rehearsing my thoughts, and what exactly I'd just seen and heard.

Then things quietened down for a while. There's not a lot going on in the far south of Serbia, and through the windows the night was unbroken darkness. Miss Battersby tried to liven things up by getting Miss Froy to read out the bit about the old Roman capital of the province of Upper something-or-other. But as the Romans hadn't left the lights on it didn't mean much. A few more passengers drifted away to their compartments.

Near the bar, the mysterious Valfierno - the M. le M. himself - nodded meaningfully at me. I'd no idea, of course, what the meaning was.

He was distracted by the departure of the Misses Battersby and Froy, whose hands he felt it necessary to kiss. He lingered a bit longer over Miss Froy's. 'The beauty of the sun it must depart', he murmured; 'but we know that the beauty of the moon will appear.' He smiled gravely at her. 'If you will permit a compliment.'

'A compliment may be gratefully received,' Miss Froy replied rather stiffly, 'but flattery must be mistrusted.' She said it as if reciting from a nineteenth century book of Advice for Young Gentlewomen - which she probably was - but it was a fair point and coolly delivered.

Again the heavy smile. 'One must worry', he said, 'if a little imposture is no longer permissible in the relations between the sexes.'

'One must worry', Miss Battersby replied firm, 'that a little imposture is too easily a large imposture. Good evening.'

The older woman took the younger by the elbow and they glided out together, an ocean liner accompanied by a yacht.

Valfierno watched them go reverentially. I was watching Miss Battersby more particularly. She was built for comfort rather than speed, but there was a toughness in her; a resilience. One would be wise not to underestimate Miss Amelia Battersby.

Then Valfierno turned to me again. 'I would offer you a drink, Sir Henry,' he said; 'but I don't wish to detain you with these foolish jovialities.'

I almost agreed for his attitude alone, but I didn't want to get into a long conversation. I just couldn't see him as the courier: too obviously mysterious, surely, and I couldn't believe that the British - or any other government - would think him reliable enough for this sort of job.

I said something manly about discipline and restraint, and he nodded. 'I have been watching you', he said. 'You will pardon me, I hope. I have not wished to push myself forwards, nor to intrude. And yet...' his face was close to mine now, the voice low and serious. 'I have the impression you are a gentleman of prudent taste. A man who might be interested in... in the discreet' - he emphasized the word - 'acquisition of items that are, shall we say, of unique character. I find that I might be in a position to oblige you.' He glanced around quickly. 'I think I have something that you might want.'

He saw someone over my shoulder, and nodded at me and smiled and moved off.

39.

What the hell had that been about?

I walked out of the dining car immediately. Partly because what the hell and enough with the madness, and partly because it was the best way to stop myself beaming him with the soda syphon.

I found Quinn, and he joined me in my compartment for a council of war. 'I'm ceasing to find any stimulation or amusement in this situation', I said, pretty grumpy. 'Entertainment value of this trip is now officially nil.'

Quinn grunted. That was about average for his conversational style, and a well-judged caution about trying to read my emotions.

'Can't have a glass of wine or a mouthful of food without worrying about the company. Can't have ten-minute's chat with an attractive woman without her trying to blow up the shop.'

His face was stone. I'd the sense he was having difficulty suppressing something.

'Nothing amusing about this, Quinn.'

'No sir.' He shook his head firmly. 'Certainly not.'

'Then don't smirk.'

'No sir.'

'Whole thing's ludicrous.'

'Yes sir.' He went to say something, then thought twice about it, which was probably wise. Then he risked it. 'You're naturally angry about it all, sir. Rightly so, that is-'

'Rightly so, Quinn.'

'Rightly so. And it's all a muddle. But...' - he was feeling his way with heavy steps - 'surely we don't... really... need to be worrying about it.'

'What?'

'You don't have to be in this, sir. You're curious about who the courier is, rightly so... But you don't need to know. And you don't need to do anything. You're off the hook, sir.'

'Try telling that to the Bulgarian mutton shunters! I'm still the one they're arresting. I'm still the one getting his valuables looted in the waiting room. I get some fat Balkan bobby rummaging round my knackers and everyone else goes off shopping!' I glared at him.

'That is… that is very distressing, sir, yes.'

'And all the bloody time, Algernon-the-bloody-innocent is swanning around out there, shiny shoes and free as a bird and no doubt having a good laugh. Sneering bastard; I'll give him something to laugh about.'

Quinn just nodded.

'Now that damned Spaniard, or whatever he is, he says he's got something I want. Is that the document or isn't it? Why the hell would he want to give it to me?'

Quinn shook his head.

I pulled out the passenger list. 'Right. Who don't we know about? The First Class I've been through and they're giving me a headache. Second Class… The Misses, surely not but we'll keep our ears open. You - you're not the secret courier, are you Quinn? Keep your ears peeled around your Sikh chum in case something slips about Sikander Ali, but I doubt it. Russian girls seem unlikely and I don't know how we'd find out… Now, Monsieur C. Chehab. Don't know anything about him and apparently he's a bit furtive.'

I glanced at Quinn. He shrugged. 'Keeps himself to himself.'

I scowled. 'And Dr Jam. Bit too smooth to be true? Oh, this is no good… Then the two maids, no. Now, Craig and his Swedish chum.' I looked up again. 'Two fit active competent men.' Quinn waited. 'If you get the chance, see how comfortable they are talking about themselves. Then the priests. Haven't had a peep out of them.' He shrugged. 'We need to do better. You're a quiet sort of chap. See if they open up to you.'

'They seem a bit… intimidated, sir.'

'Even better: intimidate them. Then Junot - I'm into him

all right. Ah, this is your pal isn't it? In with Junot. J. Munk. What's his story?'

Quinn scowled. 'The one they promote to Corporal just because he's big, but he hasn't got the sense for it.'

'Where's he from, anyway?'

'Think I heard him talking German with the French gentleman.' As a journalist Junot might be one of the rare frogs who'd deign to learn it. 'From Prague, I think. Austrian, or Austro-Hungarian, isn't it?'

'Might be. Keep your ears open.' He nodded. I considered him. 'Quinn, if I'm making bad decisions out of anger or funk, it's your job to tell me.'

He pretended to look reassuring. 'I wouldn't-'

'In this case I'm not, anyway.' He pretended to agree. 'I know I'm a bit ratty, Quinn. But I would like to know. And there's still too much that's unexplained. What happened to chummy on Constantinople railway station? What happened to the Turk - Hilmi's man? And was it Hilmi who tossed the compartment? And those unlikely bandits - whose side are they on? And what's Valfierno up to? And pretty much everyone else?'

Quinn stayed silent.

'I'm not going to sleep. I'm staying on the front foot.'

He nodded.

I felt the train slowing, and soon it stopped. Dimly, through the foggy window, I could see the lights of a station. Our first in Serbia.

I stowed the passenger list. 'Right. Back into the front line, eh?' Together we walked along to the dining compartment, and I paused by the bar to see who I ought to get pally with next, as part of my effort to find the courier.

'I suppose there's one good thing sir.' There was no one near us, but his voice was low.

'I find it hard to believe, Quinn, but have a go, do.'

'Now we're really not the ones carrying the paper,' he murmured, 'and there's really someone else carrying it, there has to be a good chance that they'll attract the suspicion.' He was actually looking rather optimistic, unusual in a Cornishman and in someone who's spent time in my company. 'I mean to say, maybe you're not going to be feeling the heat quite so much sir.'

At which point a Serbian uniform appeared in the doorway and said: 'Good evening, ladies and gentlemen. Who of you is Henry Delamere?'

40.

The look I gave Quinn was not kindly, and he had the grace to look uncomfortable.

I was used to this sort of thing now, of course, and I stepped forward. 'Good evening', I said.

There were a couple of Serbian uniforms in view now. The one who'd spoken had stepped into the dining compartment, and another had appeared in the doorway behind him. The first smiled pleasantly, and spoke again. 'Good evening to you, Mr Delamere.' He was a shabby looking specimen: average height, his uniform hanging sack-like around him. 'I am sorry to disturb you.' He spoke with that sad lilt all Slavs seem to have, every vowel deep and drawn and depressed. 'Would you come with me please?'

I made like I was thinking about it. 'Out of interest,' I said, 'what if I refuse?'

He pulled off his uniform cap, and ran a hand over the strands of thin black hair that were combed across his head. He made like he was thinking about it too. 'Ivanović here' - the faintest nod back towards the man behind him - 'and as many other men as necessary would drag you off the train.' He put the cap back on his head, askew. 'How many men would be necessary, do you think? You seem a healthy fellow. Four or five men should do.' He smiled again. 'Bit of a fuss though.'

'Quite', I said. 'Merely curious.'

'Who is travelling with you?'

Now I did some real thinking. The Serbs seemed a pretty business-like sort of outfit, and I had nothing to gain from delaying them, and less than nothing from annoying them.

I pointed at Quinn. 'This man is my valet.'

The Serb officer - I assumed he was an officer - considered Quinn. Quinn was looking large and watchful. 'And how many men', said the Serb, 'would be necessary to drag him?'

'None,' I said, 'fortunately for you. He is a highly disciplined professional.' Quinn was looking even larger, and my words were for him more than for the uniforms.

Another smile. 'I am sure of it. He shall accompany Ivanović, please.'

Ivanović stepped forwards. He grabbed Quinn by the arm, which wasn't the brightest thing he'd ever done. Quinn looked into the man's face, then down at the hand clutching his arm. 'Easy, Sergeant', I murmured.

Quinn said: 'Not Mr.' He said it quietly, and he wasn't looking at anyone.

'Excuse me?' the officer said.

Now Quinn turned to look at him. 'Not Mr. Sir. Sir Henry Delamere.'

The Serb looked at me, then Quinn. 'A highly disciplined professional.' Then back to me. '*Sir* Henry, indeed. How exciting for us. Don't think we've had a Sir before.' He opened an inviting arm towards the door. 'Shall we?'

First he got me to show him my compartment. He pointed a bony finger at it, and a couple more uniforms were immediately inside. It looked like my bags and probably the furnishings were going to get another going over. Then he escorted me to the baggage wagon, and I had to point out my luggage. He left it where it was, with another man standing nearby. I smiled. 'I suppose you'll get my man along to confirm.'

'We are relatively disciplined professionals ourselves, Sir Henry.'

He led me into a waiting room. 'Where did you pick up your English?' I asked.

He looked at me, to check I wasn't making fun of him. Then he nodded; a grin. 'I lived six months in Brighton. I worked as a barber.'

Not an answer I'd been expecting, but it's a funny old world. A minute later Quinn and his new friend appeared in the waiting room.

It was a dingy, greasy little place, with just a single wooden bench. But they'd got a wood stove roaring in the corner, and it was warm enough.

Three more uniforms came in, rifles pointing at Quinn and me.

I considered them uneasily. The atmosphere had got a lot less friendly. Once again I was resenting the real courier, who should have been going through whatever we were about to go through.

The shabby officer saw my concern. 'Something I learned in Brighton. You Englishmen are very polite, but you are even more proud.' He looked at each of us. He checked the men around him, checked that the rifles had us well covered. 'Now you will take your clothes off.'

I looked into the pleasant face. 'What happened to the disciplined professional bit?'

He shrugged. 'Our country is less than one hundred years old. Two or three times we have changed our ruling family, by violence.' I remembered hearing about the most recent coup several years back, the outgoing King and Queen hacked to pieces by plotters - plotters in uniform. 'We were born in violent contest with those around us, and we have survived in violent contest with those around us, and we shall probably be in violent contest with them again.'

'Ever stopped to wonder why?'

He smiled, jolly as ever. 'You are suspected of carrying a

document which is extremely damaging to Serbia. The one certainty this night is that we are going to search you, from toe-cap to hat-box, every stitch of every seam. You can make that easy. We're all men here, and the stove is nice and cosy. Or my men will club you unconscious with their rifles and rip your clothes off with their knives and search you anyway.' The voice was still brisk, business-like. 'We are known for our wildness, Sir Henry. The rest of the passengers will not be surprised if we dump you back on the train, half-dressed and half-dead. And they certainly won't protest. Entirely up to you.'

I nodded. 'Merely curious', I said. And I undressed. Quinn followed.

They found nothing of significance, not on us, not in our clothes, not in our bags.

Among the things they didn't find was the blank document, because a few hours earlier, before going into dinner, I'd burned it in the little sink in my compartment.

41.

I'd burned the document partly out of calculation that it was useless, partly sheer anger at the deception against me. It had been halfway burned when I suddenly wondered if there had been something written in invisible ink - if I had, after all, been carrying Europe's most secret and powerful document - and if I had, therefore, just burned Europe's most secret and powerful document to ashes in a railway compartment vanity unit. I was rather hoping not. I could always say that the Serbs had taken it from me, which they surely would have done.

They'd searched our clothes with the thoroughness they'd promised, and our bags and compartments likewise. That meant they'd had to go through Mahan Singh's digs too, and I later gathered there'd been a rather dicey moment when a Serb policeman had come close to an awfully painful death, but Sikander Ali had stood him down and the search had happened without anyone being disembowelled.

That helped me. So too did the arrival, half way through the searching of our clothes, of the conductor. He'd come into our cosy little waiting room, escorted by a policeman, to ask how long the delay would be. He found Sir Harry Delamere, Baronet, sitting bare-arsed on a bench by the stove enjoying a cigarette and chatting about the back-streets of Brighton with the Grand Inquisitor, and Quinn, also in a state of nature, standing watching closely as the police went through our kit, and he'd looked pretty startled. Quinn's a physically imposing sort of beast even when he's got his trousers on. I'd asked my scruffy friend, a bit snootily, whether he was selling tickets for this performance, and the Serb had looked genuinely unhappy at the interruption, and the conductor had been hustled out again.

Pretty rich for a frog to get rattled by a healthy bit of nudity - I mean to say, this was probably an average afternoon's entertainment in the café back in Paris - but rattled he was, and that was all to the good. The failure of the public and very thorough search of our compartments, and this now public very thorough search of our persons, would only reinforce our innocence.

The Serb officer was obviously disappointed not to have found what he was looking for, and it had taken some of the wind out of his sails. He got us dressed and back on the train and called it a day quickly enough, with a courteous 'bon voyage' and the wish that we'd give his regards to Brighton. As the train got underway, Quinn bustled off to re-stow our bags and I went for a drink.

'Rather irregular', I said to the Hungarian, the first chap I saw at the bar. 'Never had a search like that. Had to take all my clothes off.'

'Well goodness', Peg Madison said from one of the bench seats. 'You often do that sort of thing, or was this a diplomatic protest?'

'It is all most distressing', said Michel, the conductor, who'd hurried in after me. The sight of Quinn's torso had obviously upset him more than I'd realized. 'I have never heard of such a thing. The Compagnie des Wagon Lits is most sorry Sir Henry.'

Miss Madison was still enjoying herself. 'Was that why they let you go so fast, d'you think?'

For now it suited me to play it serious with the conductor. 'Don't mention it', I said to him. 'Bit of fresh air, good for the pores. I am hoping this'll be the last harassment I must endure.'

'Of course!' he said, anxious. 'Of course.' We both knew it was a long way to Paris, but now that he was at last convinced I was a truly innocent passenger he wanted to be polite. I wondered if he'd run to some free champagne.

42.

I saw Theotokis nipping out, faithful treasure-box in hand. Too early for him to be turning in, surely; the bar couldn't be dry yet. So I might have an immediate chance to carry out a wheeze I was now set on.

I grabbed a glass and Quinn, and hurried out into the corridor.

In my compartment, I spoke quickly. 'Turns out the Serbian government weren't listening to you, Quinn - bit of a blow, I know - and I'm still in the frame. That being so, I refuse to sit still and enjoy the view.' He didn't disagree. In his silent solid way, I knew that he was as annoyed as I. 'There are a few things we're going to check once and for all. Starting now.'

He nodded, and I gave him the plan. It wasn't much of a plan, so it didn't take long.

That was handy, because almost immediately we heard what we hoped were Theotokis's footsteps coming back along the corridor from powdering his nose. Quinn stepped into the corridor, and began gazing out of the window while waiting for me. Only I would have noticed his murmured confirmation that they were the right footsteps.

And only I would have noticed his three slight coughs, evenly paced. On the third I was backing out into the corridor, turning out the compartment light as I went. I backed straight into poor old Theotokis, and with the impact the contents of my glass went all down one side of my coat. 'Oh you stupid b-!' I began, turning.

I saw who it was, and stopped. 'My dear chap, do excuse me. Hadn't realized it was you.' I was still speaking crossly and he was looking rather alarmed. I turned and glared at Quinn. Theotokis was apologizing, a bit bewildered and a bit defensive. 'Not at all, partly - Oh hell, it's soaking through to my shirt now.' I thrust the glass at Quinn and pulled off my coat and thrust that at Theotokis - he held it uneasily over his box - and started to examine my shirt front. 'Yes - no - we might be all…' I re-entered the compartment. 'Bring that in here would you? Thing is to sponge it down quickly before it stains. Over here. Hold it up, would you? Quinn!' This over the Greek's shoulder. 'Stop standing there like a bloody heifer. Close the door and come here!' I knew that Theotokis would appreciate the instinctive blaming of the staff. 'You will stand right there behind Mr Theotokis. Hold this box of his, but don't move an inch, you hear? It is the most precious thing in Europe.' They were all saying that on the Orient Express this season. 'That's right old chap, hold the coat up. That's the ticket. Hold it flat and firm and that way I won't splash you. Sorry, think you got a bit there. Now, if you keep it there like that - that's right - I'll just towel it down as best I can. Really, you mustn't give it another thought. Why my man didn't warn me you were there… Got him cheap from the prison; half asleep most of the time. How's it feel now? Not too damp? Well, let's try it on. Sorry, didn't mean to catch you there. Perfect. Well now.' I took a theatrical breath. 'Right,

135

here's your box, safe and sound. Might I suggest we go and enjoy a drink together now?'

43.

The next hour included two major crimes. At the time they totally passed me by. So excuse me if I take the action step by step now.

The train rattled onwards through the Serbian night. In the dining car, a select group of passengers settled down for another drink or two and a dozy chat. Some were naturally inclined that way. Some weren't ready for sleep after the disruption of the border crossing. And some had nefarious purposes. At the time I thought that was just me.

I ended up sitting with the Bishop, the Hungarian music-man, and big Karim Bey. The latter two were on the aisle, mercifully: you wouldn't want Karim on the edge of the wagon, not going round corners. Across the aisle, Theotokis - box safely between his feet again - had got distracted onto a table of the Misses Battersby, Froy and Madison: something for everyone, there. One table farther from the bar, their backs to Theotokis, the two Russian girls had just joined Svensson. I saw Quinn pause beside them, and murmur something to the Swede. It was the usual inaudible Quinn grumble, but I knew he was expressing his new-found enthusiasm for agriculture and hoping to see the box of seeds sometime. Svensson was nodding with earnest enthusiasm and patting the box, and I saw the two women considering Quinn as if he were a Bulgarian cathedral. He wandered on to Dr Jam and Monsieur Chehab, the chap from Beirut, and cautiously invited himself to join them. Good scout. I was aware of one or two other figures down that end of the compartment.

Someone had suggested champagne - the Hungarian, I think. He seemed a light drinker, and I wanted to be this evening. The Bishop was probably on a regular diet of half a bottle of port a night, but accepted the champagne as a warm-up. I doubt Karim even noticed the stuff: you'd have to fill him from a water tower to have any effect. The conversation flowed pretty free and friendly, anyway. The Hungarian seemed to have that naive quality, which you often get in people working in a foreign language, of never understanding a joke and always pushing a point farther than necessary. And since on this train most of us were foreign to most of the rest of us, and generally desperate for good conversation, he was a positive player at any table.

This had been his first visit to Constantinople, he'd said. Did Karim Bey think the city was changing very much? 'Can we yet speak of a twentieth century Constantinople?'

Karim inflated himself - staggering idea though that was - and pronounced in his usual philosophical manner. 'In some particular areas of progress, its energy has shown the way into the twentieth century. But in many habits and values, it remains eighteenth century.'

'The bandits', I said, 'were pretty well-dressed.'

Karim beamed at this. 'Some would reverse that emphasis, and suggest that the well-dressed men of Constantinople seem to be bandits.'

We chuckled politely. 'My hotel perhaps was a good example of the mixture', Hungary said. 'The manager and the staff had the most elaborate mediaeval courtesies, but the plumbing was very satisfactory. Did you find, excellency?' - this to the Bish. - 'At the Bristol, you said.'

'Indeed. Certainly an improvement on Cairo, where the opposite is always the case: twentieth century manners and eighteenth century plumbing.'

More laughs. Hungary said something about the mixture of costumes - traditional and modern western. The Bishop made a comment about what sometimes happens with African tribesmen who spend a lot of time working with white men.

Hungary said something about the new politics in Istanbul - did Karim expect that this would change the tone of society? - and again I saw the old Karim, the one who'd been bugging me twenty-four hours earlier. First the silence. Then the big empty smile. Then big empty words: perhaps we would think him unimaginative, but he expected, as ever, change to be so slow that we would not notice, and so slight that perhaps we, with our curious western enthusiasms, would be disappointed. Mischievous smile, and we all felt as ignorant and impertinent as he intended. The Bish. asked what Hilmi would say on the subject, and Karim looked very peculiar indeed - somehow both offended and offensive. I got the strong impression that one didn't speak lightly of the domestic affairs, and particularly the domestic officials, of the Ottoman Empire when Karim Bey was around.

My focus was wandering. I was trying somehow to be aware of the whole compartment. Mr Beirut seemed to be speaking very ponderously, and Quinn was looking interested. I saw Peg Madison showing her portable camera to Miss Battersby, and answering a fusillade of technical questions. Once again, Miss Battersby was proving a more intrepid sort of bird than first glance would suggest. Shortly afterwards she and Miss Froy toddled off to bed. Svensson was being very earnest about something. The Russians were nodding thoughtfully as he spoke, one rummaging in her bag. Farther down the compartment on my side I saw Valfierno, and I was trying to work out who he was talking to. Was it Craig's shoulders I could see, or Junot's?

We'd finished the champagne, and Karim had summoned a steward: no he didn't need the cocktail menu - he would have a Bijou; gin and tonic for Hungary; brandy for the Bishop - perhaps he was still building up to the port; and whisky for Delamere. The Bishop offered cigars. Karim began an elaborate question to the Bishop comparing the paths of the Ottoman and British Empires.

By this point I wasn't paying attention. Someone had said

something, and I couldn't think what it had been, and it was echoing oddly in my head. I think I noticed the doctor wandering past and out of the compartment, medical case in hand.

I came alert when a female voice swore close by. I assumed she was swearing, though my Russian doesn't run to that sort of detail. Oksana - the particularly lovely Russian girl - had stopped by our table and was bending down and peering at something around the back of her thigh. For a moment I was still trying to recapture what Svensson had been saying about hill ranges running east-west or north-south. As she'd got up from the table - following her friend? I didn't notice the other - a thread on her dress had snagged on something and pulled away as she walked. Theotokis was happy enough, in the ringside seat by her legs, but I was cursing my broken train of thought.

Our drinks arrived. Hungary asked the Bishop what he thought British policy was in the Ottoman Empire. Both the Bishop and Karim looked uncomfortable. From the end of the compartment, Valfierno got up and walked along the aisle. He was carrying a thin attaché case. He slowed as he passed us, and nodded heavily to me.

The chat went on a little longer, Delamere not saying much. Pretty soon the Bish. decided he'd had enough of imperial strategy, and wandered out to bed. One or two others left not long after.

And then I got it. I glanced beside me at the Hungarian, who was saying something to Karim and checking that his flute case was still on the seat beside him. I remembered his interest in plumbing.

The things people say, and the things people don't say.

In that moment, I was pretty sure I knew who the real courier was.

44.

No time like the present. I excused myself, beckoning to Quinn as I made for the door.

Valfierno, it turned out, hadn't left the compartment. 'Sir Henry,' he said, just a murmur, 'I have something I'd like you to see. I am sure you would appreciate it.' He glanced around us. 'In your compartment, I suggest.' He was still holding the thin case.

I nodded, and let him lead the way into the corridor. He didn't see my gesture to Quinn; I would not be unguarded.

As soon as we were in my compartment he was straight down to business. 'Sir Henry, you are not a man for the elaborate ceremonial and the small talk.' I smiled. 'I will be direct. I noticed you quickly as a man of reserve; a man of discernment, and this is why I venture to speak. Perhaps in turn you have been wondering my business.' I tried to look like a man who hadn't. 'I am a dealer, Sir Henry, in *objets d'art*. But I have no public face; no shop.' He said the word with distaste. 'My interest is known among... certain connoisseurs, among the great families of Europe. Occasionally I become aware of a unique piece, and I am able to find a customer for it. It may be that I only make one arrangement in a year, but it will be for a price congenial to both parties, and it will ensure that some treasure of art remains in appropriate hands. How does this seem to you?'

Hellish fishy, was the obvious answer, but presumably not the one in the book. I gave a single heavy nod, the kind that a man of discernment might give.

He nodded back - that made two men of discernment - and at last opened his case. Using the case as a stand, he propped up the contents.

It was a painting.

That's about all I could tell you, but I was pretty sure about it. Less than a foot tall, a bit less than square. A chap sitting down, relaxed but grand. Good looking, and very athletic. Just a cape draped round his shoulders and discreetly covering the essentials. Perhaps he'd been having trouble with the Serb police too.

Valfierno said softly: 'It is Poussin, naturally.'

'Naturally.'

'The god Apollo. For his Apollo and Daphne, yes?'

'Ah yes.'

'From his final residence in Rome, of course.'

'Of course.'

I was going carefully. I've done a few legitimate trades in my time, and I've done a few more very suspect trades, and it never does to jump ahead.

'In his final years, when his hand was not so sure, he produced more elaborate preparatory sketches for his great paintings. As you see, it has almost the detail and finish of the final masterpiece. And of course the added thrill of seeing the master at work. The process, as it were, happening in front of your eyes.'

He watched it, happening in front of his eyes. So I did the same.

I wouldn't know Poussin if he sat next to me on the omnibus. Nor the god Apollo; not unless he always dressed that way. More civilized acquaintances confirm that my ignorance is matched by total lack of taste. But the picture was exquisite. The poise of the figure; the combination of simplicity and beauty.

'This has been in private hands - one family - for many generations. They have found themselves obliged to sell some treasures, in circumstances which they do not wish public. Accordingly, they come to me. They know they will get an adequate price, and more than adequate discretion.'

I was curious why he fancied me a likely punter for his picture. Perhaps for the same reasons as everyone else thought me a likely British government agent. Or perhaps precisely because everything else thought me a likely British government agent.

'The Apollo, perhaps, more appropriate for a gentleman of independent mind. The patron of travellers, the protector of fugitives.' A glance at me, a flashed smile.

'It's very handsome', I said, and I meant it. 'And... you seem to choose your customers with the same skill you have for your works of art.'

A little bow. 'The frame is for convenience only: it can be changed easily of course, if you prefer something more or less elaborate.' He started to show how easily it unclipped from the canvas. 'Or some connoisseurs prefer the canvas alone, I know.'

'Monsieur le Marquis, would you allow me a day or so to think about it? While we're on the train.'

'But of course, Sir Henry.'

He packed up and I showed him out. 'As to...'

He nodded. 'The price is one hundred and fifty English guineas.'

'Very fair, no doubt.' And he was gone.

45.

Quinn was lurking a yard or two off, and I beckoned him in.

He looked the question. 'Chap wants to sell us a painting for a hundred guineas.'

He nodded. He was hoping I wasn't interested.

'Meanwhile, I'm pretty sure who the real courier is.' That got his attention. The Quinn eyebrows rose.

I told him. The eyebrows dropped again; not convinced.

'Major Hilmi gave us one specific detail about the handling of the document in Constantinople: a location; an hotel. And each time it's been mentioned, the conversation has been rapidly steered away, and each time by the same person. The first time it was steered onto me, and why I'm such a good suspect. That wasn't the only time my obvious shiftiness was emphasized for public benefit. And if I wasn't already shifty enough, he encouraged me in my investigations, just so's I'd associate myself even more with the document, make myself even more the centre of attention.'

Quinn still didn't like it, but he understood it.

'Anyway, I'm popping round to his compartment for a chat. Go and block the conductor a mo, then get back in here. Keep an eye out the window and an ear out the door, in case I need you.'

The slightest nod and he was moving. I waited until his bulk blocked the conductor's view of the empty corridor, then I was out and knocking softly at compartment number 3.

I didn't wait for a reply, and it wasn't locked. I slipped in, and quickly closed the door behind me.

My host was staring up at me, eyes wide in alarm.

'You might or might not be a Bishop', I said quietly. 'But I'm damn sure you're something else too. You're the government's real courier. You're the man I'm decoying for.'

Still he stared up at me.

He might or might not have been a Bishop; he was certainly dead.

46.

I gazed at the dead face for as long as I could stomach. He'd had some sort of seizure, by the looks of him. That was my expert medical analysis, anyway.

But then, it seemed one hell of coincidence that the good Lord had chosen this particular moment to call him home, right now, when he was carrying a top secret document. You'd think the Almighty would have a sharper appreciation of the demands of British foreign policy.

I had a quick look, but I couldn't see any sign of violence on him.

Then again, I hadn't inclination or time to look too

closely. I was now, of course, in a bit of a spot. Hopefully I hadn't been seen entering his compartment. And no one except Quinn knew I was here. I very much wanted to keep it that way. I'd been everyone's favourite suspect as courier of the damn' document. The one man who could conclusively have proved that I wasn't had just, very inconveniently, died.

Being found with a dead body would only make me more dubious in the public mind, were that possible. There was no good reason why anyone should come calling, but the implications of them doing so would be bad.

I badly wanted out of there. But I'd no way of predicting when someone might be passing, and to be seen leaving was the worst outcome: either I'd have to advertise his death and draw attention to having been with him, apparently near the end; or I could not mention it, and then invite much darker suspicions when it was finally discovered.

There was more. I badly wanted out of there, but I badly needed more time in there. Time during which every second might bring discovery.

Quinn.

I stuck my head out the window a little cautiously, hoping not to find half the train looking at the stars. I was lucky: no line of spectators, just my valet, and he was alert. I beckoned to him and then, by an exuberant gesture of both hands, tried to suggest surprise or excitement.

Then I was back looking around the compartment. The late Bishop only had a couple of small soft bags in the cupboard under his bed, and they were easily stowed elsewhere. Applying an interesting variation of the standard form Delamere Patented Cupboard Rummaging Method, I wriggled in feet first, and carried on wriggling until I was all the way inside. I could close one of the little doors, and the other as near as hopefully wouldn't be noticed.

Then I lay back in the darkness, and waited.

144

47.

Partly for lack of an adequate mime for it, I'd not told Quinn to delay, and he didn't. It was only a minute or so before I heard a knock at the door.

By luck or judgement, he'd contrived to have a steward near him as he opened the door. It wouldn't have been much of an improvement to have my valet in the predicament I was trying to avoid for myself.

He started to say something about Sir Henry asking something, then I heard a word of surprise. Immediately there came the steward's muffled concern, and that was the job done nicely: dead Bishop officially discovered, and no one individual in the frame, least of all poor Harry Delamere.

There was a bit of scuffling in the compartment, the steward apparently giving the old Bish. a shake just to check he really had checked out, and then I heard hurrying feet; he was off to fetch more senior help, no doubt.

Quinn's voice was a firm murmur: 'Just me, sir; fifteen seconds only.'

Down in my cupboard, I kept shtum. Nice of him, but my calculations about being found on the spot - or, worse, being found wriggling out of a cupboard on the spot - hadn't changed. In a few moments the steward was back, and now there was the conductor's voice with him.

They all piled in, and there was a renewed bout of dead-Bishop-shaking. At some point in the proceedings, a discreet boot - no doubt Cornish - very gently pushed my cupboard door fully closed.

As a result, I heard less of what followed. At one point I caught Quinn saying that I'd asked him to deliver a message to the Bishop. Good line, I thought. Then there was something from the steward, presumably confirming Quinn's story about the discovery, so that was his alibi sorted.

Then another arrival; packing them in like sardines. More muffled conversation. There was a different character to this voice: less surprise; less discussion. I heard shuffling down by my ear, and my heart jumped. Would someone think there was something useful here in my cupboard? A blanket?

A voice said, more distinctly - commanding - 'Lay him flat.'

The shuffling and murmuring continued close by. Alarm at imminent discovery distracted me longer than it should: this was a quiet, steady voice, apparently looking closely at the body, and when I stopped fretting I realized they must have woken young Doctor Jam and got him along.

A final shuffle, and the murmuring was more distant; he'd finished his examination, and stood. A last bit of discussion, and whoever was still in shuffled out.

There was a final bit of murmuring from the corridor, and then I heard the door being locked.

Once again there was silence. Just me, locked in the compartment, in my cupboard, hands folded on my chest and contemplating the infinite. At some point I realized that, a foot or so above me, the Bishop must be laid out in exactly the same posture.

48.

I gave it a quarter hour. I had no way of telling if it was a quarter hour, of course, stuck in the pitch darkness of the cupboard with limited arm movements. More or less a quarter hour.

The opposition, somehow, had got to the poor old Bishop. Presumably they wanted the secret document he was carrying.

Perhaps they'd got it.

But he wouldn't have given it to them. There were no obvious signs of violence on the old chap; it didn't appear that they'd forced it out of him. And the compartment had seemed neat and tidy - dead body aside. Perhaps they'd been very clever or very lucky and found it immediately. Or perhaps they were well-brought up assassins who tidied up after themselves; if a thing's worth doing, and all that.

It didn't seem likely. Obviously he'd have had the thing well hidden. And they'd have been unlikely to linger with the dead body, for precisely the same reasons that had vexed me. And the Bishop hadn't come to bed all that long ago: I couldn't see how they'd have had time for a full search and then a bit of house-keeping.

So the most precious document in Europe, a document which had cost the lives of two of its guardians already, was still concealed somewhere in the compartment above me.

There was still a chance for me to get it.

To take possession of this document which, as I say, had already proved fatal to two people who'd had possession of it.

Sometimes I find life rather frustrating. He's got an odd sense of humour, God.

One further conclusion seemed to follow. The killer - killers? - might not have got the document yet, but they'd certainly want their hands on it as soon as possible. Their best opportunity would be to break back into the compartment during this night.

So if I was going to get it ever, I was going to get it now.

Very gently, I pushed the cupboard door open, and began to wriggle out.

Once I was almost free, I untied my shoes and left them in the entrance to the cupboard. No clumping or shuffling allowed on this job.

The thought of my shoes led to another thought. I bent down, struck a match, and pushed it and then my head into the cupboard. Nothing else in there: no dark wallets, no slim folders, nothing stuck to the underside of the bunk.

I wriggled back out again. At last I stood upright. I turned on the compartment light.

My sleep during the first night, however curtailed, had demonstrated that the Orient Express compartments were pretty well sound-proofed, and that meant that the doors were pretty well sealed. So even if the conductor or someone was passing, the light shouldn't show under or around the door.

I pulled the little stool out from under the table, and sat and considered the compartment around me.

I tried not to keep looking at the corpse directly in front of me.

This was the other thing I'd given a bit of thought to, while I'd been stashed in the cupboard. There were various ways of going at the search. Plan A was to take the place apart with a vengeance. But I wasn't sure how quietly I could do that, and I wouldn't be able to tidy up satisfactorily after myself, and it meant telling the opposition that the game had changed. Also, I had the vague sense that the Bishop's hiding place would be canny enough to defeat the brute approach.

Plan B was the methodical one: systematic; exhaustive. Top to bottom, left to right, light bulb to waste paper basket, examine and if possible open every damn thing there, open every single item he'd carried, feel every seam of every garment, test every fitting in the compartment for concealment. That seemed more reliable. But it would take a hell of a time. This was a well-equipped late Bishop, occupying a well-equipped First Class compartment, and that meant God only knew how many gadgets, pockets, packets, pages and well-tailored hems.

Perhaps God did know. I found the old man's bible on the little shelf above his head, and riffled through the pages and tested the binding.

Sentimental, the Delameres, in our way.

That would leave Plan C: logic; reason.

Think of the man, think of the circumstances, think of the compartment, think of the kit, and deduce where he could or must have hidden the document. Sheer brain power.

On the whole, I was liking Plan A.

My irritation at not being able to rip the compartment to

pieces was only increasing my wish to do it. I hope I'm sharp enough to get by, but I'm not really a brain power sort of chap. Just get on with it, rather than sit on your arse scratching your head and thinking big thoughts.

Uneasily, uncertain, I sat on my arse, and wondered how one summoned big thoughts.

I got up again, opened all the cupboard doors, pulled every one of his bags into plain view and opened them in front of me. Then I sat.

I may actually have scratched my head.

Boots: hard worn, good quality. Socks, I could see those as he lay there. I'd seen him in two suits: he was in one, the other was hanging up beside me. Shorts - presumably; unless he'd gone very wild among the locals in Matabeleland. Shirts… one of the cases had enough changes of the essentials for the journey. Clerical collar. Did they have more than one?

Bed: pillow, sheets, blanket, all tucked in; dead chap on top of same, obviously. Cupboard under bed (officers for hiding in), now empty. Wall, light fitting, mirror. Luggage rack; nothing up there now. Basin unit, shelves underneath, empty. Shaving kit in leather pouch, soap, not much else. Hanging space with the second suit and tomorrow's shirt.

Bible. Other books: the *Odyssey* in the original - that's a proper Bishop for you; poems of Lord Tennyson; *Lady Marjorie's Dilemma* by Gertrude Washbourne. Spectacle case - interesting; I'd not seen him wearing them. Cigar box. Matches. Binocular case. Hat: I'd seen him in a bowler, on the station, but nothing else; if he had another it was in his heavy baggage.

Would he have had the document on him all the time? Not necessarily. Fewer places to hide it, and a close search more likely.

Stashed somewhere in the compartment then. Yes. Except that he'd still have to worry about searches, and he'd have to worry about sudden emergencies. So he'd need to be able to get his hands on it quickly, and get it away.

I'd the vague sense I might be getting warmer. If he'd the faintest idea of the sort of thing he was up against - and all the rigmarole back in Constantinople and the whole business of a sneaky Bishop and a decoy Delamere suggested so - he'd have to plan for the opposition making aggressive efforts to get to the document. Even if he hadn't thought so before the bandits had turned over the train, he'd surely have done so after. And he had to reckon, too, with the routines of life on the Orient Express. He'd been willing to leave his compartment unattended. Any number of porters might handle his heavy bags.

It had to be well hidden while it was in the compartment, and not easily lost to porters and baggage-ransackers. Not in his heavy bags. At the same time, it had to be easily accessible. Not screwed or locked behind anything, not concealed in the fabric or fittings of the compartment. It had to be portable. Nothing clumsy to be carrying around; nothing unnatural. He couldn't walk about all day holding his shaving bag or a spare shoe.

He looked rather peaceful, stretched out there. The doctor had arranged him in the traditional style, hands folded together on his chest as if modelling for his tomb. If his parishioners back in Matabeleland had a whip-round for a monument, this look would be just the thing.

I wondered again if he might have had it on him. Wondered where he might have secreted it if so. Actually on his person? Taped on? I took a deep breath, and ran my hands over him, into his coat and round his arms, under him and along his spine.

He was already cold. I was feeling it myself.

I wondered how small the document could be made, for hiding. Decided there was one place I wasn't looking. Not a Bishop, for goodness' sake. If he'd been that devoted to old England and the damn' paper, he could keep it.

I straightened him out again, tidied his coat, re-arranged

his hands. Grim business.

Come along, Delamere.

Portable and accessible. I thought back to the live Bishop, remembered him sitting opposite, remembered him walking along the corridor. What he'd said; what he'd worn; what he'd carried.

I had another go at the bible. I up-ended his cigar box and checked under the lining, tapped the wood. I found his wallet, stuffed down beside the mattress at the head of the bed.

Something more. All the to-ing and fro-ing, the threat of being searched and so on, the need for the document to be portable. It had been hidden but perhaps, more than that, it had been disguised. He'd not been wandering the train with a damn' great envelope, bound up with ribbon and labelled 'secret document'. This was a document that didn't look like a document.

Discussion of Africa, discussion of Turkey. Careful about politics, sincere about himself - a touch melancholy. The conversation with me, the conversation with the Hungarian. Moments of bluster - had it all been a pose? - and moments of acuteness. Picking up Craig on his Ottoman politics - the moment when I'd thought Craig had been caught out in something, when I'd suspected Craig was trying to distract from it. But Craig, of course, hadn't been the courier. The Bishop distracting the attention away from himself - with Hilmi, with the Hungarian. Distracting the attention onto me. Stirring me up to make more fuss. Witty and, I now realized, very watchful. Remarkable nerve; remarkable calm.

And at last I had it.

Knew it; looked for it; found it.

I tidied up. Scanned the compartment, looking for the signs of myself. I pocketed a couple of cigars; souvenir of that extraordinary old man.

49.

Then I started to wonder how I was going to get out.

I'd heard them locking the door. That itself was no problem: from the inside the mechanism worked with the handle alone. But even if I could sneak out, I wouldn't have the conductor's gadget to lock it again. So it would be clear someone had been in. And in any case, sneaking out unseen even in the middle of the night was too long a shot. For all I knew, the conductor might spend the whole night on his little seat in the corridor.

I was keen to get out. The conductor, the doctor, and eventually the police would have a legitimate reason to come in. Whoever had killed the Bishop would have an illegitimate one. Being discovered by any of the first lot meant almost certain arrest. The second lot meant almost certain death. And I wasn't going to hide under the bed for the next couple of days, hoping no one thought to look.

If not the door, then it had to be the window.

I opened the window and - trying to spot trees and bridges in the darkness - stuck my head out. The roar of wind and soot had me gasping and choking immediately. I gave up any nonsense of climbing from window to window while we were moving.

I'd no idea how long it would be to the next station. There didn't seem to be a lot going on in the south of Serbia, civilization-wise. Could I stomach spending hours in the compartment, waiting for the sound of the door being opened?

Only one way to find out, apparently.

I sat on the stool, trying not to think about the door handle.

As a distraction, I tried instead to think about the various melodramas I'd been through in the previous thirty hours. The murder of the British Government chap on Constantinople station. And now the murder - I was assuming it was murder; I just couldn't believe he'd choose this very evening to peg out of his own accord - of the British Government's real courier. And the bandit attack: another extraordinary coincidence interrupting the secret document's smooth journey across Europe.

Then there was the popular suspicion about me. When I'd thought I was the courier, I suppose I'd assumed that Hilmi's people really had seen me with the Government chap at some point. Or maybe I just felt guilty and so assumed everyone else could see it. But it hadn't been true. Why did people - and some people in particular - think it wasn't the Bishop but me? Hilmi was obviously part of my problem, but was he all of it?

I didn't get very far, but it occupied my mind for half an hour or so, at the end of which I felt the train slowing. Immediately I was up, head out the window again, and thank God Quinn was still waiting for me. I went into yet another of my improvised miming routines.

A few minutes later the train stopped. I was still waiting at the window.

I glanced back at the dead body.

Once I'd realized he was the courier, I'd only thought of him with resentment. Now, as he lay there cold and monumental, I thought of his bravery, his endurance. Much of what he'd said about his life had been true, I think: its disappointments; the strange lonely compensations of life exiled in Africa. And at the end, running the ultimate risk in the cause of… it had to have been patriotism; he had nothing left to prove, no use for money. And he'd given his life for it. I remembered how much I'd warmed to him in our first conversation.

I offered him a silent promise, and a nod of regard. And then I peered down out of the window to look for what I could hold onto on the way.

From the other side of the train - the side of whatever station platform we'd just stopped at - I heard a shot. No doubt a few others did too. I began clambering through the window.

At the last moment I realized I wasn't wearing my shoes. Trying to explain how they'd ended up in a locked compartment with a dead man would have been real Sherlock Holmes stuff. The alarm at how close I'd come to that idiocy, and the rush to put them on, stopped me wasting time planning the descent. In a moment I was hanging on to the window lip with my feet flailing in the air, and then they found a wheel.

Then another shock as I remembered that the conductor and co. had left the compartment with the window more or less closed. They might not remember if it was fully closed, but they'd certainly remember it hadn't been wide open. With the fingers of one hand clinging painfully to keep grip on the window sill, I slid the window up as best I could with the other. It was almost done when my fingers gave out as well as my spasming legs and I dropped to the track. A moment later I was reversing the procedure to clamber back into my own compartment, and wrenching off most of my clothes.

I waited until I heard voices in the corridor and emerged in front of them, shoes over bare feet and coat over bare chest.

I don't know how many people the shot had woken, but most of them had stayed in their compartments. It had served its purpose anyway: anyone who had been awake had been looking out the wrong side of the train, and any noise from my impromptu exit and entry had been lost in the shuffle.

I joined a small group on the platform of what turned out to be a place called Niš. At the end of the Second Class wagon, an angry conductor and an angry station master were standing in front of a sorry-looking Cornish valet, who was explaining how he'd stepped out for a cigarette and been polishing the revolver when it had accidentally fired.

I found Peg Madison standing near me. She considered my obviously incomplete outfit. 'You expecting the Serbs to ask you for a show again?' she said, the usual soft dry drawl.

'Ready for action at any time', I said. I looked at her dressing gown; rather smart silk business, in scarlet. 'You?'

'Your pistol still loaded?'

Quinn is the least nervy man in existence, so his performance of cowed anxiety was rather good. Almost as good as my performance of bleary irritation. I pushed my way forwards, swore at him for a clumsy lunatic, confiscated the pistol, and ordered him back inside so that he didn't delay the train any longer. A nod of courtesy to the uniforms and we were gone, leaving no one else any excuse to delay us either.

As I stepped up into the train I saw Major Hilmi lurking at the connecting door to the Second Class car. He'd rather faded into the background in recent hours, which was no bad thing. He was looking at me and the pistol with equal hostility.

There were a couple of other faces in the corridor, and then we were inside my compartment. 'Best to lie low here for a bit', I said to Quinn. 'Afraid you had to swallow a bit of bad chat from the conductor, but you shouldn't have to put up with it from anyone else.' He nodded, and sat. 'Don't often see you looking all humble like that. Not sure it suits you.'

The Quinn smile. 'Any sergeant who's had to take orders from a junior officer knows the game, sir.'

'I think this is where you're supposed to say that I was the exception among junior officers. You certainly never looked that humble with me.'

'Naturally inspired by your leadership, sir. You got out from the Bishop all right then.'

I nodded. 'Grim business, but all done now. No reason for us to be linked to it.'

'And you reckon your guess was right then, sir - that he was the man?'

'He was the man.'

Quinn nodded. 'I suppose we're shot of the problem now, aren't we sir?' I waited. 'You've got rid of the decoy version of this document, and the opposition have got rid of the real courier. You're free of suspicion, and free of the burden.' For a fleeting moment he almost looked happy.

'Well…' - I tapped my breast pocket, where my new trophy was temporarily resting - 'yes and no.'

50.

There are times, just very occasionally, when I think Quinn regrets his life choices. One life choice, anyway.

He's generally pretty obliging, when it comes to my instincts for a sporting sort of existence. He's partial himself to a bit of adventure and romance. So we're fairly compatible. But every now and then a circumstance will arise - quite often the circumstance will have longish odds on soft ground, or red hair and willowy lines and a quietly cool manner of speaking - and I can see him working out if he's saved enough to retire back to Cornwall and open a pub. Or at least for the train fare.

'So this dangerous document, which everyone kills to get hold of, we've taken that back on again?' The words came slow and steady as ever, but he didn't give me time to reply. 'And before, people were wrongly assuming we were the courier, but now we really are?'

'That's right Quinn. You summarize with typical brilli-'

'This is our duty, is it sir?' He was looking very weary.

'Probably. Didn't give it much thought, to be honest. Seemed the right thing to do.'

Quinn nodded, rather sadly.

'There's no reason to suppose they know I've got it.' He didn't look convinced. 'Game's changed, anyway. I'm fed up of having to play amateur rules. We've to survive two more days on this damn' train, and that'll take a bit of preparation.' He nodded, unhappily. I gave him a couple of errands I wanted him to run next time we had a longer stop in a town, and he pushed off back to his compartment.

I drifted uneasily off to sleep, thinking of new places to hide the document.

My last thought before unconsciousness, with a lurch, was whether this one was blank too.

51.

Breakfast was a rather sober occasion. As soon the passengers were settled, the conductor announced the sad death of the Bishop during the night. We were fortunate to have a doctor travelling with us, he said, and the doctor had examined the dead man, and had diagnosed a seizure perhaps acting on a weakened heart.

He looked at Dr Jam, and Dr Jam stood up, and gave a sombre bow to the company to confirm all that. Then Dr Jam sat down again.

'In Belgrade', the conductor went on, 'we shall notify the authorities and the British Embassy, for further arrangements. Ladies and gentlemen, please to enjoy your breakfast.'

No one had known him well enough to be upset, but the meal was more or less silent: respect, as well as the macabre awareness that there was a dead body only a few yards away.

I was rehearsing some of my thinking from the night. Without any kind of facilities, the doctor had been able to do little more than confirm the old man was dead. There were no obvious signs of any other cause, so 'seizure' - which I doubt had any real medical meaning - was a good catch-all. Plenty of old chaps switch off for good after a hearty meal and a glass too many, and no questions asked.

But Dr Jam - presumably - didn't know what I did about the Bishop. And about the other British chap at Constantinople. I wasn't accepting the coincidence, and that meant… poison, presumably. Even I'd have spotted any other kind of fatal wound, and the doctor certainly would.

I glanced round the compartment. Craig opposite me; Theotokis adjacent; a murmur in a French accent behind.

If I was right about the death, then someone in the compartment was a poisoner. And if I was right about the reason for the death, then someone had unfinished business.

I looked down at my half-drunk tea and empty plate.

Everyone drifted off after they'd eaten. I saw them glancing uncomfortably at the door to the Bishop's compartment as they passed it.

That got me thinking.

I managed to bump into the conductor shortly afterwards. 'Desperately sad business, Monsieur Michel.' He agreed it was. 'Such a fine old chap.' He agreed he had been. I glanced back in the direction of the late fine old chap's compartment. 'To think of it. Alone in there...' I turned back. 'There'll be quite a bit of interest in London about this. Distinguished man of the cloth. Last words and so forth.' I produced a sad smile. 'Trying to remember if he said anything particularly significant over dinner. Did he have any visitors last night? I know Sikander Ali Khan had been in for a smoke the previous night. I think you were in the corridor, weren't you?'

Paul Michel agreed he had been in the corridor, and thought for a moment. Then he shook his head.

'You sure? I thought I saw... Well now, who was it? The Bishop left the dining car, and then...'

'A little while later the two English ladies.'

'Yes, that's right. The ladies. Then... The doctor, no?'

'Yes, he. Then the Bishop himself. Then the Swedish gentleman - Monsieur Svensson - and then Monsieur Junot.' Junot had been there? He must have been the one down with Valfierno. 'Then you yourself, Monsieur, with Monsieur le Marquis.'

'That's right.'

'Then I saw that the dining car was emptying at last, so I came to check that all had been satisfactory. I am sure that no one stopped with the Bishop. I would have noticed, because if conversations are continuing there is more chance that drinks will be demanded. I was there until the last of the diners had gone, and the corridor was empty. I wanted to be sure that I could make the final arrangements with the stewards in the dining car without interruption.' Another shake of the head. 'I saw and heard no one until... Yes, Monsieur le Marquis came out - why, out of your compartment I think Monsieur' - I nodded - 'and then I exchanged some pleasantries with your Monsieur Quinn' - he had trouble with the name, unsure whether to go for a French pronunciation or risk an English, and so falling in between - 'and then no one. It was not long after this that your - Monsieur Qu- - your valet and one of the stewards found the Bishop dead.'

He seemed sure. And from all I'd seen of him during the previous day or two he was the attentive type.

So the Bishop had gone to his compartment alone, and stayed alone, and died alone. Which was remarkable, now I started to think about it. Because it meant that if he'd been poisoned, it had to have been at dinner, and I simply couldn't see how that had been possible.

I had, after all, been at his table myself.

I was about to say something to the conductor to show how natural my curiosity had been, when we heard heavy feet coming from the Second Class car and Mahan Singh loomed over us.

With his whole hand he beckoned to me, once and definite. 'Please sir,' he said, the voice up from the train wheels, 'you must come.'

52.

I followed him into the Second Class wagon - only my second or third visit, I realized. There were a few heads sticking out of doors, and people gathered in the corridor. All moved aside quickly for the big Sikh, then at last he let me past. The conductor was hurrying along behind me.

I saw Quinn's back first. He was standing poised, facing the far end of the corridor, the front of the train. I could see over his shoulder, a couple of yards beyond him, diplomacy's friend the brewer from Prague.

He and Quinn appeared to have bumped into each other again. The brewer from Prague was propping himself up against the window, and dabbing his face, where his nose and one eye were turning a peculiar purple.

Quinn didn't turn round. 'Stand easy, Sergeant', I said in his ear. 'You doing international politics again?'

'Nothing to see here, sir.' He still hadn't turned round.

'This - this' - the brewer from Prague - Munk, was it? - was having trouble with his words, possibly because English wasn't his first language and possibly because of the state of his lip - 'this animal attacked me! I should - I should -'

'Come again if you like, chum.' Quinn's voice was quiet, solid. 'Three in a row, I win a goldfish.'

I chipped in again. 'Some kind of disagreement Quinn, apparently.'

'Not any more, sir.'

'Any reason you'd like to share?'

'No sir.'

Now I saw, through the open compartment door to the left, Madame Dewoitine's maid. She had a handkerchief to her face, but I guessed that was just for form's sake; her expression was furious. She saw me looking at her. 'He attack me!' She pointed along the corridor. 'Him - the pig - the Austrian - he force him into my chamber!'

The outrage and the pronouns were bewildering, but the message seemed pretty clear. I looked at Munk again. 'She wrote to me!' he insisted; he was outraged himself. 'She invited!'

The maid actually screamed her rejection of this. The nonsense was getting out of hand. It wasn't helped by the

160

whole exchange happening in a narrow tube and all the participants standing in a line. Only Quinn was silent, and still.

'We know what kind of woman is this now!' Munk went on. 'She in there, with the savage woman too.' This would be young Suraya's maid, presumably. 'Both of them we can say are-'

'Stand fast Sergeant!' A Cornish ocean-going fishing boat and the non-commissioned officers' cadre of the British Army both breed toughness and they both breed a fairly simple view of values and discipline. I've never seen Quinn beat a man to death, but I'm pretty sure he could and I'm pretty sure he was about to. There was movement behind me, someone trying to come through: Mahan Singh, who hadn't appreciated the reference to the savage Indian woman, and was about to do some battlefield surgery with his carving knife. 'Enough', I said. I didn't shout it but I made sure it was heard. 'Enough pantomime for one day. Mr Quinn and Mr Singh, back to barracks please. Now.' There was a moment, and they went.

Munk started forwards, rediscovering his courage now he didn't have Quinn staring at him. It takes a special kind of stupidity to annoy a large Cornishman and an even larger Sikh in one sentence, and this chap was determined to go deluxe. He started to fuss some more. 'You've had your fun', I said. 'Now take your medicine. Nothing to prove now, nothing to win. Get Dr Jam to have a look at your phiz, then pop along to the bar and have a drink on my account.' He lurched off, evil expression not helped by the after-effects of Quinn's damage.

I stuck my head into Quinn and Singh's compartment. 'Mr Singh, would you mind?' He understood, and left. I went in and shut the door. 'What the bloody hell was that?'

Quinn was uncomfortable, but unapologetic. 'Sir, you heard what he-'

'I don't remotely give a damn! I don't care if he insults you

161

and every woman in Serbia; I don't care if he wipes his arse on a picture of the King and sings Greensleeves with naughty words. We are supposed to be keeping our heads down. We are supposed to be keeping our eyes out for spies and assassins. We are not supposed to be lamping foreigners to impress the girls. Am I clear?'

There was the suggestion of a knock at the door and then it opened. 'Monsieur!' The conductor, not happy. 'You must please to understand that such behaviour by - by your servant is intolerable on this train.' I could see Quinn's face, swallowing that lot with difficulty. I don't know how train conductors figure on his pecking order of life, but he doesn't respond well to snootiness from anyone. 'This is not a horse and cart! This is-'

'He did what any man would have done', I said. 'And what you, Monsieur, should have done.'

That stopped him.

'As you were saying, this is supposed' - I hit the word nastily - 'to be a line of distinction, of the greatest comfort and security. How would it be, Monsieur, if - as well as the bandit attacks - your lady passengers fear that at any moment some monster is likely to walk into their compartment and assault them? Was the door catch even working? That poor girl was terrified; nothing to protect her at all. Except Mr Quinn here.' He didn't like it, but he didn't have a lot to say. 'Mr Quinn and I are discussing the matter. End of story.'

He still didn't like it, and he might have said so, but the train whistled and we started to slow. 'But my dear chap', I said, suavity restored, 'I'm keeping you from your duties. So sorry. Tell me, how much of a stop do we have here?'

'Belgrade…' he said, re-gathering himself. 'We must change the locomotive. And there will be some arrangements regarding the poor Bishop. At least thirty minutes.' He hurried off.

I looked at Quinn. 'Thirty minutes', I said. 'You'll have to shift a bit. All right?' He nodded. 'Don't be late, for God's sake. Doubt the conductor's in a mood to do either of us a favour.'

I left him to it, thanked Mahan Singh as I squeezed past him, and ambled back to the First Class car.

I suppose I should have been used to the strange flexibility about whose compartment was whose on this unique train journey. And I suppose I'd been in and out of more than my fair share myself, and not always officially. So perhaps I couldn't complain. But still.

While I'd been experiencing life in Second Class, Major Hilmi had apparently fancied a look at First Class. He was sitting on my bunk, his pistol pointing at my chest.

53.

He put a finger to his lips, and then used it to beckon me in. I closed the door behind me.

The pistol stayed firm at my chest. With his other hand he threw something and instinctively I caught it.

Box of matches.

'In case you are left in any doubt', he said, 'someone has entered your compartment.'

'Make yourself at home. Not your first visit, I think.'

He smiled. 'This time the results shall be more conclusive.' The old self-assurance was back. He looked neat and comfortable. 'Should you not have started your denials, Sir Henry? Your very amusing performance of innocence and outrage?'

'You haven't accused me of anything yet.'

'There is no question of accusation. It is our certain knowledge that you were chosen to be the courier.' The pistol barrel waved casually. 'The games of suspicion and investigation, these were for the benefit of the other passengers. I know' - he hit the word - 'it is you.'

'Even though I have been searched and searched again,

my clothes, my luggage, everything.'

He shrugged. 'I know.'

He knew wrong, of course. Or rather: he had known wrong, but I had now adjusted reality to make him right.

The train jolted slightly. Just for a moment Hilmi glanced over his shoulder. We had stopped in Belgrade. Immediately the bustle began: the slamming of doors open and shut, shouts, whistles.

Hilmi and the pistol were focused on me again. The stop made no difference to him, apparently. 'Mind if I sit?' I said, reaching for the little stool. I needed to start to change the situation, to interfere with the mechanism.

'Yes', he said. 'I do mind. In a minute or two we shall leave the compartment together. We only wait for the first rush to finish. No interruptions.'

'Got it all planned, it seems. Wait:' - my realization was genuine - 'that business in Second Class with the maid - did you make that happen?' Again the smile. After all his previous frustrations, today Major Hilmi really was enjoying himself. 'But how?'

'Here in First Class, Sir Henry, you think nothing of the lives in Second Class. You are polite at dinner, and then they disappear from your life again. I have lived among them. I have seen the little relationships develop. I have watched the Austrian animal undressing the French girl with his eyes; I have heard his stupid comments. And I have seen her reaction. Did my note of invitation from her to him have a good effect?'

I nodded. 'Very. Your Austrian friend now has a black eye.' He made a silent chuckle, his dapper little body shaking. 'You're lucky I went along there.'

Another shrug. 'You have a habit of being where the action is. And if it had not worked, I would in any case have called on you here. This arrangement only gave me the minor advantage of not being seen.'

'Good you mentioned that. Mind telling me what the hell

you're doing here?'

'To finish what we started, in our first conversation here.' I saw his glance wandering a moment, as he tried to catch sounds outside, or the lack of them. 'First you will lie face down on the bed, so I can get into the corridor without you trying something heroic. Then you join me, and we walk a little way together.'

He knew what he was doing. But every time either of us had to move a foot, I would have a chance.

'Let me be clear on two points, Sir Henry. So you do not become so optimistic. First, I prefer to finish our business before we are formally in Austrian territory. We are still on the less civilized side of the Danube, the old Ottoman lands, where I have much more chance of buying my way out of any difficulty. Second, I will do anything necessary to achieve my aim. If you try to escape me, or to attract attention, or to get help, I will shoot you and then anyone who interferes with me. It is of no concern if I must also kill your servant, and anyone else you care for: the English ladies, the wanton American. Anyone. I shall probably escape.' He stood, the pistol still steady. 'And if I do not, that is no concern either.'

54.

It went exactly as Major Hilmi intended. There was no one in the corridor, and no one in the dining car. A steward bustling in the kitchen area, perhaps, but no one to see us. At the back end of the dining car and beyond the kitchen Hilmi used a key to open a door, and gestured me through first.

We were in - what would you call it? - a vestibule. Bit at the end of a carriage with doors either side, and a connecting door on to the next carriage. This connecting door was blocked, because beyond was only the luggage wagon; the end of the train.

Hilmi pushed me forwards, and locked the door we'd

come through. Then he stood so that his back was blocking the window of the door on the platform side of the train. Nothing to see in here. Even if anyone was faffing around the back of the train, they wouldn't know we were here.

'I could shout.'

'You could, Sir Henry. You could shout, you could sing, you could do as you please. And I would shoot you. I prefer not to at this stage, but - please believe me - my inconvenience would be less than yours, I think.'

'Kill me as you killed the man on Constantinople station? As you killed the Bishop?'

He frowned: mild confusion. 'The Bishop? And a man on the station?'

'You described the man you said was my contact. He was stabbed on the platform, just before the train left. I assume that was you tidying up.'

He shook his head.

'Then you came and claimed he'd been taken ill. Rather ugly irony, that.'

'That was merely an excuse for the conversation.' He seemed genuinely confused, but unconcerned. 'He died? It was nothing to do with me. It would have been unnecessary. And it might have interrupted my mission before I started.'

'You weren't so cautious when your bandits were shooting at us.'

'Ah, you realized they were mine?'

'They were better dressed than half the passengers; they had to be someone's. During the attack, two doors that were supposed to be locked were unlocked, right after you'd been near them. You did everything you could to make things easier for the bandits - trying to separate us, trying to slow us. And all so that they could search the compartments.'

He nodded. 'My first efforts to find the document had not worked. If the passengers had been separated as I wished, you could have been searched more forcefully, or kidnapped, or perhaps tragically killed during the attack.' He smiled at the thought. 'But your performance interfered with that. In any case, the search was worth attempting. So no, I was not worried that someone might get shot. I have killed on this journey, Sir Henry, and I will kill. But I cannot claim those two.'

I was thrown, I grant you. As soon as he'd shown up in my compartment with his pistol, I'd forgotten all my previous speculations about mysterious poisoners. Hilmi had obviously been the danger from the start.

Now? I couldn't see why he would lie. Surely it didn't make sense that he hadn't killed them…

But of course it did. He'd always believed I was the courier, and he still did, so why would he want to kill the Bishop?

I fell silent, trying as usual to work out what the hell was going on, and as usual failing. Silent we stayed.

The conductor had said at least thirty minutes, and it couldn't have been more. We heard the usual whistles and shouts, and Hilmi braced himself and checked his distance from me. He didn't miss a thing. We felt the jolt as the train started to move, and we both swayed, eyes fixed on each other.

My hand missed its grip as I went to steady myself, and I stumbled against the window. It slid down.

'Going to jump, Sir Henry?'

'After you.'

'It would not matter so much to me, and you would save me a bullet. But… what was your word? - I prefer to be tidy.'

The train was rolling slowly forwards. Apparently the station had been on the edge of town: through the window I saw only waste ground and trees.

'Care to tell me what you're trying to achieve? Or do you just like to make your threats as theatrical as possible?'

'No threats, Sir Henry. I told you: this is the finish. You know, perhaps, what is the treaty that you carry.'

'I do not.'

He smiled. Again he seemed genuinely surprised. The little eyes were bright. 'Poor Delamere: so ignorant. But what a hero! What a man of duty! Let me explain at least this. I would choose to secure the treaty myself. I have - you must admit - given you a fair opportunity to give it to me. You have refused.' Shrug. 'So now I have only one alternative. For my purposes, it is only necessary that it does not reach London immediately - this is its nature. If you are lying dead on a Balkan railway track, my needs will be satisfied.'

I felt the sick sense of a miscalculation turning round and kicking me in the gut. I'd assumed he was still trying to get the document off me. I'd assumed I still had time.

'Is it too late to reconsider your original offer?'

'It is.'

'You're not going to search me?'

'I'm going to shoot you, Sir Henry.' He was moving across the vestibule towards me. 'Quicker and easier and more conclusive for us both. And I confess it will give me much more pleasure.'

He'd get away with it, too. Shoot me, push me out of the door in this wasteland, appear in the dining car a little later, terribly sorry to hear old Delamere's missed the train. Here at the back I'd probably not be seen going, and apparently he didn't care anyway. Cheeky so-and-so could claim he was cleaning his pistol and it accidentally went off.

It was still in his left hand, from when he'd used the right to lock the door behind us. 'Well then', I said. 'Au revoir.' Slowly I offered him my hand.

He looked down at it, glanced up at me, smiled that same damn dapper smile.

His own hand came up. It was holding a knife.

'Your last mistake, Sir Henry Delamere. In the new Turkey there is no place for gentlemen. The old order dies with you.'

'Anything you say, old chap.' My left hand was behind me, out of the window, and it turned the door handle as my right grabbed his wrist. The door lurched open and we both tumbled out into the void.

55.

We both tumbled, but one of us had been expecting it and had sneakily got an arm hooked over the window. Hilmi went headfirst into the undergrowth; I swung round on the door with my arm getting wrenched off at the shoulder. I clutched wildly and got the other hand round onto the lip of the window. The door waved back and forth of its own accord, me clinging to its outside edge, and my boots flailing over the track as it rolled beneath.

A branch smashed into my shoulders and I almost lost my grip. It got me moving, and I locked one arm and started trying to work my body round to the inside face of the door. Then a branch hit the door, and it began to swing shut. That was handy, except I'd now got my legs round and so they were trapped against the doorstep by the door as it closed on them. I yelled in pain, let go of everything, and the door started to swing open again and I went with it. I grabbed at whatever I could, the door started to close and I scrambled in, this time bringing most of my legs with me. I lurched to my feet, stuck my head out of the window, got hit on the back of it by another branch, and caught only a glimpse of Hilmi lying by the side of the track beyond the luggage wagon. I couldn't be sure if I saw him move.

Then I was in the vestibule, collapsed on the floor, aching in legs and arms and head and not sure which was which.

Slowly, I dragged myself upright. I took another, more cautious look out of the window. The ground was falling away and immediately we were rattling onto a metal bridge and there was water flowing underneath. I caught my breath, enjoyed the sense of freshness that came off the river, the gentle clanking of the wheels.

And so it was we came out of Serbia. I was going to say 'in one piece', but as I almost left my legs behind I shan't boast. Only spent the one night there on this occasion, but I think I'd packed in enough entertainment.

I brushed myself down a bit and hammered on the connecting door. Eventually someone found the conductor and the conductor found a key, and I emerged into the dining car with a mumbled explanation about a wrong door and a strong desire for a drink.

By now we'd rattled off the metal bridge and into the first stop in Austria-Hungary, and I was feeling a little more cheerful. That might only have been the drink.

Hilmi had felt freer to finish me off back on the Serbian side of the river, and - perhaps I was imagining this, but you can hardly blame me, having crossed the border clinging to the edge of the train - I think everyone felt a little easier now we were over. The border village looked pretty squalid, but all the signs were written in grand lettering with an elaborate crown-and-eagle business at the top. And even though we were still a long way from Vienna, we were on territory ruled from there, and Vienna's somewhere you've heard of - an elegant world city, with ballet, and big cream cakes. Never understood why people like ballet or big cream cakes - or indeed cities - but you take my point.

I called it Austria-Hungary. At that period - they keep changing it, and I admit I don't keep up with central European constitutional politics - it was technically the Kingdoms and Lands Represented in the Austrian Imperial Council and the Lands of the Holy Hungarian Crown of St. Stephen. I got that from Miss Froy, who of course was reading out the details to Miss Battersby. Basically the centuries-old Habsburg Empire - all the bits in the middle you always lose track of, name-wise. Still under the rule of Franz Joseph, who, now about a hundred and thirty, having only the second most spectacular moustache in Europe, had had to become Emperor instead of a Bulgarian secret policeman.

The Hungarian bit was now bolted on through the most elaborate set of arrangements - I was told - but as it took them a revolution and a lot of lawyers to settle it, there's no point me trying to explain.

My Hungarian friend had certainly perked up, now that we were on his home turf again. He had invited himself to join the English ladies and ordered champagne, and was correcting Miss Froy's guide book, and she was making tiny pencil amendments. Everyone picked up some of the same spirit, and it was nearly lunch time. The compartment filled, and some of the sombre atmosphere from breakfast had passed. The Bishop's body had been taken off the train, apparently, and with him went the sadness. Peg Madison was interrogating Karim Bey about something, Theotokis was sitting down with the two priests, it apparently being their turn to have a look at his precious golden cup. Junot the journo was chattering to the Russian girls. Sikander Ali Khan and Suraya were with Madame Dewoitine.

Quinn came in among the last, as I stood at the bar, and I could tell from his expression that my brush-down in the vestibule hadn't been adequate. 'You all right, sir?' he murmured. I had another go at patting my hair down. 'Look like you've been under the train.'

'Off, but not under, thanks.' He looked the question. 'Hilmi tried to kill me.' Still the question. 'He lost.'

He nodded towards the back of the train. 'Any… tidying up needed?'

'No thanks. He went over the side. I can't be sure he's dead, but for the first time in forty-eight hours I can be sure he won't be in my compartment. You do what I asked while we were stopped?'

He nodded, and murmured: 'My compartment, luggage rack, plain bag.'

'We'll leave it there for now. Thank you. Drink?'

He didn't have a chance to reply. There was a shout - a curse, I guess - in Greek, and Theotokis yelled across the compartment: 'It's gone! The chalice of Colchis - it has been stolen!'

56.

So that was the end of the good cheer. Poor Theotokis went through the obvious ritual - checking the empty box, the seat, under the table - then he ran, absolutely ran, down the aisle and out of the dining compartment. The conductor had heard the shouting and was hurrying in just as Theotokis went racing out, so there was a bit of doorway business in the farcical style before the former was following the latter to his compartment.

We all looked at each other. I guess everyone had found Theotokis a bit of a nuisance - though inviting the ladies to look at your golden chalice is an improvement on the collection of French postcards - but no one believed he'd simply mislaid the damn thing, and there was no doubt how serious a matter theft would be. Eventually, table by table, a low murmuring started up.

I got Quinn his drink.

A couple of minutes later, Theotokis was back through the doorway in a rush, the conductor trying to keep up. 'Gone!' he announced. 'Someone here must-'

The conductor managed to get round into his vision and interrupted him. Furious passengers rampaging around in the middle of lunch he didn't need. I guess he was also a bit more used to this sort of thing, compared to bandit attacks and naked Englishmen. Certainly wouldn't be the first or last time a passenger had lost something valuable, and I assumed it wouldn't be the first or last time a serious crime had been committed on the Orient Express. He was talking fast and firm to Theotokis. Commitment, reassurance, all well done and trying to show the Greek how to talk in a normal voice.

Theotokis wasn't having it. Asked quietly when he could

last remember actually seeing the cup, he yelled: 'I do not know! But yes! Yesterday - at lunch - I showed it… To her!' He pointed at Peg Madison, whose face showed exactly how much she appreciated being pointed at by angry Greek men. 'And you!' Junot, wounded dignity. 'And Arab! Where is Arab?' The chap from Beirut - Chehab - stood slowly, and made a little uncertain bow, and sat.

It was all foolish, of course. If it had been taken, the people least likely to be able to do so were the ones in front of him when he had it in his hand. The conductor checked that he had not seen it since, and Theotokis's face twisted in the pain of remembering. At last: 'No!'

So, the conductor began, we were discussing the last twenty-four hours, perhaps twenty-two. He had another go at the quiet voice, trying to get Theotokis to remember where he'd put the box, when he might have taken his eyes off it. I doubted he'd get far: I'd seen how carefully the box was guarded. Always in Theotokis's hands, on his table, between his feet. Never out of his sight. The Greek, eyes and hands wild, was rehearsing the previous day and night.

Quinn murmured to me. 'Happy bit of distraction for us though, sir.'

I looked at him, not happily. 'You've not finished thinking this through, have you?'

He was wary. 'You mean we can help him? We can narrow down when it was still in its box?'

'Keep going, Quinn. Almost there.' I shook my head. 'As usual, things have just got worse for us.'

57.

Theotokis marched up to me, unhappy conductor in tow.

'You!' he said, finger rigid under my face. 'You stole the chalice!'

'I beg your pardon?' I said, trying to sound affronted. I

knew what he was thinking, but I couldn't afford to explain why.

'Last night, you get me to compartment when I knock your drink. You distract me. Your servant take my box. This is only time it is not in my hands! In one second, he opens, and - pouf!' He gazed triumphant at the conductor, then back at me, anger doubled.

And here was the snag: everything he'd said was true.

Quinn and I had done exactly that, right down to Quinn opening the box and having a rummage. But we couldn't explain and he wouldn't believe that this was only part of our little campaign to check all the odd hand luggage to see if it hid the secret document. This had been in the lull between when I wrongly thought I was the courier and when I knew who really was. We couldn't explain and he wouldn't believe that I'd also had a beak in the Hungarian flute box, and that Quinn had talked his way into Svensson's agricultural specimens, and that I'd accepted Valfierno's invitation into the attaché case even once I was pretty sure the Bishop was the courier, and that I'd been planning similar expeditions against Miss Madison's camera case, Dr Jam's medicine bag and a couple of other likely spots.

And he certainly wouldn't believe that, having opened the box and got his hands on the damn chalice and picked it up to look underneath, Quinn had carefully replaced it. I could swear that Quinn was innocent, and I could indeed swear that the chalice was safe fully twelve hours later than he thought. Except I couldn't.

Batting off false accusations was becoming second nature. Batting off entirely true accusations is harder. Unfortunately, what Theotokis was saying was entirely true.

'What you're saying is entirely false', I said, dignified but sympathetic. 'Sorry to say it. My man was standing right next to you all the time; you know that. He had no chance to remove the chalice, and nowhere to put it, while you were there with him. We left together with you. The suggestion is impossible, as well as…' - I softened my voice, trying to sound understanding-but-sad - 'rather offensive.'

What I was saying was entirely true too. And it got a similar response. 'You stole it!' He was camping on what he thought was firmer ground.

'No,' I said. 'I did not. Your shock and your anger are entirely justified, and for what it's worth you have my sympathy, but-'

'No sympathy! I want police. I want back - this - great - treasure. You understand? You are thief and you are arrested.' He turned to the conductor, waving his finger near me. 'Arrest this man.'

Poor Monsieur Michel was looking horrified. This was not the sort of pantomime that the high-paying travellers expect over lunch. And his powers of arrest were probably rather limited.

'I'm sure the conductor could arrest me if he wanted.' I looked at Michel, who was usefully wearing the look of a man who was sure that he couldn't. 'But the idea is offensive and unnecessary. The conductor is in charge here. If he suspects that the chalice is stolen rather than lost, and if he suspects that one of the passengers has stolen it - rather than one of the staff, or someone at one of the stations, or customs officials - then I'm sure he can search us all. Search me by all means.' I made a gesture of openness, pulling open my coat a little. As I did so, my thumb felt the document still pinned under the lapel. Damn. 'But…' I went on hurriedly, 'I don't know if the conductor feels he has the authority to search the passengers. The ladies, I mean to say…' For once Theotokis wasn't thinking of the ladies: he was ready to search me himself, right there. Damn, damn, damn…

If I'd been mixed up in just the one complete lunacy, life might have seemed a little easier. Juggling two was hard.

Mercifully the conductor was thinking of the ladies, and of all the other passengers, and of how the reputation of the Orient Express would suffer if he let a furious Greek go through everyone's kit. Let Theotokis get anywhere near Karim and there'd be a Balkan war by teatime; and what Madame Dewoitine might do to European stability if he so much as gave her a funny look didn't bear thinking about.

'I shall search!' Theotokis hissed. 'And if I don't find… I know! Your servant left station in Belgrade. He gave it to other spies and thieves there.' Again he looked triumphant.

And again he had me. It was perfectly plausible. It was arguably more plausible than the truth.

'Conductor,' I said, cold, 'I've had enough of this nonsense. I'm sure all of us here are very ready to co-operate with the proper authorities on this or any other matter. But I expect the company to shield passengers from insult and scandal.' The conductor was looking very unhappy, as well he might at my pomposity. 'That is all. I suggest you get this gentleman a drink and help him to calm down.'

I turned away before Theotokis could continue his tiresome habit of telling the truth, ordered the first thing at the top of the cocktail menu, and led Quinn away. He found a seat with Mahan Singh and the Indian and French maids, so he was all right. I found a seat among the Khans and Madame Dewoitine and Karim and Peg Madison. 'I recognize', I said stiffly, 'that an adventurous life makes one a suspect when something adventurous happens. But I won't tolerate cheap insults. Not' - I added with extra stiffness - 'from a foreigner.' And the two Indians and the Frenchwoman and the American and the Turk all politely nodded their agreement.

My drink arrived, and I took a healthy slurp and sat back amid the chatter.

At last, my mind was getting round to the much more interesting question. I - perhaps I alone - was sure that I hadn't stolen the chalice of Colchis. So who had?

58.

Lunch and coffees and whatnot took us most of the way to Budapest. We didn't see much of poor Theotokis. Unable to arrest me or otherwise vent his frustration, he understandably felt incapable of sitting and enjoying a genteel luncheon. He let the conductor get him back to his compartment for a stiff drink, and no doubt some additional orders and complaints.

The land was flat - really, Hungary seemed to be one vast plain stretching out of the window for ever - and the line was straight and we had a fair bit of time to make up. Only one or two brief stops, just long enough for Theotokis to chivvy the conductor into sending a message ahead to Budapest about the theft. So the locomotive built up a good speed and we raced northwards.

The sense of progress, the sense that the roughest parts of the journey were behind us, and not having Theotokis yelling in the corner, all improved the mood again. The Hungarian kept the wine flowing and lost a bit of his reserve.

I stayed sitting with Miss Madison. She seemed to feel as bruised by the chalice melodrama as I was. She was naturally a person of such poise - a coolness; a calm - really among the most attractive qualities in a woman - and Theotokis's rant must have been irritating. Whatever it was, we were neither of us in the mood for chatter or jollity, and so were perfect company for each other. Kind of sociably anti-social. We muttered of this and that: she asked me more about my travels, and Africa; she talked about what Theodore Roosevelt's model of politics and leadership might mean for Europe. A pleasant, adult conversation with an intelligent and attractive person: it was welcome relief after all the previous nonsense.

Budapest is supposed to be a charming city, but even our Hungarian patriot was subdued by the sight of the police who were waiting on the platform. As we slowed to a final stop, a man stood in front of each door. The conductor was immediately out to speak to them, and they were clearly expecting him. A chap in elaborate uniform appeared in the dining car and told us we were staying on the train. Very polite, very charming, but not for discussion.

The message was relayed to those elsewhere in the train. Then the conductor and Theotokis got off and disappeared. The uniforms stayed in front of the doors. We looked set for a long stay. I excused myself and wandered off to find Valfierno and have another peek at the painting.

I was in Valfierno's compartment ten minutes later, holding the painting and admiring it, when there was a knock at the door. Valfierno didn't like being interrupted when he was discussing brushwork in the Baroque period, but they weren't waiting for an invitation. The door opened: the conductor, a uniform, another couple of uniforms crowding behind.

The conductor started to apologize and explain, but the lead uniform took over. 'Gentlemen: a serious crime has been committed on imperial territory' - I suspected it hadn't actually been on their imperial territory, but it wasn't a point to argue - 'and we are searching the train. Thank you for your co-operation.' Bland, competent sort of face and manner, and again no debate just get on with it.

Valfierno looked alarmed, and I gave him a performance of weary irritation. 'I'm sure we're happy to help', I said to the policeman. 'Don't forget to look in this case.' I waved the attaché case, obviously too thin to hold the missing goblet. 'Check it's not hidden in the frame here?'

As they came in, I saw Theotokis eager behind them. Poor chap, someone was taking him seriously at last. And I was his favourite suspect. Valfierno was fussing around the policemen as they started to look in each of his bags, and I told them I'd look forward to their visit and slipped out. They were knocking on my door a few minutes later, and my helpfulness was sincere. The theft of the chalice was a serious crime, and one did have to feel for Theotokis however tiresome he might be, and I had no reason not to co-operate with the police. They had just a token look at me myself - realistically, no one was hiding the thing on their person, not without a hollow wooden leg. Then they went through the cupboards and bags. They were methodical and brisk, and if I did have the loot in there they'd have found it.

I didn't, so they didn't. The briefest thanks and they were gone. I wandered off to check that Quinn was behaving himself. As I went, I got a sense of how the search was going in the other compartments. I think the conductor was having to do some extra diplomacy to get access to Madame Dewoitine and Miss Suraya, neither of whom had much respect for men, uniforms or Hungarians.

They had a few search parties working at the same time, and they were mostly done in First Class: I saw Karim Bey and Peg Madison closing and re-stowing bags, and the Hungarian tidying up after the official welcome home. In Second Class a policeman had made the mistake of opening Miss Battersby's hat-box without permission, and was getting a summary of English Common Law as it applies to rights of property. A thud further along was a policeman dropping a hat-box, and Oksana the Russian girl was swearing at him, opening the box for him, demonstrating its obvious and complete emptiness, likewise the hat it contained, taking it on and off, offering to swap hats, in a performance of most charming grumpiness that must have had the poor lads very confused. They were into all the bags I'd wondered about, and into them more effectively: the medical case, the seed samples, all of it. Craig was swearing at them for clumsiness with some pottery he was bringing home. Chehab was looking unhappy as they went through his bags, and Dr Jam was looking unhealthily het up as they rummaged among his professional kit.

Then a shout of excitement: a policeman had unwrapped a bundle in a bag hidden under the bunk of one of the priests, and the contents gleamed. The priests looked very unhappy, and there was much passing of messages to and fro and then the senior chap was hurrying in with Theotokis trying to get past him.

An elaborate metal cup it was, but it wasn't gold and it wasn't Theotokis's - as he had, reluctantly, to admit. The priest had acquired it for godly purposes, and hidden it for reasons that were now entirely obvious. The search went on: boxes, bags, basins, bunks.

I turned up at Quinn and Singh's compartment more or less as the police did. Whether through discipline or cheek, the two ex-soldiers had decided to treat it as a barracks inspection: their bedding was immaculate, their bags were arranged squarely and symmetrically and opened ready, and the two of them were standing at attention. The standard patter from the policeman died before it started. He looked into the room in awe and a certain amount of alarm. Eventually he raised a cautious arm and went to touch the first of Singh's bags, watching for the reaction as he did; the expression on the big Sikh's face was terrifying. I left them to it, and ambled back to the dining car.

Peg Madison was chatting to Junot, and then the Hungarian joined us from where he'd been leaning out the window.

'They searching the luggage wagon?' I asked.

'No', he said. 'The conductor swears he has the only key, and it has not been opened since well before the cup was stolen. I understand that they went through the kitchen and the other parts of the train very thoroughly though.'

He wasn't looking too happy. Perhaps he felt that Hungarian hospitality wasn't coming out of this too well. Or maybe this was the imperial Austrian side of things throwing its weight around. 'Most impressive, your police', I said. 'Polite and efficient.'

'Sir Henry…' he said, pained, and beckoned to me. Not looking at all happy. I followed him a yard away from the others. 'I happened to hear two of the officials talking on the platform. No doubt they guess that you and the others do not speak Hungarian. Mr Delamere…'

He glanced over my shoulder, and behind himself. He looked hot and ill. His message and the after-effects of a morning's drinking were mixing to uncomfortable effect. He took a deep breath and went for it.

'Sir Henry, they are about to arrest you.'

59.

I felt weary more than angry. 'But I haven't stolen the damn cup!' I hissed. 'They've just proved that for themselves.'

He shook his head. 'No, it is not that, I think. It is some other matter, which they take up now that the search is finished. They will arrest you and stay with you on the train to Vienna.'

Well, for God's sake… 'Thank you', I said. 'Very kind of you to mention it. See you at tea, I hope.'

I didn't run, because one tries not to. But I was in my compartment very quickly, aware of uniforms moving on the platform as I passed. The compartment was only instinct, just to buy a moment's breathing space, perhaps a moment's thought.

The door knocked behind me. 'Just coming!' I said. I locked the door and jumped to the window. 'Come in!' Please let the window open… The window jammed. I heard the door rattling. I took a breath, had another go, and this time it slid down. I heard shouts from outside, summoning the conductor and his key. This side of the train, away from the platform, there was only a blank brick wall. I swung my legs over the sill, got my hands on it and dropped clumsily to the trackside.

I needed to be on the train when it left: presumably very soon if they were planning to let the journey continue and hoick me off at Vienna. I needed to be free on the train; that meant hidden.

I started moving along beside it. Quite a few windows had been opened by passengers wanting some fresh air while we were stopped and confined. I was trying to remember the sequence of compartments. I got to what I thought was my first choice, and sure enough the window was as I'd left it when I climbed out the night before. Feet on wheel spokes, fingers on window sill, up and catch window, down she comes, over and in, easy. I scrambled into the late Bishop's compartment, half closed the window, and bent to see if my usual accommodation under the bed was still available.

I heard the door handle. A smart policeman realizing there was one compartment they hadn't searched for the chalice? The door started to open: no time, and I was at the window again and scrambling out and falling to the track. Then scrambling over the stones towards the next option, trying to remember…

Faintly, I heard a whistle. Not long now. Were the police still in my compartment? Would they follow me onto the track? Wheel spokes, window sill, window down and up and in, clumsily over the table space and stumbling down.

'Delamere!'

Wrong. I knew that voice. He'd got up from his bunk and he was between me and the window now.

I really hadn't wanted to choose Theotokis. 'Just helping the police with the search', I said, took a breath and opened the door to the corridor. He yelled something after me.

I couldn't wait. Out I went, and for a fickle moment the corridor was empty. Move! Were the police following me in through windows? Trying another compartment? Surely I couldn't reach Quinn this way. I saw a rifle barrel appearing round the end of the corridor, heavy boots. I knocked and opened the door beside me and went in.

Wrong. Once again the momentary frisson as Miss Suraya Khan sat up in bed. But this time it was her own bed, and she hadn't got any poetry ready. She opened her mouth to scream. 'No!' I blurted. 'I'm just here to check - That is, I need-'

There was a knock at the door behind me, and we both jumped. 'Suraya...' said an Indian voice.

'Told you you could do better', I said. As her father started to open the door I was at the window. Down it came and over and out I went, collapsing between the wall and the side of the carriage. Move! Scrambling over the stones and steadying myself against the train.

The whistle was clear and long. I had moments only before the train and my freedom and the damn document slid away from me. Open window: spokes, sill, window, down and up and the wheel started to turn with my feet still on it and I was swinging and scrambling over the window sill and my knees and ankles were hitting everything and I rolled head over heels over the table top and in.

I came up on hands and knees and pulled myself up against the lower bunk and found myself staring wildly into the face of... Miss Winifred Froy. Her eyes were frozen in alarm, the little jaw clamped rigid.

'Sir Henry', she said at last, and she'd clearly gathered all her pluck to control her emotions and react coolly. 'Are you here to check my ticket, or should I ask to see yours?'

60.

I stood. Brushed myself down. Listened for shouts or knocking. Our eyes were still locked on each other: God only knew what she thought I was about to do; I knew that what she was about to do could finish me.

I had to think fast; whatever fantasy I produced, it had to be exceptional.

'Miss Froy', I said. So far so good. 'I am carrying a secret document for the British Government, and I am hunted. I apologize for busting in, but I need you to hide me.'

It certainly wasn't what I'd planned to say. But you know how it is when you've spent the afternoon clambering in and out of train windows. I stood there, gazing at her and waiting for the scream or the policemen knocking at the door.

The pause went on for an age, and still we stared at each other. And then 'Sir Henry:' - again the sense of her fragile courage - 'are you a good man?'

Dear God... 'No', I said, weary. 'I suspect I'm really not. But... But I do believe that for once I am doing a good thing in a good cause.' I had to hope she didn't know the British Government as well as I did.

'Very well', she said at last, and I could have kissed her, but the thought of Miss Battersby was too large in my mind. Say what you like about the English - and I do, because I've seen and felt my fair share of the hypocrisy and mean-spiritedness and insularity - but only England could have produced this young woman: prim but practical, virtuous but brave, calm despite her alarm, decisive and cool even in a madness beyond her imagining. 'But where exactly do you propose to hide? We're a bit hugger-mugger in Second Class.'

'Cupboard under the bed', I said, and I was already opening the door and pulling bags out.

'But it's not so big. Are you sure you'll fit?'

I paused an instant. 'I'm sure.' I started to slide in.

'Sir Henry-'

'Please stop calling me that. Harry.'

She tried the word. 'Well, er... Harry' - she looked more alarmed at herself than when I'd fallen through her window - 'you're a very strange man.'

'Miss Froy, you have no idea. Bye for now.'

And that was that. After a moment, she pushed the cupboard doors fully shut.

And there we were, in the silence. I can't say I felt comfortable, lurking in a cupboard in this innocent girl's room.

184

But what a girl. I wasn't thinking about her romantically at all - really, that didn't come into it - far too correct a woman to interest me, and too young, leaving aside that she would find me far too scruffy and chaotic, and that the kind of cautious god-fearing parents who would give her a companion like Miss Battersby would welcome the bubonic plague before they welcomed me as a son-in-law. But some day in the not-too-distant future, some bland provincial lawyer or minor rural gentry bore was going to take her, indifferent to her looks and thinking of an heir and good housekeeping, and he'd be tripping over a rare prize. Not that he'd realize, as she faded into domesticity. I wondered if she might instead escape all that: if this mad journey might become a beginning rather than an end, a glimmering idea rather than a faint memory.

I heard her moving around. She'd thought to re-stow the bags so that the disorder wouldn't be noticed. Bland provincial lawyers and minor rural gentry bores get all the luck.

She was just in time. A courtesy knock and Miss Battersby was back, bringing cups of tea - I'm sure the stewards would have delivered, but Miss Battersby was never one to be fussed over. She sat beside Miss Froy on the bunk, and it creaked painfully above me. Then a few minutes of the genteel rattle of tea-cups, and some useful chat about the policemen still searching the train.

It was reinforced by a knock at the door, and a new voice. 'Your pardon ladies, we are still searching the train. Have you recently seen the Englishman Delamere?'

'I saw him,' Miss Froy said. 'In the corridor, I think, when you were searching our bags.'

The policeman tutted. 'Since then?'

The two ladies said not.

'He has not come in here? He was trying to climb into windows.'

'What a foolish question.' Miss Battersby's scorn was equal

for foreigners and illogicality. 'We confirmed to you that we have not seen him.'

'Quite', Miss Froy added, rather faintly.

'We suspect he is still somewhere on this train.'

'I think I would know', Miss Froy said, 'if he was hiding under my bed.'

The police left, no further courtesies. Their frustration was satisfying, but I knew it meant continued trouble for me.

Then tea-time was over - 'I thought not biscuits, dear: one is so sedentary on a long train journey, and we are eating too heavily; we shall be dreaming about French prisons again' - and another creak and she was up and away. 'Now then, I've finished my Gertrude Washbourne, and you're still in the middle of Mr Wells, aren't you? Not uncritically, I trust.' Her voice was suddenly louder, nearer. 'I think my Carlyle is in the bag under the bed here.'

The cupboard door opened.

61.

'No!' Miss Froy's alarm was instinctive.

'I beg your pardon, dear?'

'No. Not down there.'

'Whatever do you mean? I remember distinctly where the book is and where the bag is.' The shaft of light was sharp through the crack in the door and across my leg.

'I moved it. Them. The bags.'

'But why?'

'I don't know. A whim. Just sorting, you know. And I thought it must be so uncomfortable for you - to have to bend down - like that. So unnecessary.'

'But up there they're even less...' Miss Battersby stopped. 'What's the matter, Winifred?'

'Nothing. Nothing at all. Sorry for the inconvenience. I'll just get the book for you.'

'You'll do no such thing. Why are you looking so..?' Miss Froy might be the pluckiest girl in the world, but apparently she didn't have much of a gambler's face. 'Winifred Froy, what is going on? What is the matter?'

'Don't', Miss Froy said feebly. 'You mustn't.'

The bed creaked mightily again. There was a pause.

'Winifred, my dear: do you remember our conversation, at Folkestone? About sins and misadventures?'

Miss Froy, quiet, shy: 'Yes, Amelia.'

'About curious cats and alley cats? Our little agreement, our book of rules?' Christ, that must have been a conversation and a half.

'Yes Amelia.'

'And then our discussion at the gallery in Paris, in the reserve exhibition?'

'Yes.' Perhaps I ought to be buying the picture of the god Apollo after all.

'Look at me, my dear.' I'd the idea they were holding hands now. 'Is this a misadventure of shame, or a misadventure of self-possession?'

A pause, but the reply was clearer. 'Self-possession.'

'Disregarding the usual hypocrisies and pedantries - as we may safely do when abroad - as women dignified and free in ourselves, should you feel any regret or embarr-assment about whatever it is you have done, or should I?'

Pause for reflection, resolution. 'No, Amelia. We should not.'

'Very well then.'

There was another knock at the door. Miss Battersby added: 'Oh… I see; of course. Come in!'

My cupboard door closed.

'Our sincere apologies, dear ladies.' The conductor. 'But the police…'

The police: 'We must check. Perhaps the young woman was asleep, she did not notice-'

'Don't be ridiculous.' Not a woman to truckle to foreign

policemen, Miss Battersby.

'A man escaped from one compartment and then was climbing in and out of other compartments. He was seen climbing into one of the windows at this end of the carriage. Almost certainly the criminal Delamere.'

'Nonsense. No English gentleman would behave in such a disreputable and disorganized fashion.' Ouch.

'Perhaps he hides in the basin cupboard, or under the bed.'

'Unnoticed? You silly little man.'

'It seems unlikely', Miss Froy added, more naturally the diplomat. 'Because with the train moving and you patrolling so effectively, he would be trapped. With you here, surely it is more likely that he wanted to leave the train.'

Baffled, the police left.

I heard the door being locked. Then Miss Battersby's voice, a firm murmur:

'I don't propose to pass the rest of the journey with you lurking in the cupboard like the family ghost, Sir Henry. I think it would be best if you came out now.'

62.

Speaking as softly as I could, sitting on the stool, I told them the whole story.

That's not true. I gave them a short and somewhat adjusted version of the whole story, in which from the start I was the heroic government agent rather than the blundering decoy, and in which I knew what I was doing at every step. I didn't mention that the document wasn't actually on me at the moment, but hidden elsewhere. 'Can I just add..?' I said once I'd got them up to date. 'I'm a bit cynical about humans, and a lot cynical about England. But I've rarely seen the kind of pluck and resolve and sympathy you two just showed.'

They pooh-poohed this in the sturdy English style, old

and young versions thereof, and I loved them a bit more.

'Honestly,' I said, 'I must give you fair warning. I am truly not the knight in shining armour. The baronetcy is my only inheritance from the bankrupt and drunkard who was - for a few seconds at least - my father, last of a long line of increasingly pointless burdens on humanity. I'm at least as desperate and amoral as the Austrian and Turkish police think me. I know fractionally more than you about what I'm doing on this train, but not much, and what I do know doesn't inspire me. If you seek a gallant hero and a worthy cause, Harry Delamere and the British Government are the wrong place to look.'

'We don't do it for you, Sir Henry. We do it for ourselves.'

'Miss Battersby, you seem… remarkably determined to believe in me. London polite society, and the police of quite a few countries now, would say you're backing the wrong horse.'

Her substantial frame stiffened. 'You have a most curious idea of where I should seek my moral compass, Sir Henry. Polite society and foreign policemen, indeed. And - if I may - your understanding of the realities and motivations of an English spinster - anonymous, impoverished, ageing and never exactly an oil painting - is at least as ignorant as my understanding of your diplomatic affairs. The very most a woman may hope for is that now and then she may be allowed to make her own decisions.' She was looking rather pink. Miss Froy reached for her hand. 'Today, we exercise our right to do so.'

'Miss Battersby: I think you're rather magnificent.'

'Calm yourself.'

'Sorry. You're taking… quite a punt, on a set of values that has shown itself pretty tawdry over the years. Isn't it possible - isn't it more likely - that I'm just a wrong'un, as false and corrupted as they say?'

'Perhaps I am not so foolish. Perhaps I am, after all, an adequate judge of a man.' Miss Froy's expression suggested

I'd said the wrong thing. Still the formality from Miss Battersby, the emotion restrained within it: 'My younger brother went to South Africa with your army, Sir Henry; Jim. With the horses - Jim was a farrier - he always loved horses; always good with them.' She shook her head. 'He died there. With his horses. I may be a foolish old woman, Sir Henry, but I choose to believe that there was something noble; something worthwhile. If you are false, then everything might be false. If you are true... then something might be true after all.'

I took a deep breath. Not a lot I could say to that.

'But we are becoming sentimental.' The moment had passed, and Miss Battersby was all practicality again. 'You can't hide in a cupboard all the way to Paris.' I had considered doing exactly that, but she was probably right. 'And next time the search might be more rigorous.'

'If I can just get to Vienna - I think that's the next main stop - I'll have more room for manoeuvre, another chance to shake their rhythms a bit. Please do exactly what you would do anyway. If you do choose to leave the compartment and you can catch Mr Quinn alone, you might tell him that you've got me safely stowed. But that's not essential - he bides his time, doesn't flap; probably forgotten me by now. Otherwise, if you don't mind, I'll keep you company for the next couple of hours. If you've finished with it, Miss Battersby, I could make a start on your Gertrude Washbourne.'

63.

In the end I didn't get much reading done, except when they were out at dinner. I started on the book - and she writes brisk racy prose, old Gertrude Washbourne; I could see why the late Bishop and Miss Battersby were connoisseurs - but I wasn't in the mood. Instead I chatted with one or both of them, over the next couple of hours. They got an honest version of me: my family, my travels, my brief stint as a soldier in the Cape, one percent uncontrolled chaos on the battlefield and there's your medal, ninety-nine percent uncontrolled chaos on the thunderbox with dysentery. I heard more about them: the family; brother Jim; Miss Battersby's strange wandering endurance; Miss Froy's thoughts on Mr H. G. Wells's thoughts on socialism.

If England has a chance, in this new American and German century - and even I wouldn't put money on it - it is in women like those two.

We were at racing speed again, thundering over the great floodplain of the Danube, then soon enough we were slowing for Vienna. The buildings of the Habsburg capital rose around us. Miss Froy had popped out for a chat with her Hungarian musical friend and expressed her curiosity about what the police were up to, and he'd been anxious to impress and shared a cigarette and a chat with his compatriots. She was back in the compartment just a minute or two before we stopped.

'There's to be a full search of the train', she said, rather alarmed. 'Every cupboard and corner. They'll hold us here until they're sure you're not on it.'

'Right-ho', I said. 'Nice to be popular. Miss Froy, could I ask one more errand of you? I need you to find Mr Quinn, right now. Tell him that at Vienna station I'm going west. That precise phrase.'

'Going west?'

'Then wait where he can find you again.'

She nodded, uncertain, and left. A minute later the train came to a stop, and my head filled with the whistles and shouts of Austrian officialdom, and I knew they were mostly about me.

I had to get ont the front foot. Quinn had to act in time, Miss Froy had to get back in time, for me to have a chance.

Miss Battersby and I sat quiet. I think she was humming. It might even have been a hymn.

Miss Froy was back in time.

'Can I suggest you both leave the compartment first?' I said. 'Different directions down the corridor, just a few paces. Block the corridor a moment, chat to anyone you meet?' They looked surprised. 'If at all possible I'll try to slip out of your compartment unseen. I've disrupted your journey enough. Better you don't suffer any after-effects from my visit.'

I shook hands with them both. 'Miss Battersby:' I said, and took a breath. 'You and I know, from our different points of view, that England is a shabby place in many ways. The war in the Cape was a clumsy, dubious and inglorious affair, and I still don't know who won. But the Army that fought it was full of men like your brother: essentially good men, who believed they were doing something good, however misguidedly. Those were the men Jim fought with, and for. That's all we have, and it'll have to be enough. Miss Froy…' I smiled, still uncomfortable at having over-heard a private conversation. 'May your misadventures always be misadventures of self-possession.' She smiled at me shyly, a little pink, and then she and her splendid companion were gone.

64.

I had to get onto the front foot. If the Austrian police were going to search the tight confines of a train, in the middle of the Austrian capital, they were certainly going to find me. If they got me cornered - if they got me cuffed - I was finished.

As long as I was moving, and able to keep moving, I might have a hope. If the police thought things were going their way, they might just relax enough to allow me to move. Always the knack, with policemen and with criminals: let'em think they're winning, and there's a chance you'll get off more lightly.

I stood on the doorstep of the train, taking in as much of the view of Vienna station as I could manage in the second of immobility which was all I could allow.

It was evening by now, and dark. That might help, but for the fact that the station was probably the most magnificently illuminated structure in the city. It was heaving with people; again that might help, but for the fact that most seemed to be in uniform, and therefore presumably on tonight's anti-Delamere excursion. Uniforms were lining the other side of the train - no sneaking out of windows here - and uniforms were lining this side. The nearest of them stepped towards me as I stepped down onto the platform, gesturing me back with his rifle.

Keep moving. I pointed to a couple of other uniforms a few yards away and pushed my wrists forwards to suggest being hand-cuffed. I kept moving, and chummy came with me, keen to control but not needing to restrain. I picked the most senior-looking chap - age, hat, pistol not rifle, talking not doing - and hesitated in from of him. 'I'm Henry Delamere', I said. 'I'm the man you're looking for. I surrender.' And I shook his hand. Funny how people instinctively let you. A moment of doubt, and then he was nodding and almost smiling. One of his easier evenings in the police force; he'd be home for cocoa. 'It's this way, is it?' I pointed away from the train, to what looked like the main entrance. The big cheese barked an order to the man he was with, no more searching required. I started walking towards the entrance, beckoning to the chap with the rifle and nodding and smiling at the boss. I seemed peculiar, no doubt, but as long as I didn't seem to be resisting they'd let me move.

Keep moving. We strode to the entrance, my escort slightly behind me and in step. Two more uniforms stepped forwards to block my way. I nodded politely, earnestly, indicated the escort; all under control, all going terribly well for the home team. Then I pulled the identification card from my pocket, and handed it over. One of the policemen looked at it carefully. More co-operative than the average citizen; nothing they could complain about.

The policeman nodded and handed the card back to me, and looked over my shoulder. Not interested. He was looking for an Englishman called Delamere, and what he'd just got was a Turkish would-be bandit named Yıldırım Akbulut. The card had come in handy after all. The two policemen stepped aside. They had no reason to stop me. The chaps behind still had no reason to panic. They'd found me, and I was farther from the train every moment.

Keep moving. My escort weren't sure what had happened with the identification card, and hesitated a second and that gave me a yard. I lengthened my stride and that gave me two. A skip to avoid a handily-timed luggage trolley about to pass in front of me gave three yards and a momentary obstacle for the escort. I was through a set of double doors into the station building and a nudge set one of them closing slowly behind me.

Keep moving. I ducked down and to the left a couple of paces. Anyone in the crowd who noticed this surprising move would have been immediately unsurprised when I started fiddling with my boot-laces. That made me inconspicuous for another second, another scurried pace sideways, and for taking my hat off and skimming it through the legs around me into the centre of the hall. The eyes of my escort just coming past the door would follow the hat for at least a further second, and now I was up and walking off to the side, head down, and through the first door I saw.

As I mentioned, it was vital that they didn't corner me, didn't confine me. I knew that at some point I would run out of luck. I hadn't counted on shutting myself in a six foot square windowless cupboard inside thirty seconds.

I wasted a few moments swearing silently at the universe. I wasted a few more checking that there really was no other way out of my brilliantly-chosen hide, no windows, no loose floorboards, no open drain, nothing. A cupboard for the cleaning staff, by the looks: mops and buckets and boxes of cleaning products, a step-ladder, a tiny basin, a couple of broken chairs. I wasted a final few moments balancing the benefits of staying and going. There was a chance they hadn't seen me come in and wouldn't find me; but it wasn't a very big chance and, above all, time was on their side. I needed to be back on the Orient Express; they only needed to keep me off it.

A minute later, a figure in a workman's coat and hat, pushing a wide broom and carrying a bucket, slouched out of the cupboard and began to trudge past the crowd. Every nerve I had was screaming at me to run. Every cell of my brain was urging calm. I'm not saying the brain cells are in the majority, but they're persistent. Out of the corner of my eye I glimpsed uniforms, movement, back and forth.

Keep moving. I reached the edge of the main hall and turned, still trudging, still slouching.

This was a long arcade of shops, now all shut up for the night. In other words it was a tunnel, with my pursuers close behind me and a long way to go before I had any options. Trudge trudge trudge.

Two uniforms appeared at the end of the arcade, turned into it. I kept my head down. Ten yards off, to my left, a door between two shops. One of the uniforms pointed in my direction. They were closing fast. Had he pointed at me, or beyond me? I could trust to my disguise. Or I could duck through the doorway, see what new options it gave me - and still trust to the disguise. Another few seconds and the uniforms would meet me. From somewhere behind, in the main hall, I heard orders shouted. Head down.

I barged through and dragged my broom and bucket in. Then I pushed the door to and leaned against it, took a breath.

No one tried to follow me. There was no hammering on the door, no immediate pursuit. The room I was in was large.

Although they were small and high out of reach, there were windows. That was all to the good.

On the other hand, there was no getting away from the fact that I had just trapped myself in the ladies' lavatory.

65.

Come along, Delamere. What are the advantages? What are the resources?

One tries to be positive, but I couldn't see any. I'd given myself flexibility about when I moved again, but it had to be soon to get the train, and I'd no way of knowing who might be outside at the moment I opened the door. The cleaner's coat and hat might excuse me being in here. Or they might not.

I carried broom and bucket into the far cubicle, and closed the door behind me. Shelter. Concealment. Now if someone did come into the room, I could choose if and when I appeared, and who I appeared to be.

I wondered how long the Orient Express was due to wait here in Vienna.

The door from the arcade opened, and footsteps tapped into the room.

I'd been uncomfortable at the idea of listening to what went on in the Battersby-Froy train compartment. This promised to be considerably worse.

'Hubertus?' A woman's voice, cautious. Then again, this time lower but with the middle syllable high and teasing: "Hu-BERT-us!'

I swore, silently. I had to hope that the woman would disappear into a cubicle and stay there long enough for me to get out once the coast was clear, or that she would...

And then at last I asked myself why a woman would be calling a man's name in a ladies' public lav.

Lord, this I really did not need.

Rough old place for a lovers' rendezvous. I felt a kind of pity for her. It was swallowed by enormous frustration.

She had me trapped better than any policeman. If she was waiting for her paramour - and, god forbid, if they were going to do the deed here on the spot - my incarceration was as good as permanent.

There was silence outside my cubicle. Then, very faintly, I made out the woman's breathing.

We stayed that way for a minute, perhaps two. Me trapped in the jakes. The woman lurking outside. Beyond her, a gang of police, or killers, or killer police, hunting me.

A vague rustling suggested she was moving around. Then, softly, she started to hum.

God only knew what the tune was. I didn't get the impression she was hitting it all that closely.

In my somewhat over-complicated life, I've hidden out in a large and rather diverse set of places. Umpteen trees, wardrobes and rooves, of course; all the classic spots. And a cross-section of more exotic choices: in a clock in a French château, the Royal Box at Covent Garden, Sarah Bernhardt's dressing room, a cart of straw behind Boer lines during the war.

There can be a thrill about it: a sense of heroism in the concealment; pride, or skill; even wit.

Not on the present occasion, of course. Trapped in this third-rate Habsburg railway privy, I felt angry and pretty damn' foolish. Hardly an exploit for my memoirs. About the least glamorous billet imaginable, and more importantly not very effective.

I wondered optimistically if she might just go away. Hubertus had clearly got a better offer, or the wrong address - as we spoke he was no doubt lurking round the back of the tramway stop - and it would be the most natural thing in the world for her to give it up, go home, send him a grumpy telegramme and read some improving book.

Instead she called again: 'Hu-beert-us...' But it was

different this time, the pitch seemed... 'Was machst du da?' It was coming from down nearer the floor - under the -

Christ, the damn' woman had actually got down on her knees and peered under the door. Now she tapped on it, insistent, whispered the name again. She'd seen a pair of man's boots, and naturally assumed I was her beloved.

We stood there, either side of the door - a flimsy, plain panel it was - each waiting for the other.

Well, for God's sake. Of all the stupid, maddening, ridiculous situations. Why couldn't the whole damn' world just -

She tapped again.

I opened the door.

66.

'Nein, ist nichts Hubertus,' I said, and I made it sound as despairing as I could.

She screamed. Not in the grand style, but enough of a shriek to make me jump and wonder how deaf my pursuers could possibly be.

Resisting the urge to throttle her, I raised a finger, and with as much restraint as I could manage I placed it against her lips.

Shock at being confronted by an unknown man - the wrong man, in the wrong place - combined with confusion. Her eyes were wide, staring, uncomfortable. She'd a perfect right to be where she was, but she was feeling the foolishness of her liaison.

I switched to English. I've German enough for the essentials: picking a horse, ordering a sandwich. But not for this woman, not now: it was impression, emotion, that would save me; not vocab.

'I am a stranger in this country, Madame! Alone, lost. And no one will help me. Help me, dear Madame, I beg you!'

She was staring at me, stunned and uncomprehending.

I had one hope: that a relationship based on rendezvous in railway station privies - badly-organized rendezvous in railway station privies, at that - wasn't the most formal or deep. And the hope that she didn't have enough English to know how much nonsense I was talking.

I pointed to myself. 'Harry. Ha-rry.'

I pointed at her, eyes wide and questioning.

She stared. Then she said 'Jo-hanna.'

'Johanna' I repeated. Grateful smile. 'Johanna.'

She smiled at this foolishness.

'Help me, please. Spare me just one moment of kindness.'

I had to get out. The hunters could wait indefinitely; I could not. Now that the police thought I wasn't on it, my train could be leaving at any time.

I offered her my arm, and a hopeful smile.

I might not be as attractive a prospect as the mysterious Hubertus, but at least I'd turned up. Her original plan looked like it wasn't happening, and even if it was it probably wouldn't be as jolly with a madman sharing the room. If I was suggesting we go out into the arcade together, I probably wasn't planning anything awful. Johanna was human, and curious, and we all need a bit of warmth and company sometimes.

Cautiously, faintly amazed by me and by her own daring, she tucked her arm under mine.

I got my own coat out of the bucket and, arm in arm, we strolled out.

In the arcade, I walked us back towards the central hall of the station. I kept us in the centre of the passageway, and I tried to keep smiles on our faces, jollying Johanna up as best I could with exaggerated expressions. Only a couple of men on the platform had seen my face and knew it as Delamere, and only for a moment. If I didn't seem like Delamere, I wouldn't be. Two policemen appeared ahead. Keep moving. I contrived a laugh as we passed. No solitary hunted fugitive here.

We made the main hall, and I celebrated with another laugh and big smile. I was keeping us in space, obviously a couple, and at the same time looking for my next stop. There must have been a dozen policemen in view, and out of the corner of my eye I thought I saw the chap I'd introduced myself to on the platform. Another laugh. No one was noticing us.

Wrong. A man was striding through the hall, and his first glance passed over us, all good, and then his second turned into a stare and he stopped still. Not good. Not good because this looked like trouble, not good because trouble would transform how the rest of the hall was looking at us. I tried to turn.

But Johanna had stopped too. 'Hubertus!' she squawked.

Ah. I confess I've gone through versions of this scenario a few times in my life - when a lady's Plan A turns up just when I'm flagrantly getting down to Plan B - but never as publicly or dangerously.

'Mein lieber Herr!' I called, cheerfully. Big smile, and steering us towards him. 'Ah, sehr gut, sehr gut!' He was a little chap, wire glasses and greased-back hair. He was bewildered, shading to angry. Johanna was obviously uncomfortable, and trying to get her arm free of me. 'Sehr gut! Wie geht's?' That got us to him, and I grabbed his hand and shook it boisterously. 'Spät und ohne Blumen?' I said more quietly. 'Must try harder, old chap.' I clapped him on the shoulder, kissed Johanna on the hand, and left them to it. At last I'd seen the left luggage office.

It couldn't have been more than five minutes later that the whistle blew to herald the departure of the Orient Express for Paris. Policemen still lined the platform, watching for any sign that I might be trying to sneak back on. The conductor was hastily welcoming a new passenger - a chap with an ill-matched peaked cap and green coat, spectacles and a tiny moustache that looked as if it been drawn on in the Valfierno style - 'No, there was no trouble, Monsieur Somerset: we received your telegramme and happily we had a space for you - compartment 10 in the Second Class. Just this small bag? Please to hurry now.'

Monsieur Somerset did as he was told, and the whistle came again more insistent. Paul Michel caught the eye of the policeman near him, and shook his head. The policeman nodded and gestured conductor and train out of his city, and good riddance. The whistle squealed one last time, and the steam began to thump harder.

It seemed that I would not now be catching the train.

67.

Mr Somerset settled into compartment 10 of the Second Class car. Because he had it to himself, the upper bunk was still folded up out of the way, so the space was similar to what he'd have had in First Class. And though the fittings weren't as extensive or shiny, they were still better than most places he'd ever lived.

It was fully night now, and compartment 10 was at the end of the corridor. So there'd been few other passengers around to see Mr Somerset's arrival, and there was no expectation that he would make an appearance for another ten hours. Half an hour after the train left Vienna, a soft knock called him to his door. On the floor outside, in the silent corridor, he found a plain bag. The valet of the former occupant of compartment 2 in First Class had repossessed the baggage there, and was thoughtfully passing on a few essentials.

I'd removed Mr Somerset's hat as soon as possible, because it looked like an old pudding had died on my head, and his spectacles because they were giving me a headache. The silly moustache would have to stay for now, not least because the ink was probably permanent.

I settled back and smoked the last of the Bishop's cigars. I threw the stub out the window, thinking of the old man as it went, and enjoying the night air rushing past my face.

I had disappeared, and it felt wonderful. More than a few times in the last couple of decades I've felt how much of an improvement it would be to not be Harry Delamere. Now I was trying it, and I'd been right. Delamere - suspected, harassed, hunted, blown up, chivvied in and out of windows - he was lost somewhere back in Vienna, no doubt keeping the Habsburg police busy. But Somerset... Somerset was unknown and unnoticed. He had little baggage, in more ways than one.

There was another knock at the door. Again brief and discreet. I wasn't expecting anything more from Quinn, and he knew not to advertise the link between us. But no one else had reason to call, not at this time of night.

I put the spectacles on again. I listened at the door. Silence. Then I opened it a fraction.

'Say it ain't so...' an American voice drawled very softly; 'Harry Delamere in Second Class.' And, carrying a substantial handbag, Miss Peg Madison pushed past me and into my compartment.

68.

'The ears are the problem', she said as I closed the door and locked it.

'What's wrong with my ears?'

'Nothing's wrong with your ears. That's the problem.'

I took off the specs, and blinked her into focus.

She stood in front of me, close. 'You can steal someone's coat and fool around with spectacles and funny hats, and - Lord, is that ink on your lip?'

'It is.'

'It's not straight.'

'It was done blind, in ten seconds, crouched in the corner

of a left luggage office while I appeared to be tying my boots.'

'Yah, the boots were the giveaway too. And the ears. Very distinctive, ears.'

'Obviously I'll visit the false ear shop next time. And the coat was not stolen.'

She hesitated, and I could see her thinking. Peg Madison was as frank in her facial expressions as in everything else. No delicate lady-like musing. When she thought, she thought hard and cold and it showed. 'Belgrade', she said after a moment. 'Mr Quinn, that big lump of granite of yours, left the station. He doesn't do sight-seeing and he doesn't do souvenir-shopping. He bought the stuff for you then.'

'Yes.'

'And… that's when he wired to book the ticket from Vienna. You always plan it that way?' I waited. She thought. 'No… No, the telegramme booked the berth from Vienna, or maybe even Budapest, but said you'd join wherever your business commitments left you. Is Mr Somerset an international arms dealer or writing a book about European churches?'

'Mr Somerset is discreet about his business. That way he doesn't have to bone up on cannons, or… canons.' She scowled; not a fan of the word-play, apparently. 'I'd invite you to sit, but I'm sure you're too discreet to visit strange men in their compartments at night, and I'm sure Mr Somerset is too discreet to receive strange women.'

She sat. 'Look at that:' she said; 'wrong again.' There was no joviality to her wit; always cool, always the same confident gaze.

'And because you could give the game away, you have me over a barrel.'

'That doesn't sound very comfortable. And…' - she shook her head - 'what benefit would it bring me?'

I shrugged. 'Amusement?'

'Because I've finished my needlework and my three-volume novel and what else is a woman to do except play social games?'

'I value your skills as a bodyguard, if that's any consolation. But in the absence of Turkish bandits I don't seem to be in any danger.'

'That's what you think.'

'What benefit does it bring you to stay?'

'Material for writing my own three-volume novel, maybe.' She opened the handbag, and again I had a moment's interest at the remarkable diversity of luggage on this trip. She pulled out a bottle of champagne. 'I thought', she said, following it with two glasses placed very precisely on the table, 'that we should have a little talk, Delamere.' Her eyes were sure, severe.

'You've probably gathered that I'm not the talkative type.'

'Many men might appreciate a woman bringing them champagne.'

'I'm not many men.' I eased the champagne cork out with my handkerchief, and it came with a faint gasp.

'Mmm. No, you're not many men. But you are one; and one in particular.' She held up the glasses for me to pour. 'Mr Somerset's funny hat is off, and his ink is fading. The one, the only, the always Harry Delamere is here, and it turns out he's been here all along, the clever fellow.' She addressed her champagne glass. 'And we ask ourselves: what in Hades is he up to?'

I raised my glass to her, and tasted the wine.

'I'll admit it', I said, and her eyes snapped onto mine; 'I do appreciate a woman who brings '98 champagne and the right glasses.'

I sat at the opposite end of the bunk, and waited.

'It's a start', she said. She leaned forwards, and began counting with her fingers. 'One: the Turkish police are hunting some secret document. Two: a Turkish policeman disappears, apparently murdered. Three: we are attacked by bandits. Four: that sweet old Bishop, and he looked pretty robust to me, ups and dies in the night. Five: the holy grail of the ancient Greeks gets stolen. Six…' She ran out of fingers. She leaned even farther forwards and took one of mine in her own finger and thumb, and waggled it gently. 'Six: Sir Henry Delamere starts doing the damnedest things.' She released me, and sat back. 'Is it my imagination, or is there something just slightly out of the ordinary on this trip?'

'You're right', I said. 'I'm a lunatic spy assassin thief, and that explains everything. Except the bandits; chalk them up to local colour.' She waited. Still so sure, still so cool. 'The simplest explanation, as you imply, is that I really am a lunatic spy assassin thief. And you've just invited yourself to my compartment. You know that in some cultures that makes you responsible for anything that happens now?'

'You know that in some cultures women are allowed responsibility, even if it means inviting themselves into a man's compartment?' I waited. 'God… if you weren't so damned… so damned you. Most men, you give 'em a drink and a respectful look, they talk their heads off. But you: it's like trying to flirt with an oak tree.'

'Ah, I wondered what you were doing. No one's ever respected the Delameres: we get a respectful look, we know someone wants something.'

'I'm scared, Delamere.'

We were silent a moment. She gazed at me. She didn't blink.

'You're one of the calmest, steadiest, most self-assured people I've ever met. I don't think you do scared. Let's call it intelligent concern, shall we?'

'You call it what you like; I'm scared.' I was curious. She really wasn't a woman to scare, and she didn't look scared. 'You're not bothered? You don't wish this journey had gone rather differently?'

'I've got a very handsome woman on my bunk and a free glass of wine: for the first time in forty-eight hours I wouldn't change a thing.' I refilled both our glasses. 'But yes, since we're being honest: of course this is madness, and of course

I'm worried. Any of you might get caught in the crossfire, but they're actually trying to kill me.'

She looked up from her wine. 'Really? A straight-out go at you?'

'Major Hilmi got bored of playing the wounded bureaucrat and tried to shoot me.'

'Yah, I wondered what happened to him.'

'Oh, and there was a small incident with a bomb.'

Her eyes went wide, but she didn't ask any further, and I was grateful. 'And where did you get to at Budapest, and Vienna?'

'You really don't want to know.'

'Worse than your show for the Serbian police?'

'Yes, I think it was.' Poor Johanna. 'Even if I manage not to get murdered, eventually one of these policemen is just going to throw me in the local clink for ever. That's if I don't break my neck clambering in and out of windows.'

She took a slow sip of wine. 'And that's why I don't think you're the bad man in all this. All this nonsense you've been up to' - she pronounced it non-sense, which at least made it charming as well as irritating - 'it would have to be the most spectacular misdirection in history, or you'd have to be the most incompetent spy.'

'Let's not rule that out too fast.'

She topped up our champagne. 'So what are you going to do about it all?'

I felt like I'd been doing things non-stop since we left Constantinople. 'Do? I'm just trying to survive. Not very competently, I grant you, but I'm trying awfully hard.'

'Your plan is to hide out in here and... avoid the crossfire?'

I was going more careful now. I really had been the harassed innocent for a time, but now of course I was busy guarding the document, and that meant I did want to find out what was going on. I raised my glass again. 'As long as the wine lasts, it's a smarter idea than anything else I've done.'

'And all the other stuff that's happening? What'll you do about that?'

I shrugged. 'Surely it can't be a coincidence that Theotokis's cup gets stolen around the same time. And how many people', I added, watching her, 'have the dash to steal a priceless relic from under its guardian's nose? But I can't see how it's related. In my experience - which is mainly reading cheap newspapers and hanging around the wrong kind of nightclubs - spies and thieves are totally different breeds. Different values, different ends. You don't set off on some desperate diplomatic mission, future of Europe in your hands, and halfway along take a fancy to your neighbour's pocket-watch to make a bit of money on the side.' I poured more wine for us both. 'Then the Bishop. Again surely not a coincidence, but again I can't see how killing a Bishop achieves anything for anyone.'

'Did he know something? Did he see something?'

'Good ideas', I said. 'But what could he have known or seen that none of the rest of us did?'

'Perhaps we're all in danger.'

'I'm sure you've nothing to be afraid of down here in Second Class.'

'Is that so?'

'Far too cramped.'

'Perhaps that's what I'm afraid of.'

I sipped at the wine. 'You'd think that no one could do anything sinister because there are a dozen pairs of eyes watching everything. We're all more or less on top of each other.'

'Perish the thought. But if you're fast, that's exactly when you could make something happen. In… in the crush.'

I nodded; she was right, but still… 'If he was killed, I guess it means he was poisoned. There wasn't - They didn't mention any wound, and they thought it was natural. I don't know about poisons, but I guess if he was poisoned it had to be sometime during the evening. We don't know exactly when he died, but we were all up and about for the Serbian police-'

'Some of us more than others.'

'Thank you, yes. Anyway, the Bishop didn't die until several hours after dinner.'

'Aren't some poisons pretty slow-acting? I've read of people taking days to die.'

'True, but I think you'd start to feel bad rather quickly - wouldn't you? - however long you then hang on. The Bishop was pretty chirpy during the evening. I can't believe he'd been poisoned at lunch, felt fine for twelve hours and then suddenly keeled over at midnight.' She nodded. 'You were with him at dinner, weren't you? He seemed jolly enough.'

'Well naturally he was', she said, and I remembered the cigars. 'But only because I hadn't poisoned him yet. Do you know who was sitting with him last, later in the evening, after the stop at the Serbian border?'

I looked at her uncomfortably. 'As it happens I do: the Hungarian chap, Karim Bey and… me.' I emptied the last of the champagne into our glasses.

'Oh.' She looked at the wine, then me, then sipped. 'You again.'

'You having second thoughts about coming here?'

'I always have my second thoughts first. Let's for now politely assume you didn't poison him… I'm guessing you didn't see either of the others drop anything in his glass.'

'Obviously not…' I was doubting myself now. 'Surely I'd have seen it. Anyway, looking at it the other way round, our Hungarian friend or Karim would need a reason to kill the Bishop.'

There was one hell of a lot I wasn't telling her, of course. Even so, I still couldn't see the motive for either of those two.

Madison said: 'Karim was pretty upset about his death.' I looked interested. 'At Belgrade he was fussing around the conductor and the police, when they were getting the body out.' I'd missed all this, of course, being Shanghai'd by Hilmi instead. 'I guess he felt it was kind of an insult to Turkish hospitality or something. Or at least that some official courtesy was needed. He went off the train with the body, and I think he was trying to get the Turkish Consulate in Belgrade involved.'

'Odd. But that's all long after the event, anyway.'

'You're right.' She was looking dissatisfied. 'So that's it? We just keep our heads down and survive the journey?'

'Seems enough of a challenge.'

She looked at her glass, only a mouthful of wine left in it. 'And is Mr Somerset going to insist on throwing me out now?' She looked up.

'Mr Somerset insists on nothing, being a gentleman despite the hat. Mr Somerset would strongly prefer that you spend the night here.' Her eyebrows rose slightly. 'Each time that door opens it draws attention to me.' I considered her. 'I'm trying to lie low. I feel I'm rather at risk of being... exposed.'

She nodded. 'Glad to know your motives are honest and pure.'

'Honest, yes.' I drained my glass. 'Pure, no.'

She drained hers. 'Is there any chance you could clean that ink off your lip?"

'What possible interest could you have in my lips?'

She showed me.

69.

I woke twice.

The first time was magnificent, because beauty on the pillow beside you is an absolute truth. In a fancy hotel or in a pile of straw, even squeezed in a railway bunk which you're occupying under false pretences because the Austrian police are hunting you, that still form has its aesthetic power and it has the memory of happiness and it has the promise of all the character you know to be preparing to wake. And Miss Peg Madison, she of the pistol and she of the champagne, had character and to spare behind the delicate strength of the jaw, under the dark gold mane that spilled onto the linen.

The second time there was someone hammering at the door.

Madison took in a great breath and, without opening her eyes, said: 'You order the maid to bring breakfast?'

'I think we're probably crowded enough.' I was looking out the window into a grey morning. 'We've stopped.'

'You've done enough moving for one night. Border.'

'The time's wrong.' The train began to clank forwards again.

'We were already running late. Must have got held up again during the night.'

The door hammered again. I called 'Good morning', without enthusiasm. Outside, a French accent started to babble something.

It was interrupted by another voice: 'Good morning. I apologize for disturbing you at this ungodly hour.' A different accent. Almost certainly - given the border we were crossing - German. 'What the poor conductor tries to say is that I invite you to open the door at your convenience, or I shall instruct the conductor to open it, and if the lock is jammed I shall merely shoot it out.'

I stood, pulled on my trousers, and opened the door.

Standing there was a tall, slender man in impressive and immaculate uniform. 'You selling souvenirs,' I asked, 'or just excited that we're in Germany at last?' There was no doubt in my mind that he was German.

'I am sure we are all excited by that, mein Herr.' He gave a little bow, stiff and elegant. 'Major Von Eisen, at your service. The conductor informs me that you are Mr... Somerset.'

'That's right: Somerset.'

He seemed to see Madison for the first time, over my

shoulder. I saw his eyes flicker a moment, the poise momentarily less sure, and I glanced round. She was sitting up in the bunk, her body emerging from a swirl of sheets, her expression cool as ever and a little haughty.

He wasn't looking at her expression. He eventually managed a little bow to her too, and dragged his eyes back to me. 'And the lady is…'

'The future Mrs Somerset.'

He smiled. 'How charming. My compliments to you both; I do hope you will favour me with an invitation to the happy event. And if I were so crude as to insist on seeing your passport, what… spelling of the name would I find there?'

'Delamere.'

He nodded, smiled in understanding. 'Sir Henry, you are most welcome.'

Madison said from the bed: 'The brilliant deception didn't last long, then.'

'It brilliantly got me out of Austria, which was all I needed.' My eyes were still on the German major, so correct in front of me, and so calm. 'Besides, you shouldn't complain: moment ago you were a future Mrs; now you're a future Lady.'

'Nah, I think I'll pass.' She had reached into her bag, and was pulling on the dressing gown. 'Don't think either of us can carry off that kind of dignity.'

The Major gave me a look of commiseration. 'Sir Henry, might I invite you join me in the dining car in - shall we say ten minutes? We have… certain points to discuss.'

'My pleasure', I said. Then I got it. 'Von Eisen: I saw a Von Eisen riding at Liverpool, year or two back.'

He smiled. 'My cousin; little Hansi. A lovely sport, but myself I got too tall for racing when I was fourteen.'

I turned to Madison, who was now standing behind me and gathering the last of her clothes into the bag. 'Keeps getting better', I said. 'The Major here is a Count, I believe.' The Major tried to look modest. 'Hang around another ten minutes, who knows what you'll end up with.'

She stopped in front of me, always that handsome sure gaze. 'One knight was probably enough', she said, and she kissed me and was gone.

70.

The train was winding along beside a river. Through the window, to the south, the land rose and kept on rising towards the distant Alps. Nearer, a fairy-tale castle appeared, perching on a hill.

The conductor had made a little announcement explaining the further delay during the night: there had been a land-slip, and the Orient Express had had to wait for the last of the debris to be cleared.

Major Von Eisen gave his orders for breakfast in fluent French, and refused to discuss business while we were still eating. The classiest kind of Hun. He was a splendid and intimidating figure, and the other passengers kept clear. With the exception of Madison who, as she was walking past, gestured that I still had a bit of ink on my lip. None of the rest had noticed my temporary absence: I had missed the train as Delamere and then had to resume my identity as same while they were asleep. Again with one exception, none had the pleasure of making the acquaintance of Mr Somerset, during his brief existence. And there was the conductor, of course, but I think he was now so confused he was keeping quiet out of sheer exhaustion.

The stewards were pouring coffee, and I thought it only polite to kick off myself. 'You're very patient, Major. You had something else you wanted to discuss, besides East Africa.'

'I do, Sir Henry. And I hope your courtesy indicates that we may resolve the matter in the quickest and most civilized manner.' Hope all you like, chum. I smiled. He took out a cigarette. I lit it. You can see why I was glad we'd left the

Balkans behind. 'To that end', he continued, 'I shall be as frank as possible. Cards on the table, yes? We should be in a position to enjoy a drink together in Munich, if not before.'

I say that the rest of the passengers were keeping clear. They were certainly watching pretty intently, and more than a few could probably hear us.

Von Eisen took a puff of cigarette, breathed the smoke out through his nostrils, the most aristocratic dragon you ever saw; just right for the fairy-tale castle. 'Well then, it is known - I emphasize the word - that you are the British Government courier of a secret treaty recently signed with the Ottoman imperial authorities. This treaty - we shall not discuss our respective governments' perspectives about its fairness - but it is certainly disadvantageous to Germany. The treaty - and again I emphasize that I present to you a fact - it will not leave Germany.'

I decided on second thoughts to have a cigarette. I liked the way he was using his for emphasis. He lit it for me.

'That's very clearly put', I said.

'Then perhaps you could you see your way clear to handing over the document without any… fuss?'

I took a long drag of cigarette. 'You won't be surprised to hear that you're not the first official to say I'm the courier. I have been searched several times, and nearly killed. My compartment has been searched officially and unofficially, and once almost blown up.'

He nodded, as if thinking about it. 'Does this not perhaps make you think you could make your situation easier?'

'Does it not make you think you could be wrong?'

He looked serious for the first time. I wasn't sure what was more offensive to him: the idea of being wrong, or the idea of being in the same class as the Turks and Bulgarians. 'Sir Henry, you are no longer among the barbarians, with their superstitions and guesses. Germany has the most effective intelligence apparatus in Europe. I do not say that we suspect or we believe you are the courier. I say that we know.'

For a rare and brief moment, I had a bit of respect for the British Government. Von Eisen wasn't to know that I'd only recently and unofficially become the courier. His certainty meant that the sneaky sods in the Embassy in Constantinople had deliberately leaked the news that Delamere was the favourite for this race, knowing that the likes of the Germans would pick this up. Can't say I liked it, but you had to admire the skill.

'Major, I thank you - sincerely - for the very fair way you've set it out. I'm afraid that I... cannot oblige you.'

He looked at me gravely. He expelled a last jet of smoke. He stubbed out the cigarette. 'The treaty will not leave Germany. I have said this and you understand. Yes?'

'You have and I do.'

'And the only question is, within my legal authority, how... aggressive are the measures I am required to take to achieve that.'

'Yes.'

He nodded; shrugged. 'Then may I suggest that we go to your compartment?'

71.

It was a pretty odd proceeding, but in no way uncomfortable. Von Eisen had one last expression of regret - only doing this in case it avoided more tiresome business later on - which I thanked him for and ignored. I stripped down to my birthday suit, and he had a quick check that I wasn't concealing anything screwed up between my toes or whatever. He then handed me my dressing gown, while he went carefully through my clothes.

He was just finishing that, when there was a knock on the compartment door. I glanced at him, and he hesitated. Von Eisen had a plan, and he didn't like interruptions.

The knock came again. A muffled 'Quinn, sir' followed

the knock. 'You needing reinforcements?'

'Better let him in', I said to Von Eisen. 'He's less patient than you, and even less polite about locks.' Von Eisen nodded, and I called the invitation.

Quinn came in poised for anything. Beside him was a German soldier, pointing a rifle at his head. 'You all right sir?' He moved towards me a fraction, and the rifle jerked anxiously. Quinn glanced to the man. 'Simmer down, chum. You'll hurt yourself.'

'This is Major Von Eisen, Quinn.' Smile from Von Eisen, wary nod of courtesy from Quinn. 'The Major is just going through my kit. He's a neat sort of chap, so we should be all right. Major…' Von Eisen looked up again. 'As you can probably tell, Quinn is… gentleness itself. A pussy cat. And a very disciplined one. As long as you don't trouble me, he will not trouble you. Your man can probably stand easy.'

Von Eisen considered this, then barked a word. The soldier lowered the rifle.

'Quinn, the Major is convinced that I'm carrying a secret document. He is exercising his authority to search me and the kit. When he doesn't find it - as of course he won't - he'll look elsewhere, I'm sure. Determined fellow. Provided he and his men show you the same courtesy they've shown me, you will allow them to search you. Clear?'

'Sir.'

Von Eisen smiled. 'I might', he said. 'Then again, I might not bother. Partly because you seem so willing, which would be a risky bluff. More because I do not think you are a man to push such a risk onto your servant instead of taking it yourself.'

'As you wish. You'll have a rootle through the luggage, presumably.'

He nodded. 'That will be the next step, yes. We shall open the luggage wagon at Munich.'

'Then if I can have my trousers back, I'll pop out for another coffee and a cigarette.'

As I was entering the dining car I bumped into Valfierno. He murmured a good morning, and I didn't disagree because it would have taken too long. He added: 'Not to press you, Sir Henry, but I must leave the train in Munich. Should you still be interested…'

Funnily enough, I was still interested. I made an appointment to visit.

I didn't get much farther. Madame Dewoitine raised two perfectly drawn eyebrows into a subtle but irresistible glare of command, and then glanced at the chair opposite her. I sat.

She offered me a cigarette. I refused. I had an aunt like Madame Dewoitine; and indeed a Regimental Colonel. One did not relax.

'The Germans' - she swallowed the word like a foul-tasting medicine - 'seem to take an interest in you.'

I shrugged. 'He's polite enough. He has his duties, Madame.'

'As do you, I think.'

'All those uniforms, they have to keep them busy somehow.'

Her lips tensed, thinned. Apparently I hadn't been joking - or funny, anyway. She nodded. 'There are German uniforms on French soil. They have occupied Alsace and Lorraine for forty years now. It is an open wound.'

'I sympathize, Madame.'

She nodded again. 'For you English, the Germans are a rival, a competitor. You challenge them for empty corners of Africa, just as you would challenge them in a game of football. For the French… They have been an enemy, an invader, for a thousand years. One must do business with them, of course.' I hoped her legendary profits helped her tolerate the burden. 'But…' Her eyes snapped back to me. 'That little corner of territory between us, it passes one way and then the other, like the tide.'

'After forty years, Madame, you must hope that the tide turns soon.'

Again her expression hardened, became more guarded. Alsace-Lorraine had been French much longer than it had been German, until Bismarck kicked a bit of discipline into the Germans and they marched into Paris. It's also full of coal and iron. I wondered at Madame's patriotism. 'But this is populist chatter merely', she said. 'I should save it for little Junot. Sir Henry.' She made the name sound like an accusation. For once she hit the H; it came out like a kind of gasp. Always impossible for the French, but Madame would do impossibility rather than imprecision.

'Madame?'

'I find that your man is…' - I waited; Quinn can be many things, not all of them charming to refined European sensibilities - "e and my maid - they are… What would be the English phrase?'

'It would be… much less elegant than the French phrase.' The faintest smile touched her lips. 'I understand, either way.'

She paused; considered me, yet again. 'She is a good maid, Monsieur.'

'No doubt. He's a good man.'

She considered this too, even more doubtfully. 'I 'ave spent a great deal of time training 'er. I very much 'ope… that she leaves the train in the same condition in which she entered it.'

I nodded. 'As they say in the advertisements: nothing taken away, nothing added, yes? Quite so, Madame.'

She smiled faintly; nodded. I stood. 'Oh yes…' she murmured. I waited. She was looking past me, and her voice was low. 'I understand that you have been talking to that… Is it Valfierno?'

'The Marquis, yes.'

Again the eyebrows, and a souring at the mouth, as if I'd just told a dirty joke. 'A man may call 'imself many things.' Then, slyly: 'May 'e not, Sir Henry?' I just smiled. "E tries to sell you a painting, I think. A Poussin. No doubt for a significant but credible figure.'

'One hundred and fifty guineas.'

She chewed this, still looking away. At last her eyes came back to mine. 'Sir Henry, 'e does not 'ave a Poussin.'

I leaned a bit closer. 'I don't have a hundred and fifty guineas, Madame.'

She considered this a moment, and then at last that ruthless grip relaxed: she laughed, and well. It was a deep, rich sound, a happiness precious and private. She looked at me again. 'Si méchant', she said to herself; 'si charmant…'

The interview was over. As a family motto for the Delameres, that would have to do.

72.

As we got close to Munich I was in Valfierno's compartment with him, enjoying a last look at the fake Poussin.

Speaking as a fake courier, even an impostor can be as effective as the real thing. I liked the picture, anyway.

There was a knock at the door, and Quinn's voice outside. I had my hands full of painting, and it was Valfierno's compartment, so it wasn't inappropriate to encourage him to open the door.

While he did so, I had time to retrieve the treaty from inside the back of the frame, where it had been since just before my train window steeplechase at Budapest.

I was now thinking of it as a treaty, following Von Eisen's insight. He'd know far more about it than I. He could hardly know less.

Quinn was sticking his head in, as arranged, to say we'd shortly be in Munich. Final regretful farewell to the doubtful marquis, and a more sincere one to his doubtful picture, and I hurried off to find somewhere else to hide the treaty.

As Von Eisen had promised, at Munich the Germans went to war on the luggage. They didn't search individual passengers: Von Eisen was still sure I was the courier, and that I couldn't or wouldn't get someone else to carry what I wouldn't carry myself. His focus was the places where I might have stowed it: that meant a quick look at everyone's compartment just in case I'd snuck in while they were out, and a long look at all the heavy baggage in case I'd found a temporary spot in there during one of our stops.

The Orient Express had been directed to the most secluded platform at Munich, farthest from the station building and exit. As we came to a stop, we saw uniforms all around the train. Valfierno got away with difficulty and a search of all his kit in the waiting room. Everyone else was escorted to the luggage wagon for their bags to be searched. Von Eisen oversaw proceedings with immaculate courtesy and total indifference to complaint.

Only one person stayed above it all. Madame Dewoitine could be seen at her table in the dining car, gazing straight ahead into space, as if determined not even to see Germany or anything German as she passed through it, and obviously fuming at the assault on her bags.

'I wouldn't like to be the next German businessman trying to get a fair deal with her', I said to Junot, my journalist friend.

'My friend, there is a very real chance that we will be at war with Germany by tonight.' I smiled at this. He shook his head. 'Sincerely, at a minimum there will be a telegramme from Paris to our Embassy in Berlin. Almost certainly a diplomatic protest. Perhaps my government cannot achieve anything in Berlin like this; it certainly cannot fail to take Madame seriously.'

Von Eisen knew who Madame Dewoitine was, and had made an effort at extra courtesy with her. She wasn't having it, and it didn't make any difference to him, so they agreed to disagree.

I should add, of course, that they didn't find the treaty in any of the compartments or bags. The van was re-packed and re-locked, Von Eisen dismissed his troops, and the train was allowed to proceed. Not a single raised voice or hurried movement in the whole business.

I was careful to avoid any hint of triumph or humour when I bumped into Von Eisen, as we were gathering speed and heading westwards through the late morning.

'I have told you, Sir Henry.' The accent was still crisp, the voice still calm. 'There remains the possibility to make it easier for me to retrieve the treaty. There is no possibility that it leaves Germany.'

73.

He was a lot more confident than I was.

We were rattling through southern Germany, and I was having a solitary smoke as the stewards cleared away the remnants of lunch, and I was mulling on table settings, and therefore where people sat, and therefore who could have poisoned the Bishop. Quinn was sitting with me, always a good companion in solitude.

He helped himself to a dribble of wine from the bottle, and poured out the rest for me. I watched this, then sat up.

'There's no other way he could have been poisoned.'

'Sir?'

'Everything else the Bishop ate or drank that day was served from a common dish or poured from a common bottle or pot. It could only have been put into something that was definitely his, and that meant it had to be fast hands at the table.'

Quinn nodded.

'And they weren't worried about finding the treaty. I was wrong about this before, wasn't I? They only needed to delay it. That's what Hilmi said. Killing the courier, the Bishop, meant his body and kit was taken off the train. All they needed.'

'It also means it had to be someone who knew you weren't the courier, sir.'

'Good point…' And then my thoughts switched tracks with a jolt. 'Hang on, this is what Von Eisen's thinking as well, isn't it? I'm feeling terribly pleased with myself because he hasn't found it yet, but he doesn't need to.' I shook my head. 'That's what he keeps promising. Not that he'll find it, but that it won't leave Germany.'

I drifted into thought again. Never a pretty sight. I think someone tried to stop and make conversation at one point, but got a look of such hostility from my valet that they hurried away to make their peace with God.

At last I began to see it. Quinn registered the change in my expression. 'We really' I began, still clutching at thoughts, 'need to get a wiggle on.' He was watchful, still, ready for the charge. 'But… The one person who might be able to make this work is Madame. I need to call on her. Now. And I'll need the conductor there too. If you can't reach her yourself, then her maid must be able to dig her out. I gather you are… making a positive impression in that direction.'

'Friendly, sir. You know me.'

'Apparently everyone knows you, Quinn. Especially the little dark pretty ones. I also gather that if you get careless, the government of France will declare war on me personally. This would be inconvenient, certainly for the next twenty-four hours. Any chance you can restrain yourself?'

'I'll try, sir.'

'Cold showers. Innocent walks among the flowers.'

'What shall I say you want to talk about?'

'Tell her… tell her it's about the tides.'

74.

My charm - or more likely Quinn's - turned out to be adequate, and ten minutes later I was in Madame Dewoitine's compartment. She didn't invite me to sit, and she didn't like having the conductor in the conversation, but we were in.

'Madame, I hope you will prefer directness and honesty to courtesy and persuasiveness, because we haven't time for them.' She didn't say what she preferred. She continued to glare at me. 'From the beginning of this journey, you have heard about some mysterious document, a treaty, being taken secretly from Constantinople to London. Various policemen have suspected or accused me of being the courier.'

Still she glared.

'They were quite right. I am the courier.'

I heard movement from Paul Michel behind me, but Madame Dewoitine didn't look surprised; didn't react at all.

'I confess that I have no idea what the treaty is. I suspect you, Madame, with your familiarity with European politics, will have a much better idea. You have heard Major Von Eisen say that the treaty is disadvantageous to Germany.' I took a breath. A lot depended on the next sentence. 'I suggest that in the current European balance, a treaty with Britain that is disadvantageous to Germany is a treaty that France would support, or at least tolerate relative to the alternative.'

Her mouth stiffened. For a fraction of a second her eyes wandered away from mine. Someone in there, a very fast calculation about the grand strategy of all the great powers had just been completed.

'Von Eisen also said that he is determined to keep the treaty here. I didn't understand at first. I think I do now. Major Hilmi said that he didn't need the treaty itself; he only needed to stop it getting to London, or even just delay it. Von Eisen thinks the same. If he wanted the document he'd have grabbed me as soon as we crossed the border and beaten the truth out of me inside five minutes. I'm not such a hero, and he's not such a gentleman. But he prefers to avoid drama and scandal, and he knows he can.'

A fine eyebrow flickered.

'He's going to stop the train. Block us.'

This further insult to his train was too much for the conductor. 'How?' he said. 'Where?'

'Now I'm guessing, Monsieur Paul. We're running - what - six or nine hours behind at the moment?' I turned to Madame again. 'He will wait until it's night, and he will wait until we're out of a station. It will be harder for any of us to get away, or get a message out, and at night it will take longer for us even to notice. It will be much longer still before anyone else notices. That delay is all Von Eisen needs. He'll have found the document, or forced it out of me, or just delayed it long enough not to matter anymore. He will wait until he's in a place where there are already plenty of German police and soldiers, to give him total control.'

She nodded. She knew where I was going.

'After Strasbourg, Madame. Von Eisen is going to seize the Orient Express in occupied Alsace-Lorraine.'

75.

Another flicker of calculation from Madame. Then she realized that I was done.

'I do not think, Sir Henry, you only came to tell stories. What do you propose?'

Straight to business, no fretting or faffing. Splendid woman. I leaned closer to her. 'How well do you know the French people, Madame? How well can you guide them?'

Very slightly, Madame Dewoitine smiled.

'I suggest you'll need to send some telegrammes, Madame, at the next stop. Stuttgart, isn't it?' A grunt of agreement from Paul Michel.

I outlined my idea. I saw her eyes widen, and glance away another moment as the cold brain considered it all. It was fantastical, of course - what hadn't been on this trip? - and it depended on her arrogant certainty that her nation was hers to command.

'And shall I be permitted to send telegrammes,' she said at last, 'by… these people?' Millions of Germans dismissed, in one slight curl of the lip; sorry, Hermann.

'Von Eisen thinks he doesn't need to be aggressive yet. For now he'll continue to wait for me to give up the treaty without extra pressure. And while I chat to him, Mr Quinn and Mr Singh will accompany you. They should be a big enough distraction for anyone who gets too interested.'

She nodded. Decision; agreement; end of discussion. Conductor Michel and I left.

I pulled Quinn into my compartment to give him the plan. He had to wait a bit, because yet again my mind had wandered away from where it was supposed to be.

I was puzzling over the idea of distractions.

Once Quinn had ambled off to be ready for Stuttgart, I went along to Second Class. Happily the two Russian girls were at home.

They were surprised to find me knocking, and a little apprehensive: the reputation of the solitary English traveller working its magic as usual, and during our very brief acquaintance they'd heard me accused of pretty much every crime under the sun.

It didn't help that I insisted on stepping into their compartment, and closing the door behind me. I settled myself on their stool, and they waited uneasily, glamorous Oksana standing stiffly against the table, dark Mariam watchful as ever on the bed.

'I wanted to ask you three questions, and then to ask your help', I said. 'That's a very smart-looking pen, by the way.' I'd just caught sight of it behind Oksana's hip, a regular nib on an elaborate metal shaft.

'It… was my father's', Oksana said. 'One of my few treasured things.' She adjusted her weight, and the movement rippled up her body, and the pen had gone and she flashed an amused smile at me. 'Was that one of the questions?'

I smiled right back, though I don't pretend it was half as

charming. 'I can't deny I admire it,' I said, 'but as a distraction you're a bit late this time. Question one: Miss Mariam, the night that the Bishop died, and we were having drinks in the dining car after we'd crossed the border into Serbia, did you drop something, under your table?'

She stared at me. 'I - I do not remember. How is this important?' I waited, still smiling in the friendly fashion. 'Yes, I think perhaps I did. I forget what.'

'I'm sure it didn't matter. Two: your surname - sorry for my pronunciation - Chichinadze; it's not actually Russian, is it? Georgian, by the looks.'

She nodded. She was wary now, the dark face bleak.

'Question three, then: what is the attitude of two modern, intellectual, forward-thinking, politically-aware young women, one of them Georgian, to a Greek archaeologist taking an ancient artefact from Georgian territory, to boost his reputation as a Greek expert of ancient Greek culture?' My eyes moved between them. A grand couple, handsome and confident. And, as I sat before them, a little intimidating. 'I'm interested, you see, if that was why you two stole the sacred cup of Colchis, or whatever it's called.'

76.

Slowly, elegantly, Oksana pulled out a cigarette and lit it.

She breathed out a long line of smoke. 'That is rather offensive suggestion', she said at last.

Mariam was sitting upright. She folded her hands in her lap, composed. She smiled. 'And rather hard to prove, I think.'

'Oh indeed', I said. 'I'm just naturally fascinated by the cultural politics of the Black Sea region. Purely academic interest.'

Another thin jet of smoke from Oksana. 'The man Theotokis is a barbarian, a nationalist, a bigot, a lecher and a thief', she said. 'Academically-speaking.'

Apparently this was still too positive for Mariam. 'He is also a second-rate archaeologist and a third-rate historian.'

'Reading between the lines,' I said, 'you're not enthusiasts then.'

Oksana laughed faintly, another ripple in the willowy body. 'Mr Delamere, you have already understood that in the twentieth century it is no longer appropriate to smuggle out a country's treasures only because you think they look nice in your European museum. That cup is the property of people of Georgia, in Empire of Russia. This Theotokis may not raid our land, like Jason taking Golden Fleece.'

I vaguely remembered the story from school, whatever its relevance here. Mariam was pressing on, anyway. 'The irony, of course, is that ancient Colchis was a far more sophisticated society than his arrogant Athens.'

'Just as modern Russia is a far more sophisticated society than modern Greece', went on her friend, and they both shrugged at the obviousness of this statement.

'Theotokis's excavation breaks terms of his agreement with our government.' Mariam again. 'And because of his amateur obsessions it overlooks many elements of more significant relevance to proper understanding of ancient society and culture, in favour of items of superficial glamour. His theories are of course based on outdated Greek hegemonistic picture of ancient civilizations, and total ignorance of the development of culture and government in the eastern Black Sea. That cup-'

'Wherever it is'; Oksana.

Smile. 'Wherever it is, was stolen first by him, for false purpose.'

'As if - Oksana - 'he would steal your crown jewels to play marbles, or first manuscript of Hamlet to prove that Danish people spoke English.'

'That might all be true', I said. Indeed it might, though half of it had gone over my head so I was in no position to judge. 'But the police hereabouts might still object to it being stolen from Theotokis.'

Another shrug from the pair of them, European trains and European property laws as irrelevant as European museum policy.

Oksana: 'If it is returned to where it belongs, our government will be happy to debate right of ownership with Greece and anyone else.'

And Mariam: 'And poor Theotokis did not see it for twenty-four hours before he missed it, and it has not been found. So this is still academic discussion.'

'Mm. I was never that strong at the academics', I said. 'But I do know one thing that no one else on this train does, not even Theotokis. I know that the cup was still in its proper place in the box late that evening, well after we crossed into Serbia. I know because I checked, or at least my man Quinn did.' Their confident eyes were a little wider now. 'I also know that we didn't steal it. And it's very unlikely anyone could have got to it later during the night, when Theotokis had taken the case back to his room. So suddenly there's not a twenty-four hour gap when it could have been taken, but one or at most two hours, when some of us were in the dining car with Theotokis. Mind if I sneak one of your cigarettes, Miss Oksana?'

She passed one over. I had to light it myself.

'I think you two would have appreciated our scheme. Lots of noise and fuss from me to keep his attention, while Quinn had a good rummage.' I focused on Mariam, sitting watchful on the bunk. 'That's the thing about Quinn: such a quiet, undramatic chap, and everyone's too snooty to look at a servant; and all the time he's the most capable, determined of men.' I took a puff of Oksana's cigarette, though I couldn't pull it off as elegantly as she did. 'I got to thinking about distractions. I knew the trick must have been done while we were all in the dining car, and so I knew it had to have been one hell of a distraction.' I glanced up at Oksana. 'I hope you won't think me coarse for mentioning it. But then you played on our coarseness and your own beauty boldly enough, didn't you? A loose thread hooked somewhere by your seat, and then your skirt awry and you bending over so strained and vulnerable. We're not a very sophisticated species, are we? Every eye in the room sure to be fixed on you. And where was Miss Mariam in that moment? I couldn't see you. You were under the table, retrieving whatever it was you'd dropped. Theotokis and you were sitting with your backs to each other, so his case would have been easy to reach down there.' Another thought: 'And you'd been shopping in Sofia: you'd seen his little case by then; were you buying a handbag that looked similar enough to stand in for ten seconds?'

They were silent, watchful. I could see Mariam, typically, thinking ahead and preparing to speak. I pressed on: 'So - academically-speaking - I cannot logically prove that you took it, but I know that no one else could have taken it. As you say, it hasn't been found, but I wonder... If I was to borrow that pen of yours, and show its extraordinary craftsmanship to my good friend Theotokis, would I learn that you had dismantled the cup into its three components to defeat a search, and stuck the nib of a regular pen on its shaft?'

Mariam wasn't thinking about speaking now.

'I don't know where you hid the other two bits, but - Wait up... I do. During the search at Budapest, there was a bit of bother when a policeman dropped one of your hat-boxes. That one, was it?' I pointed up to the luggage rack. 'Lovely bit of business from you, of course, Miss Oksana - showing that the box was empty, hat on and off, very amusing, very convincing, impossible for the cup to be there. But the bowl of the cup would fit very nicely into the crown of the hat, wouldn't it, and you'd be able to wear it as normal? So I think I could point the police towards two-thirds of it, at least.'

We smoked at each other for a few moments. Watching; waiting.

'Now', I said, 'perhaps you two are so convincing that the

police would refuse to search you, and I'm so unconvincing that I'd only reinforce Theotokis's suspicion that I stole the cup when I looked in the box. Perhaps I think he's a bit of a boor, and don't much care for his attitude to women, let alone to cultural artefacts. Perhaps your passionate arguments have convinced me what you did was fair. Or perhaps I want something in return.'

Two pairs of eyes widened, just a flicker of watchful interest. Damn but they were cool about it.

'Perhaps', said Mariam.

'You see - being so ignorant - I care about something more than your blasted cup. Something else was happening while you were taking it. Someone else in that car was doing something even worse than you, and their best chance would have been while you created a distraction.' They were curious now. And they knew my price was easily paid. 'Simply this: everyone else was looking at you. But you - both of you - must have been aware of everyone else. Your senses would have been fiercely alert, screaming. You'd planned this, you must have practised it. As you glanced round us for help, Miss Oksana, you must have been counting every eyeball to make sure they were pointing in the right direction. You Miss Mariam, you must have checked that everyone was ready before you ducked under the table.'

I stubbed out the cigarette. 'So: tell me, please. Who did you see? I need to know exactly who was there.'

It was remarkable how precise they were, how vivid their alertness must have been. Oksana's eyes froze as she re-captured the scene. 'Your table, first to my right', she said, the hand flickering. 'You. Nice Hungarian boy. Fat Turk. Bishop. Left is Greek, eyes dripping over poor Russian girl in difficulty. He ignores two poor Englishwomen. Behind him is Svensson, Swedish scientist. Then…' Remembering the image rather than the theory, she had of course missed her companion, in that moment ducking down to do the dirty deed. 'There is Doctor, and…' Her face screwed up in the effort to fix the picture. She shook her head. 'Then in right corner South American art man.'

She let out a breath. She gazed at me, waiting for my response. I looked to Mariam.

'All this', she said, pointing at her friend. 'Also, with Doctor is Arab man who imports cloths and spices, and also your companion Mr Quinn. Can we take him home with us?'

'I'll ask.'

'Art man… something is wrong with him. He is - uncomfortable. With him is Junot, the French writer.'

They waited. I didn't look happy.

'You expected more?'

I shook my head. 'I just wondered. And no one was… was doing anything that seemed unusual? surprising?'

A moment to reflect, and they both shrugged.

There was nothing more to be said. We left each other to reflect on our sins.

I'd been wondering about something more elaborate for the poisoning. But given all the other limitations, it really did seem to come down to the Bishop's table.

As I was going, Mariam the dark dangerous intellect pulled out a pocket mirror to check her make-up. The gesture seemed very unlike her. Her eyes came over the top of it, and stared into mine. The mirror, balanced in the palm of her hand, had a very substantial golden back to it.

77.

Shortly before Stuttgart, I managed to bump into Von Eisen. Helpfully, Madison was nearby at that moment: I needed an ally to help the conversation go as I wanted, she was naturally inquisitive, and he was as human as the next man and so happier talking to her than to the next man. So a very contented table we were.

I said: 'Major, can we expect any more police actions at

Stuttgart?'

He offered Madison a cigarette, and pretended to be undecided. 'You would enjoy another challenge, Sir Henry? Or like the good soldier, you want to learn more of your enemy's manoeuvres before the battle?'

'I was never all that good a soldier. I'm just wondering how much time I have to enjoy the sights of Stuttgart. Lovely churches, apparently.'

He treated this with the scorn it deserved. 'Alas no one may leave the station', he said, mock regret, 'but I should gladly point out some of the most important features from the platform.'

'Major, you seem pretty sure Sir Harry is your man.'

He smiled pleasantly. 'Miss, ah, Madison, I am entirely sure he is my man. All this…' - his cigarette circled between him and me - 'is merely courtesy. Sir Henry is naturally determined to do his duty and take home his prize - they probably give him a hearty clap on the back and three cheers, eh? - and I have made clear that he will not succeed. We need not get so emotional about it.'

She shook her head. 'No wonder it takes you Europeans so damn long to finish your wars.'

'I suspect it's really just one war', I said. 'Occasionally we adjust the sides, or the rules, or take a breather.'

Von Eisen chuckled at this, the genial host and official. I didn't buy it for a moment. There wasn't a drop of sentiment in Von Eisen, or a second of wasted thought: he was as ruthless a man as I've met. He'd said he wasn't letting the document out of Germany, and he'd stop at nothing to achieve this.

But then we were through Stuttgart, without obvious disaster. Madame Dewoitine had been one of those who fancied a stroll on the platform. By chance, Quinn and Singh had been nearby when she stepped down. Only someone looking for it - someone looking occasionally over Major Von Eisen's shoulder, for example, then trying to restrain himself -

would have noticed how their big dour presence tended to create a space around them, a space through which a woman might move unhindered. I lost sight of them, and then the Orient Express was clanking into movement again and there were a horrible couple of minutes when I thought they might have missed it. At last Madame appeared in the dining car again, and I tried to control my breathing and listen to what Madison was asking about the direction of Germany policy in the new century.

Once or twice another German uniform appeared and murmured in Von Eisen's ear. His eyes stayed on me all the time.

We were nearing Karlsruhe when my increasingly desperate effort to keep the conversation going got unexpected assistance. I hadn't seen Karim Bey for some while - and he was hard to miss - but suddenly he was lumbering past our table on the ever-present stick.

Von Eisen was immediately standing and giving his courteous little bow. Again, I had to admire the preparation that had made him familiar with the passengers. I wouldn't have known what he'd think of Karim. Splendid, was apparently the answer. Great honour to meet him, great honour to be able to welcome him to Germany, hope the wine's adequate and so on. Madison and I were rapidly forgotten, and Karim had joined us at the table.

Watching the long exchange of pleasantries, I remembered Germany's enormous influence in Turkey. For these two men, being polite to each other was a matter of the highest national strategy.

At last they ran out of pleasantries. 'So', Karim said, turning away from Von Eisen to look at me for a moment, 'you are going to arrest poor Sir Henry at last?'

We all laughed.

None of us was finding it funny. Though I think we were finding it unfunny in different ways.

Eventually Von Eisen overcame his fake polite laughter,

and said that he hoped this would not be necessary, but that he would of course be as ready to oblige me in this way as any.

Karim switched to a more serious and respectful question about politics in Berlin, and Von Eisen gave a serious and respectful answer, and they were off again. This time Madison was able to throw in the occasional intelligent question. I even tried one comment, though I think I got the chap's name wrong.

My anxiety was growing as we got closer to Karlsruhe, the next stop. I was gambling that I'd read Von Eisen's intentions right. And not only his intentions but how, precisely, he planned to carry them out. I was gambling that I would have time. Just enough time.

Then the whistles and the steam and we were in Karlsruhe station, with the usual shouts and doors - and the usual heavy police presence on the platform. Again I was glancing over Von Eisen's shoulder, again I was trying not to.

A uniform bustled up, murmured in Von Eisen's ear, got an instruction, bustled off. Then another.

Von Eisen excused himself a moment, and went and stood in the corridor. He seemed to be having a conversation with someone on the platform. I realized I was staring at him.

Then he was back, pleasant, settling himself. He said, conversationally: 'Madame Dewoitine sends many telegrammes, it seems.'

Whistles, and doors, and thumping, and the Orient Express was moving again.

'Yes', I said. 'She's been doing a lot of that.' I'd not seen her go, and I'd not seen her return. There must have been some snag, some change... 'Not a world I know well, of course, but her empire must take an awful lot of co-ordination. Bit of trouble in Paris, perhaps.'

I smiled at Von Eisen, and he smiled back. A bit of trouble in Paris was more or less German foreign policy page one. That and pretending to be nice to Turkish big-wigs.

Soon our little party broke up. The stewards wanted to set the tables for dinner. I got the impression that each of us was feeling the strain of all that politeness.

I went and stuck my face out of the corridor window, relishing the roar of the wind against it.

When I glanced back into the dining car, I saw that Karim was murmuring something to Von Eisen. At one point both of them looked at me. No one was laughing any more.

I wondered again about Hilmi's story that the Turkish authorities hadn't wanted the document to leave Turkey.

Karim and Von Eisen hadn't realized that Peg Madison was close behind them. Shortly afterwards she was beside me again.

'I don't want to worry you', she murmured.

'Worry? On this trip?' I tried for the light-hearted laugh, and failed.

'Karim and your German friend are discussing the circumstances in which you might safely be arrested.' Her smile was an attempt to be reassuring, but it just came out as pity. 'Apparently they still don't trust you.'

'They can join the queue. As long as they don't arrest me yet.' I glanced to where the two men were still chatting, all so polite. 'Not yet...'

She gazed at me. 'You're up to something.'

'Always. My ears giving me away again?'

She leaned very close to one of them, and her whisper was a breathy roar to me. 'Harry Delamere, I don't trust you either.'

78.

By Strasbourg, we were nearing the crisis. I had a fair idea what Von Eisen had to be planning, and I thought I could see a slight change in his manner. He jumped off the train as soon as we stopped, and I was watching him all the way. If the Germans made their move now, in the station, I was sunk. In some ways it would be more convenient for them here - all the station facilities, not so unusual to have a big detachment of uniforms. I had to hope that in this restive territory, Germans ruling over a grumpy and significantly French population, Von Eisen preferred discretion and isolation for his coup.

The minutes passed. I thought of the treaty in its hiding place. Twice the conductor appeared in the dining car, trying to catch my eye. I ignored him. Madame Dewoitine had already been seated when I came in, and I made a point of not looking at her either. But I saw that her gaze was still fixed forwards, towards France, and whatever was about to happen.

Then I saw Von Eisen's distinctive height in the corridor, and then he was in the door of the dining compartment. He was smiling.

From outside, whistles and steam.

'So, dear ladies and gentlemen,' he announced; 'it is time for our dinner, I think.'

We had dinner. I can't say I noticed what I was eating.

I didn't drink. Not because I was afraid of following the Bishop across the final border, but because I wanted my head clear.

Fortunately I didn't have to sit with Von Eisen. I'd made sure I had Quinn beside me, and that he had the revolver beside him. Opposite us, Peg Madison was watching and worrying about me, and Junot was chattering enough for all of us. The status of the territory we were passing through gave him plenty to discuss. Across the aisle, Von Eisen and Karim were keeping up the courtesies, and he'd also met Sikander Ali Khan and recognized him as a legendary hunter. Once or twice I glanced at their table, and I could tell that Von Eisen was on edge.

The Orient Express was rolling and clanking slowly through the twilight, and we'd just finished eating, when Von

Eisen stood, stepped with difficulty round Karim and into the aisle, and asked for everyone's attention.

'I have an announcement, dear ladies and gentlemen', he said.

And so it begins.

'You will have to accept my apologies for the inconvenience, but very shortly I will be stopping this train.' There was the confused murmuring you'd expect, the beginnings of concern and irritation. 'Regrettable but unavoidable', he went on. 'There is on this train an item of... contraband. It cannot be allowed to cross the border into France. If it comes into my hands, then the train will be free to proceed. And I am pleased to report that in any case you will able to leave Germany no later than tomorrow at midday, because at that point the item will be irrelevant.'

A few voices began to speak: Junot opposite me, obliged to represent the wounded voice of all those delayed in getting to Paris, had turned and started to rise and to complain. Von Eisen spoke over them. 'I urge you to restrain your emotions, dear ladies and gentlemen.'

It was about now that the ladies and gentlemen noticed that a pair of German soldiers had slipped into the compartment just as Von Eisen had been starting to speak, and were standing behind him, rifles held alert across their chests.

'Your protests will achieve nothing. I assure you that this action is guided by the German government at the highest level, and the government is ready to endure any slight diplomatic discomforts to defeat the conspiracy that is attempted against us. Honestly, I do not think anyone will know or care about another slight delay in the timetable. Extra supplies were loaded at Strasburg, so you shall enjoy the usual luxuries of this train.' He turned to Paul Michel, hovering unhappy nearby. 'Conductor, please to remind me the stations we pass through now.'

Michel licked his lips, and spoke uneasily. 'We are not

scheduled to stop before the border, but we pass through Saverne, Sarrebourg, and then Avri-'

'Good. Just past Saarburg station the track runs beside a lake. You will stop there.'

A lake. Further restrictions on our room for manoeuvre. He'd thought it all through, of course. I guessed he was right about the diplomacy, too: a night surrounded by German soldiers might be alarming for us, but if no one got hurt the incident would be quickly forgotten.

The conductor had his duty. 'Major, this is an outrageous interference with the line, which is an international standard.' His voice was quiet, sad, uncomfortable. 'I must protest.'

'Yes', Von Eisen said. 'But my dear fellow, I urge you to do so without passion or risk to yourself. You will stop the train by the lake after Saarburg. There is a detachment of the German army there to ensure that you do not forget, and also they have blocked the track. You will notify me when we pass Zabern station - Saverne, you would say Monsieur. I suggest you should be communicating with the locomotive now.'

Paul Michel retreated unhappily. Von Eisen looked at me. 'You lose, Sir Harry, I'm afraid. At noon tomorrow the validation period for the treaty expires. If it is not in London to be endorsed by your politicians in the presence of Turkey's representatives there, it is automatically abandoned. The status quo ante in Constantinople will be re-confirmed, which some of us will find more agreeable.'

I gazed at him bleakly.

'Tomorrow', he said, 'I shall allow you to proceed into France and then home. But you will be carrying no more than a curiosity of history, a path untaken; your paper will have no more meaning than if it was blank.'

Still the train rolled and clanked through the darkness. We were into the foothills of the Vosges, I think, and the track was winding more and more, and our progress was painfully slow.

79

A wooden sign drifted past the window in the gloom, the name clear at our lumbering pace: ZABERN-SAVERNE.

The conductor, hoarse and unhappy, mumbled to Von Eisen. The German didn't need the prompt: he was looking for the name, he saw it. His train and his plan were on track. The station was silent at this time of night, just a single light, and then its ghostly outline was lost behind us.

'I trust there'll be no… unpleasantness when we stop, Von Eisen', I said.

He managed a smile. 'You know me by now, Delamere. I have said: all that I need is to hold the train for this night; I shall hold the train for the night. You and your companions will be unmolested, and free to do as you please provided you stay on the train. Drink by all means, dance and celebrate, for tonight is the last night of your journey together, and the last night of your diplomatic intrigue against Germany.'

I nodded. I believed him. He didn't need violence, and he wouldn't use it unless he had to.

I stood. He was in control, he was playing it calm, but he was immediately alert as I moved. 'Might take that drink', I murmured. But I didn't. I stood at the bar, glanced at the cocktail menu without inspiration, smoked a cigarette.

The minutes passed. I'd never known the dining car this quiet. Most of the passengers were here, my companions of the last mad days, but all felt the strain of the moment. None of us knew what exactly would happen when we were stopped in the middle of nowhere by a special detachment of the German army.

We started to slow again. Von Eisen glanced out into the night, and then to the conductor.

Another platform rolled before the window, another sign: SAARBURG-SARREBOURG.

Von Eisen stiffened, looked at the conductor again, gave a nod of command.

Paul Michel nodded back. 'The locomotive has been informed, Major. They will stop at the lake.'

'They had better' - Von Eisen, peering into the darkness - 'otherwise we all suffer a big bump and your beautiful train will be badly damaged.'

Conductor Michel's face was not kindly.

A minute passed. Two. Everyone was looking out of the windows now.

After three minutes, Von Eisen turned to Michel again: 'How far from the station to the lake?'

The conductor shrugged. 'For distance I do not know, Monsieur. Normally some several minutes.'

'We're going rather slowly', I offered.

Another minute. 'I was told the lake is only one kilometre maximum after the station!'

We shrugged.

Von Eisen was staring out again, eyes straining. A moment later he was back, angry and accusing. 'There is no lake!'

'Not on this line', I said quietly. 'Hope you weren't looking forward to the fishing.'

80.

Von Eisen's face was deathly.

'Germany rules Alsace-Lorraine', I said. 'Your laws, your police, your army. But you can't control the minds and hearts of the local French people. In particular, you can't control the local railwaymen. The head of the most powerful industrial empire in France, she can.' His eyes veered to her, then back to me. I nodded. 'Madame Dewoitine's telegrammes: after Strasbourg, we were routed onto a different track through Alsace-Lorraine. Your chaps are going to have a long wait.'

'The stations…' he said vaguely.

'Madame's people can change a sign as well as a signal. Right names, wrong places.'

'Schirmeck and Fouday', the conductor murmured.

'But still we will stop at the border.' Von Eisen spoke in hope only. The sense of command had gone.

'No Monsieur.' Paul Michel was still uncomfortable. An unhappy passenger, even a German one, was never a good thing. 'As in most points along the present border, on this old line there is no physical barrier. The bureaucracies will be administered when we reach Saint-Dié.'

Von Eisen didn't even look at the conductor. He glanced around the compartment, until he saw Madame Dewoitine again. She allowed her eye to be caught only for a moment, and then she resumed her stiff poise, the glare into the distance. Her bleakness had turned, very subtly, into triumph.

Von Eisen gazed into me for a long time.

'Regrettable', he said at last, and there was none of the charm now. 'It seems there must be some unpleasantness after all.' He took a cautious pace back, pulled out his pistol, and pointed it at my chest. I was very still. I'd feared this. I couldn't give him any more surprises; I needed the old calm Von Eisen. 'A company of soldiers and an obstacle on the line may not be necessary: one single bullet may serve. I am confident I will still find the treaty, or delay it enough.'

My attention was fixed on his face, his eyes. 'You're aiming at me,' I said, 'but that means you've turned your back on Mr Quinn, and put yourself between him and your two riflemen.' Very slowly, I opened both sides of my coat. 'And he has my revolver, and he will make sure that you won't find or delay anything. If I don't get the treaty to London, he will.' The shoulders stiffened, as he thought of the pistol aimed at his back. 'We'd go together, Von Eisen. I wonder if we'll both be on the right track, across that border.'

The eyes were searching me, searching his own instincts and values. He was a truly loyal committed officer and, speaking as a pretty dubious indifferent officer myself, his kind are always dangerous.

'You know diplomacy', I hurried on. 'You know that this

treaty is either formalizing what's happening anyway, or a futile effort to stop it. Is it really worth both our lives, whichever town it ends up in?'

I had to read him; I had to convince him.

'You're a gentleman, Von Eisen, and I'd hate to see you treated without the courtesy you've shown me.'

Somewhere at the edge of my attention, the conductor gave me a single clear nod, and a desperate smile, and I saw the tension dropping out of him.

I only just caught it. I had a good argument against Von Eisen; but since it involved me getting shot in the chest it was, as my Russian friends would have said, a bit academic.

'I hoped to succeed without scandal', he said, with some of the old suavity, 'yet I am confident that my authorities here will give me a little flexibility, if I have saved German diplomacy.'

'But as of ten seconds ago', I said, 'we're in France.'

81.

Von Eisen didn't shoot me. He was seriously consid-ering it; that I could see in those very blue very hard eyes.

In the end, he'd known I was right. Shooting me, however appealing an idea in itself, wouldn't have helped Germany any, or him.

I bade him a polite goodbye at Saint-Dié station, and silently we shook hands. No triumph, no jokes. I hadn't won anything, I'd only survived, so far; and that only because he was essentially a decent chap and a professional.

There'd been a bit of delay while the conductor gave the authorities an edited version of how the most famous train in the world had unexpectedly turned up at their station, and asked them politely to get us back to the main line at Nancy. They'd been happy enough to believe that the German occupiers a few miles away in Alsace-Lorraine had made trouble, and happy enough that French patriotic solidarity had won out.

We were well into the evening now. After our various delays we'd be into Paris in the small hours. Some of the passengers were getting what rest they could; others had obviously decided to stay in the dining car and push on through until the bar ran out. Craig was there, my comrade-in-arms from the bandit fight. Sikander Ali was there, elegant and courteous as ever. Miss Suraya had her back to me, fortunately: we'd managed to avoid each other most of the time, our relationship based entirely on unwanted appearances in each other's bedrooms. Miss Battersby was tackling an enormous glass of port; I was confident she'd win through this time too.

I'd found a discreet moment with Madame Dewoitine.

'I can't thank you enough, Madame. I hope there wasn't too much... cost, or inconvenience.'

She gave a little lady-like shrug of indifference, and shook her head. 'There is a man called Labiche - a demagogue of the workers, a brute - who will now consider that I owe him some favour. A temporary irritation, but I am confident he will be disappointed eventually.'

'I hope you will consider the outcome acceptable. For France.'

'I think we may safely guess the contents of the treaty', she said. Speak for yourself, I was thinking, I couldn't even tell you who the government are this week. 'As you suggest, in these days what is beneficial to Britain, in the European balance, is beneficial to France. And if, as I suspect, there are implications for the movement of Persian oil... I think my investments will prove adequate.' She produced a tiny, guarded smile. 'The telegrammes that I sent, Sir Henry, were not only about railway logistics.' I had to smile at that. The subtle bravado, the amusement, the quiet relishing of life: magnificent woman. Old Monsieur Dewoitine had been a lucky fellow; until she'd pushed him down the stairs.

Now that we were in France, the end of the journey so close, and my various threats and inconveniences had passed or faded, I was feeling some relief. Not celebrating, exactly, but… in the home straight.

I'd made an appointment to call on Madison, and was ambling down the First Class corridor with a couple of bottles of champagne when I met Quinn coming the other way. He was carrying one of my few bags, the smallish leather overnight one - where the pistol had once been, back when this had been a peaceful journey. What with the confusion of the last twenty-four hours, the poor chap had spent much of his time ferrying my kit back and forth along the train - depending on who I was being at that moment, and where.

Behind him, I saw Karim Bey. If there was one man to sour my mood, it was he.

I didn't like the look of him. He, clearly, didn't like the look of me. He was hesitating at the end of the corridor, where it led on to Second Class. His expression as he gazed at me was edgy, watchful.

Quinn waited until I'd refocused on him. 'Bit of kit for tonight, sir.' He glanced at the bottles. 'Or perhaps you're not needing your nightshirt.'

'One of these is for you, so less of the comedy. Your little friend's just come home to the mother-country, safe and sound after all her adventures: might want to celebrate.'

Quinn doesn't do emotion much. Or perhaps it's just I don't do generosity much. 'Very thoughtful', he mumbled. 'Sure she will. Thank you.' He hefted my bag. 'I'll just-'

'No, I'll drop it in: don't dawdle.' I took the bag and put one of the bottles in, and gave him the other. 'Enjoying the feeling of being able to go into my own compartment, under my own name, with a reasonable chance I'll have it to myself.'

You'd think I'd have learned.

Grappling clumsily with the bag, half-opened and now more ungainly with the wine bottle jolting back and forth in it, I fiddled with the door and stepped into my compartment.

You've probably guessed: Major Hilmi was sitting on my bed, pistol pointing at my chest.

82.

In that whole mad journey, that was the one moment when I seriously thought I might have gone off my chump.

Surely I'd seen this before. Surely this had already happened. Surely I'd survived this.

Apparently not.

Again the finger to his lips, and an indication to close the door. I closed the door.

'Bloody hell, Hilmi', I said. 'I once had a bad dose of the Piccadilly Itch like you. Kept thinking I'd got rid and could enjoy myself again, and back it came.'

There was a hint of triumph in his face, but also desperation. He wasn't here for the chat. 'This time I shall be fatal for you, Delamere.'

'Funnily enough I picked that up in a ditch, whereas I thought I'd got rid of you in one.'

'Too often you have not seen me, Delamere. The one who was not here.' He stood, a yard away from me, far enough that I couldn't reach him, close enough that he couldn't miss. 'A special train from Belgrade to Zagreb and Graz, and then a car to Munich, and a train again. But already I was ahead of you. There was some extra confusion at Strasbourg, and I got on to this train unseen.' Von Eisen's efforts had had an effect after all. And all our delays: it shouldn't have been possible to race the Orient Express across Europe, to find a short cut, but the Bishop's death, and the stolen cup, and the landslip in Austria, and all the damn police checks had enabled this extraordinary little man to win a unique race.

'And now?'

'Now you die, Delamere. Goodbye.'

He squeezed the trigger.

You see it in the eyes, not the finger. I threw my bag at him. At least, I started to. Bullets are a bit faster than clumsily thrown half-open leather cases. Perhaps it made him flinch. Perhaps the bullet was deflected.

What definitely happened was that the case exploded in his face. A burst of vintage champagne and shattered glass and my socks engulfed us both, and I was on him.

I claim no special skill, no clever tricks or superiority. Two desperate men, him with his cause and me just trying to stay alive another five minutes. I was on him and he was flung back and down into the corner. I was bigger than him, but I'd found out too late that he was one of the most driven men I'd ever met. And he had the gun.

I had to focus on the gun, on grabbing it, grabbing his wrist, trying to keep his arm up and away. That meant he could focus on punching me in the head and kicking me in the Balkans and all across Central Europe. I managed to get both hands clutching his wrist, my weight on top of him, and his punches had no momentum. Then he got his other arm round my throat and started to squeeze.

I was choking, I couldn't find breaths, I started to lose strength in my arms. I grappled desperately at his gun hand, wrenched it in then flung it back and there was another explosion of glass. The barrel had smashed a hole in the window, and now Hilmi had lost his weapon.

And he'd gained a free hand. That made two he was strangling me with. I twisted, tried frantically to shift the weight, to change our positions. I kicked out against the side of the bunk, and smashed my head back into his nose, and rolled and his grip slackened and I was gasping in great grateful breaths. Now he was behind me, on top of me, and I swung an elbow back into the side of his head and turned.

There was a fraction of a second when we stood motionless, a yard apart. Then I saw the blade in his fist, held low, and he took a step forwards and thrust it towards my gut. Frantic, my hands closed on his driving wrist and with all my strength I slowed his momentum and the knife scratched against my coat and wavered back a few precious inches. I clutched it there, my two arms straining to hold back his one, then his other arm was up at my throat and I could do nothing.

Dimly, I heard a hammering at the door.

The knife straining towards my gut, his hand clenched around my throat. As my breaths became weaker, so did my arms, and that blade heaved ever closer to me.

The door smashed inwards, and a large shadow was vague behind Hilmi. Thank God, thank God, Quinn had made it after all…

But no. It wasn't Quinn. The man now moving in behind Hilmi to share the triumph was his compatriot Karim Bey. Big, dark mysterious Karim Bey, who had been at me since my first hours on this damn train and was now here for my last, the only man who could have poisoned the Bishop. The Turks: from the start it had been the Turks… My eyes were closing and I had nothing left.

I heard a ghastly choking, and my discomfort seemed to drop away, and if death is release from all of the madness then fine with me.

'Delamere!' My eyes flickered open. Hilmi was still perched in front of me, over me. His eyes were grotesque, he was gasping for air, and a slender blade was emerging from his chest.

'Delamere, the window!'

Slowly, stupidly, I twisted round and pulled on the window.

It jammed, naturally. Dumbly, I glanced back at Karim, and he gazed at me like I was a child, and I had another go and it opened. Together, we wrestled Hilmi's dying body onto the sill, and up, and over, and he dropped away into the night.

83.

I collapsed back onto the bed.

Karim looked down at me, still pitying. 'The sedentary life of the train, Sir Henry. You are badly out of shape', said the largest man in the Ottoman Empire. He wiped his blade on one of tomorrow's socks and threw that out the window. He slipped the blade back into his stick. One-handed, he slid the window up. Then he propped a pillow against the hole in the glass, and the noise of the night was muffled.

'You look a little surprised, Sir Henry.'

I was rubbing my throat and checking my head was still attached. 'You...' I croaked, 'I thought you were the opposition.'

He settled massively at the other end of the bed, took out a handkerchief and began to dab delicately at his forehead. 'Most amusing', he said. 'For a long time I thought you were.'

'But...' I started trying to think, to speak. '...What?'

'My government is making a treaty with yours, Sir Henry. Not a very great treaty, certainly not a treaty we are proud of. But a necessary treaty, in these difficult times, which will maintain stability in Constantinople and the near east for a little longer. It was a British responsibility to courier the official version to London for validation there, and your British representatives in Constantinople called on the most trusted of men, the most experienced in these affairs:'

'The Bishop.'

'The Bishop.' He bowed his head a moment, shook it sadly. 'A splendid man. I agreed to come on the same train, to... have a discreet Turkish eye on the matter. To ensure fair play, you would say?'

'Probably not. That was fair play?'

'The British told us that they would make arrangements to protect the Bishop, including spreading misinformation, but we were not told the details.'

'I was the details.'

'I was looking out for a potential threat to the Bishop. And from the first moment, Sir Henry, you seemed the most threatening of all. A man of adventure, a man of uncertain loyalty, a man of desperation, a man of bad name...'

'Steady on-'

'You understand why I was so quick to challenge you when we started. To test you and your motives.'

'I was their damn' decoy! They must have let my name leak deliberately. Sent messages they knew would be intercepted.'

He beamed, nodded in appreciation. 'Very shrewd! Most amusing!'

'Damn' hilarious.' My throat still ached and my head still stumbled. 'Wait... So if you're the home team, and you wanted the treaty to get to London all right, who the hell was Hilmi, and what was he up to?'

He was suddenly sombre. 'Our empire is unsettled, Sir Henry. There are forces of radicalism and sedition. One group in particular, with many supporters among our own soldiers, is determined that the existing system must be overthrown completely. The treaty is intended, among other things, to counter them - to make them less popular and less relevant, and to enable their destruction. Of course they were passionate against it, and determined to stop it. I did not know of Hilmi particularly, but I was looking out for men like him. I was immediately suspicious when he began searching for the document, because I knew that there could be no truly official requirement for that. I telegraphed back to Constantinople, and confirmed that he has been under great suspicion for some time.'

'But you still let him go on with his performance, all that stuff about it not being allowed to leave Turkey? His harassment of me?'

'His harassment of you, Sir Henry, was most helpful to our cause.' The big smile again. 'I am grateful, truly.'

'And he felt comfortable saying it in front of you? He

wasn't afraid that you would disagree or stop him?'

'But Major Hilmi was right, Sir Henry: officially the document should not leave Constantinople. He knew that; and he knew that I knew it. If the Turkish public knew that we were allowing it to be sent to London, as schoolboys submitting our homework to the professor, it would be a great embarrassment to our government - a humiliation likely to cause the collapse of the state, and the further rise of the radicals like Hilmi.'

'Then that's why he preferred to wait for his bandits, rather than searching me publicly: if he'd called my bluff and found the document on me, you might have taken it off him. The bandits were a justification for getting it away from you, as much as from me.'

He nodded, grave again. 'That episode was most alarming. That their group has such boldness, such resources... He killed the other policeman - at Çerkezköy. Obviously the man was not of his movement, and Hilmi thought he would be an obstacle.' Another shake of the head, the great jowls trembling. 'But this is merely chatter and speculation. Sir Henry, we have stopped Hilmi, but it is essential that we find where the dear Bishop hid the treaty before he died.'

Another thump of understanding in my straining head. 'That - that was why you were fussing around his body and his compartment, at Belgrade.'

'Of course.'

'I thought that was you being the opposition. After he was poisoned-'

'Ah, and I had been watching so closely... I was so pleased to be able to confirm that neither our Hungarian friend nor you had been near his plate or his glass.'

'I thought that you'd poisoned-'

A great tut. 'Come come, Sir Henry! We are being serious.'

'Gosh, I hadn't realized, between getting shot by your radicals, blown up by the Bulgarians, and arrested by everyone else. I am delighted to announce, Karim Bey' - I didn't feel or sound very delighted - 'that your damn' treaty is safe. I broke into the Bishop's compartment after he died. I found the document. I have tucked it away.'

For the first time, I'd surprised him. 'But this is splendid, Sir Henry.' He was all jolliness again. 'And the Embassy made you out to be such a rogue!'

'Yes, I'm going to have a few words with the Embassy. If I ever go back, which is unlikely.' I sat up, trying to stretch and straighten myself out. 'More important, don't we have a bit of a problem now? We've been trying to stop disruption to the journey, and you've just thrown a passenger out the window. Bound to be a drama; they'll have to stop the train.'

'My dear Sir Henry: as the passenger list will confirm - he was never on the train.'

Hilmi's name had only been pencilled in, and now it would be as easily removed. 'Like he said himself: the one who wasn't there... And leaving bodies with stab-wounds lying around the French countryside? That the Turkish way of doing diplomacy is it?'

'You were the one having the knife fight with him, Sir Henry; the French authorities shall come to your door long before they come to mine.' He smiled, complacent and sinister. 'And that', he said, 'is the Turkish way of doing diplomacy.'

He was right, though. Poor Hilmi, being neither an official passenger nor a gentleman, had never registered as more than an irregularity, an irritation; a shadow. And now the shadow had passed.

We both stood. Neither of us did it that elegantly. 'So half the train thought I was the courier,' I said, 'and half thought I was the assassin.'

The big smile. 'So boring to be undistinguished, Sir Henry.' Everything all right in Karim's world: Delamere a good chap, the treaty safe, no reason not to sleep well tonight. He rolled out.

And that was that.

Wasn't it?

The one who wasn't there…

84.

Last time I'd got cosy about being on the home straight, a vengeful Turkish revolutionary had immediately jumped out of my bed and tried to shoot me, stab me and strangle me.

But still: home straight, surely. We were so close to Paris now, the Orient Express hurrying through the night towards its destination. Turkey, and Bulgaria, and Serbia, and Hungary and Austria or whatever you're supposed to call them, and Germany, they were all behind me now. All their bandits, and assassins, and policemen.

Might be time to investigate holidays in England. Nice genteel seaside resort, old ladies and cream teas. Except that after Miss Battersby I'd never think the same way about Englishwomen of a certain age; and apparently half the barbers in Brighton were Serb.

Now it was just me and Miss Peg Madison, in her compartment, and the smooth mighty roar of the train beneath us. I'd brought along a bottle of champagne to replace the one that had exploded during my fatal struggle with Hilmi, and she was opening it.

Mutual respect and intimacy. What more is there?

'The treaty was in a cigar,' she said, 'wasn't it?'

I nodded: 'Which was why the Bishop got so ratty when the box was knocked over; I got there eventually. Fine paper, folded once and tight rolled.' I considered her a moment - the handsome face, the cool expression - my admiration unconcealed. 'You worked that out by sheer brain power?'

'I'm not saying I couldn't. But the Bish's cigars had a rather distinctive flavour, which I… tasted on you, long after he was in any condition to have given you one willingly. You'd decided to hide the treaty somewhere else, just in case someone worked out where it had been, and then you smoked the evidence.' She must have seen my irritation, and smiled. 'You can't think of everything.'

I shook my head. 'I was thinking of my Uncle Robert. Godfather. He'll be turning in his grave. "A gentleman should always brush his teeth before calling on a lady."'

'D'you think he could kiss as pleasantly as you?'

'There must still be a few ancient courtesans of Paris who could tell you, and Constantinople: he got about a bit, Uncle Robert. Was that when you knew it was me - that I had the treaty?'

'That was when I was sure. I assumed you'd been up to something that night. Your Mr Quinn is about as competent as they come; if he fires a pistol it's because he wants to. So I was immediately wondering what we'd all been distracted from, and sure enough you appeared late, rubbing your eyes and bless-my-soul-old-chap.' She shook her head, smiled without warmth. 'I'd have burst out laughing if I hadn't been thinking so hard.'

I nodded, and turned away. I opened the window - hers seemed to go very smoothly - and stuck my head out into the wind. I let it scour my face and my mind. So many other faces came at me out of the night: the Bishop, and the fair-haired chap at the station, with their strange and fatal versions of duty; and Hilmi and the dead bandit, with their wild ideals; all the policemen, each having a go at me in their own style; the good Johanna and her peculiar romantic arrangements; and of course the passengers, my companions during these extraordinary three days and nights. They all appeared before me, and were instantly blown away into the darkness.

I hadn't heard the knock at the door. When I turned, Madison was opening it and talking to Quinn. She closed the door and turned back to me, holding the cocktail menu from the bar.

'You're lucky with him.'

'I know it.'

She waggled the menu. 'In case we wanted another drink.'

I looked at our open champagne bottle. 'This one might see us through.' I raised my glass to her. 'My thanks and my compliments. You're much the most exciting thing that's happened to me on this train.'

She considered this. 'That's... some competition. Likewise.'

We drank, and sat near each other on her bunk. Dimly, in the darkness through the window, I could see the ghosts of buildings; the end was near.

'Harry...' She still held the cocktail menu, and pretended to skim it. 'Where have you stashed the treaty?' She looked up at me. 'Satisfy my curiosity, before we get to Paris.'

'You're holding it.'

'I'm what?'

'It arrived in a cigar, it was under my lapel, it was briefly on a signboard on a Bulgarian railway platform, it was in the back of a painting, and for the last day or so it's been tucked in behind that menu card.'

Her mouth came open before she could think of anything to say. 'Damn but you're bold', she said at last.

'Everyone got so obsessed with me, they stopped looking intelligently anywhere else.'

With one elegant finger, she pulled at the menu card, and looked down between it and its backing board. She looked up, nodded.

'Worth it?' I said.

She frowned. 'How d'you mean?'

'That treaty comes at a hell of a price. It's almost killed me a few times. It effectively killed that lad on Constantinople station. It certainly killed the Bishop.' I sipped the wine. 'As I said, he must have been poisoned later during the evening. More convenient for him to die in the night, and with some slow-acting drug earlier there'd have been the risk that an older chap would keel over too promptly; cause a bit of a scene. At night there was more chance to get in and search the compartment before the death was discovered, except I got in the way of that. And everything else during the day had come from a common plate or bottle, until our evening drinks. I was fairly sure it wasn't the Hungarian, or me. So I'd assumed it had to be big Karim. But it turns out he was the last person who'd want the Bishop dead and the treaty delayed. So apparently no one could have poisoned him.'

The old watchful Madison was back again.

'From having bust into Theotokis's box myself not much earlier,' I went on, 'and from having thought about distractions, I realized that the Russian girls had stolen the cup.' Her eyes widened a little. 'Wonderful, ain't it? Anyway, I then realized that while everyone else was distracted by them, they had a unique view of everyone else. They saw Theotokis and the English ladies, Svensson and Jam and Chehab and Quinn, Valfierno and Junot. And they saw the Bishop's table, with Karim and the Hungarian, and me. They didn't see anyone do anything suspicious. Again, apparently no one could have poisoned him. But then, a little while ago, Hilmi - yes, he popped up again; I'm pretty sure he's dead this time - Hilmi referred to being the one who wasn't there; the significance of the person you don't see.'

Silent. Lethal. Magnificent. I've met lionesses less proud and less sure of how dangerous they were.

'You, Peg. You'd been at the table with Theotokis and the English. And suddenly, at the moment when not only were the Russians playing their distraction, but also the stewards were preparing the drinks for our table - the first time that day when the Bishop had an individual and specific drink - you're not at your table anymore. That was the one moment when his food or drink could have been got at with certainty, and there was only one person who could have been loitering near the bar to do it.'

'It's in your hands at last', I went on. 'Does it feel worth it? - worth what you had to do to get it? Kissing me, of course. And also killing two men.'

She was relaxed again. She took a large sip of wine.

'Yes', she said. 'I shan't tell you my fee, nor who I'm working for. But yes, it was worth it.' She watched me, looking for my distaste. But I'd only taken my part of the job for money, so I could hardly complain. 'That was when you knew?'

'That was when I started thinking straight, anyway. It was why you got more interested in me after the Bishop's death. I ain't that charming.' She managed an expression of mock disagreement. 'Why you started spending more time with me, trying to worry me about what Von Eisen and Karim were up to. You were hoping for a clue about where I'd stowed the paper. And you were one of the few passengers still on the platform when the British Embassy man was stabbed. Why did he have to die, by the way?'

A little shrug, looking into the wine. 'I saw him at the station, and I fancied he might have seen me at a reception the previous evening. There was a very slight risk he might have drawn the connection, and wired ahead to warn the Bishop or Karim about me. And… he was a loose end.'

I considered this.

'Like me?' I said quietly.

She considered me. Call me a sentimental old fool, but I swear there was a kind of fondness there. 'Sorry Harry.' A little shrug. 'I guess you know it had to be this way.'

I nodded, sadly.

I looked at the champagne bottle. Such a waste of good wine. But what a way to go.

'What was it about?' I said, my voice still low. 'Little Hilmi, he was fighting for a new kind of Turkey. All those Balkan policemen: their governments are fighting for the old Turkey, or a different one, or none at all. The Germans wanted their own version too. But you? What or who are you working for?'

She smiled, and leaned forwards. 'I'm working for me', she said. 'Only and always.' She sat up, rather formal. 'Cheers', she said. And we toasted each other, and emptied our glasses.

'I don't suppose there's an antidote', I said.

She shook her head. 'Sorry.'

'Is the poison quick?'

Definitely fond: 'It's quick.'

'I'm glad.'

'An extract of water hemlock, ginned up by a chemist acquaintance of mine so it goes down faster and smoother. A unique mix of the wonderfully traditional and the distinctly modern.' She smiled. 'Kind of an appropriate cocktail for this compartment.'

She tapped the cocktail menu. 'Sweet of you to have this delivered.'

'I had to get Quinn to come here on some excuse or other.'

'How's that?'

'I knew I'd need the distraction - always the distractions, on this train.' I gazed sadly at her. 'So I could swap our glasses round.'

Once I was sure she was going, I left her in peace: a last dignity for that extraordinary woman. As an afterthought, I remembered to retrieve the damn' treaty, from the card she still clutched. Very softly, I placed a kiss on her forehead, and then closed the door firmly behind me.

Quinn was in the corridor, bags packed and ready at his feet, and the Orient Express was creeping ever slower to a stop. The locomotive gave a last long dying gasp of steam, and for the final time the whistle shrieked.

EDITOR'S NOTE

There have been many different Orient Expresses, from when Belgian entrepreneur Georges Nagelmackers invited guests on a pioneering return trip from Paris to Vienna in 1882 to the truncated tourist experiences available today. When Harry Delamere made what was probably his one journey on it (one can't imagine they'd have let him on a second time), the train journey all the way from Constantinople to Paris had been possible for just over twenty years; before 1889 the journey started with a boat trip up the Black Sea to Varna in Bulgaria. It gained rapidly in complexity, with parallel routes and different feeder lines and alternative destinations incorporated within the one brand, served by different Orient Express trains during the week or different sleeping cars on one train, coupled on and uncoupled as it made its way across Europe. The luxury is incomprehensible to the modern commuter; there are a few photos on the internet to show just what a grand experience it must have been. When people weren't trying to kill you.

Speaking of legendary luxuries, those with Delamere's schoolbook memory of the tale of Jason and the Golden Fleece may be interested by the theory that the pre-Christian inhabitants of ancient Colchis/Egiri - modern Georgia - may have used sheep-fleeces to pan for gold particles in their streams: so the treasures may have been real, however fantastical the adventures of those who tried to steal them.

By contrast, the Marquis de Valfierno's association with treasure was dubious in the extreme, and so perhaps was his association with reality. An account two decades later claimed he was an Argentinian con-man who had masterminded the 1911 theft of the *Mona Lisa* from the Louvre, having commissioned half a dozen copies to sell discreetly once the original had disappeared; as there wasn't a single other piece of evidence for his existence, he has always been interpreted as a sensationalist bit of embellishment of the more banal truth about the robbery. Delamere's account suggests that, however shady, he existed and might well have been involved in such a scheme. (He also features in the records of the UK's Comptrollerate-General for Scrutiny and Survey.)

Connoisseurs of *Murder On The Orient Express* (a generation later) and *From Russia With Love* (two later) may feel that their creators took one or two points of inspiration from the experiences of Harry Delamere. Meanwhile, those who know *The Wheel Spins/The Lady Vanishes* will know that - as Delamere hoped - Miss Froy's brief encounter with him was indeed the beginning and not the end of a life of adventure.

By the end of the first decade of the twentieth century, the Ottoman Empire was in a condition of terminal decay. The power that had terrified the countries of Europe for centuries was now propped up by them, sustained only because this suited their interests in their jostling with each other. Its extraordinary reach and diversity now only meant exoticism and fragmentation. The struggle between the Sultan's traditional authority and those demanding a dramatically updated political system, and the competing models of secular and religious authority, fostered prolonged instability and a series of coups, leaving Constantinople further weakened and dependent on foreign support. All of which is to say that the kind of treaty Karim Bey described to Delamere sounds very typical, as Britain and Germany and the other powers manoeuvred for advantage in the near east. It also reinforces Delamere's point to Von Eisen, that the document that caused so much chaos and destruction may quickly have become irrelevant, and forgotten by history. We can only hope that his fee was enough for some new socks.

Bolsheviks
at the
Ballet

The execution was beautifully managed.

The doomed man, standing noble and defiant. The five members of the firing-squad at an elegant diagonal, so those of us watching could see each of them and admire the discipline as the rifles came level as one. The tension rising to its unavoidable climax, the volley of shots, noise and smoke and the man gasping, staggering and dropping.

I don't know if you know *Tosca*, and if you don't I'm the wrong person to try to introduce you. Broadly-speaking, the chap's been condemned for some political business - I didn't get that bit; something about Italy and Napoleon, all rather a muddle - and the chap's lover - Tosca, hence the name - makes a deal with the Chief of Police, who's a brute, that if he replaces the firing squad's live rounds with blanks then she'll let him have his filthy way with her, he being a toe-rag as well as a brute, albeit one with good taste, for Tosca's damned handsome. Chief of Police understandably agrees, and makes the arrangements, and comes back with his tongue hanging out, at which point Tosca stabs him to death, which is hardly playing fair but serves the dirty old so-and-so right. She watches the boyfriend's execution feeling rather pleased with herself, but when she sneaks back later to compliment him on faking it so well and lead him to safety, she finds that Chief of Police double-crossed her while she was double-crossing him, they were real bullets after all, and so the chap's dead, and for her this really puts the tin hat on a trying day and she chucks herself off the battlements. General message seems to be that you shouldn't trust policemen, Italians, or women.

In this case, it was all happening against a unique backdrop. Old friend of mine has done very well for himself, and he and his wife like to annoy the rest of us by organizing evenings of opera and the like so they can show off their enormous garden. Tosca's life and death and a bit of the other bargain with the policeman was sung among the old trees and rich shrubs and flowers of a summer evening in Surrey. I pretend to be unimpressed, but it's very lovely.

I should add - and here you really shouldn't take my word for it, for I have no artistic taste whatever - that the music is wonderful. You never know what's going on story-wise, but the sound is magnificent.

A lot of those story details I had to get afterwards. I watched the execution, and then Tosca's impatient wait for the firing squad to pop off for their tea, and her discovery of the cruel trick, the body lying there really dead after all; and finally her defiant shriek for the enemy she killed but whose posthumous revenge she could not avoid, a shriek to a cruel God, and then she was gone over the castle walls. Or, in our case, sort of crossly flinging herself away behind a rhododendron. Dramatic musical climax and we all clapped. It is grand stuff, as I say.

We were still applauding, and the singers began to gather in front of their audience, forty or fifty of us in best evening wear. Then things broke down. There was hesitation on the grass stage, confusion, and then a scream.

I was wondering what I'd misunderstood, and some of the audience were still clapping and others were rather giving up, and now there was obviously trouble on the stage area, the performers gathered in a huddle. A few more moments of raised voices and everyone looking around uncertain and then our host was getting up from the front row of the audience and walking the dozen steps to join the discussion.

He was there less than a minute, and then he was walking back towards us. Towards me. As soon as he'd caught my eye he was beckoning me.

I've always had a horror of this - at the music hall, which I visit rather more often than I do the opera, they usually pull some chump out of the audience; and I'd throw myself off the battlements rather than go through that. But the look on my friend's face had me out of my seat and following him back to the group of singers, gathered in the middle of the stage.

He turned to me. 'He's been shot', he said, very quiet.

For one stupid moment I stared at him, still not sure how much of this was normal business at the opera and not wanting to show my ignorance. 'Well, yes-'

'Really shot. Real bullet.'

Now I looked at the chap lying on the ground. I bent down beside him. The crimson stain in the middle of his white shirt looked very real; the sickly grey complexion on that empty face was unmistakeable.

And the brilliant madness of it - the trick in the opera become the trick in reality - struck me only then.

The execution really was beautifully managed.

For advance notice of Bolsheviks at the Ballet, *and other bits of historical chat, pop by www.robertwilton.com.*

Death and the Dreadnought

'I've seen chaos in my time: the great bazaar in Constantinople; the retreat after Magersfontein; Frenchmen trying to put up a tent.'

London, 1910: Harry Delamere is wishing he hadn't agreed to a midnight meeting in the shipyard where Bri-tain's newest battleship is being built.

Now the police want him for murder, the workers of Europe have declared him their enemy, he's hiding out with a burlesque dancer called Annabella Bliss and everyone's trying to kill him.

Murder, mystery, melodrama, skullduggery, derring-do, international espionage, dangerous liaisons, villainous foreigners, the British class system, a couple of sentimental music hall numbers, significant incidents on battleships, thrilling chases in motor cars, desperate escapades on railway trains, fights to the death armed with only a duck pâté sandwich, all in correct gentleman's attire.

The Adventure of the Distracted Thane

'So we rode again into Scotland, Sherlock Holmes and I; only this time we came at the head of an army.'

A beautiful woman comes out of a storm to tell her macabre tale. And thus the legendary detective is confronted with his strangest case: the murder of King Duncan of Scotland, and the ascent to the throne of the haunted Macbeth.

Dr Watson's narrative reveals the untold story behind Shakespeare's play: a kingdom in chaos, a man possessed, and bloody murder. At last, literature's greatest detective gives his explanation for its most infamous crime.

The Case of the Philosophical Prince

A mysterious death. A castle of spirits and superstitions. A royal family of fierce and unnatural passions.

Prince Hamlet of Denmark believes his father was murdered, and he's determined that Sherlock Holmes will help him prove it.

But Holmes and Watson find the palace of Helsingør gripped by suspicion and fear. The spirit of the dead king lingers in unhappy minds, and rival interests are jostling as the new regime tries to settle. Holmes's investigations uncover buried secrets and betrayals, and Hamlet's increasingly deranged obsession is shattering the stability of his family. The royal court of Denmark is heading for a violent climax, and not everyone will survive.

'Was this an end to the blood and to the chaos?'
Holmes gazed at me. 'An end?' he said, and his voice was deathly. 'My dear Watson: it has not yet begun.'

From the secret archive
of the Comptrollerate-General for Scrutiny and Survey
edited by Robert Wilton

Traitor's Field

1648: Britain is at war with itself. The Royalists are defeated but Parliament is in turmoil, its power weakened by internal discord.

Royalism's last hope is Sir Mortimer Shay, a ruthless veteran of decades of intrigue who must rebuild a credible threat to Cromwell's rule, whatever the cost.

John Thurloe is a young official in Cromwell's service. Confronted by the extent of Royalist secret intelligence and conspiracy, he will have to fight the true power reaching into every corner of society: the Comptrollerate-General for Scrutiny and Survey.

'A new benchmark for the literary historical thriller.' – Manda Scott, President of the Historical Writers' Association

Treason's Spring

1792: the blood begins to drip from the guillotine. The French Revolution is entering its most violent phase, and Europe confronts chaos. The spies of England, France and Prussia are fighting their own war, for a trove of secrets that will reveal the treacheries of a whole continent.

At the height of the madness a stranger arrives in Paris, seeking a man who has disappeared. Unknown and untrusted, he finds himself the centre of all conspiracy.

When the world is changing forever, what must one man become to survive?

'A rare clever treat of a novel.' – The Times

From the secret archive
of the Comptrollerate-General for Scrutiny and Survey
edited by Robert Wilton

Treason's Tide

1805: Britain is militarily weak, politically divided, unsettled by her rioting poor. A change in the weather will bring Napoleon's forces across the Channel and destroy the British Empire for ever.

Only a dead man stands in the way – Tom Roscarrock, unwitting agent to an obscure government bureau of murky origin and shadowy purpose. Behind the clash of fleets and armies, there is a secret world of intrigue, treachery and violence. His life in danger and his motives increasingly suspect, Roscarrock must pursue the conspiracy from England into the heart of Napoleon's France, there to confront the greatest mystery of all.

'Beautifully written, wonderfully clever, this is a triumph.'
– Daily Telegraph

The Spider of Sarajevo

1914: Europe is on the brink. As Britain's enemies grow stronger, the Comptroller-General must confront the man with whom he has struggled for a generation – a man he knows only as the Spider. In a desperate gamble, he sends four agents out across the continent, on a mission they do not understand...

The future of British intelligence – of the British Empire – is in their hands. Not all will return. Unique and resource-ful, hunted and deceived, they have embarked on a journey that will climax in Sarajevo on the 28th of June 1914.

'A learned, beautifully-written, elegant thriller.' – The Times

The Silver Thread:
a journey through Balkan craftsmanship
by Elizabeth Gowing

From the mines in the cantos of Dante, to the prizes stolen in
the wars of the 'nineties, follow the silver thread through
Balkan history and culture to the new generation of
craftswomen facing their uncertain future.

The Rubbish Picker's Wife:
an unlikely friendship in Kosovo
by Elizabeth Gowing

How can you find the best rubbish pastures for scavenging?
How can you free children to go to school rather than to go
out begging? Can mayonnaise deal with headlice? An account
of an extraordinary charity, and the challenges and delights of
finding your community a long way from home.

Edith and I:
on the trail of an Edwardian traveller in Kosovo
by Elizabeth Gowing

In 1900 Europe's last wilderness was explored by a stout,
stubborn English-woman who travelled in her tam o'shanter
across Albania's Accursed Mountains. One hundred years
later, Elizabeth Gowing follows Edith Durham's trail into
Kosovo, finding not only an Edwardian heroine but also a
guide for today.

Also from Elbow Publishing:

Two Summers:
Nixon and Trump by Greyhound Bus
by Tim Albert

In 1969 the 22-year-old Tim Albert spent three happy months travelling 12,000 miles around the United States on Greyhound buses. Half a century later to the day he set out to revisit his trip, armed with his original 30,000-word diary.

Mostly We Had It Good:
a baby-boomer's journey
by Tim Albert

Teddy Kennedy, EM Forster and Saddam Hussein: an idiosyncratic and insightful look at the second half of the twentieth century, combining recollections, family material and journalism.

Albania and The Balkans:
essays in honour of Sir Reginald Hibbert
edited by James Pettifer

A century of Albanian and Balkan history is seen from an unusual variety of perspectives in this collection of essays in honour of a man who parachuted into the country during the Second World War.

About the Editor

Robert Wilton was Private Secretary to the UK Secretary of State for Defence, advisor to the Prime Minister of Kosovo in the years before the country's independence, and acting head of an international human rights mission in Albania. He's co-founder of The Ideas Partnership charity, supporting the education and empowerment of marginalized children in the Balkans. Author of the prize-winning Comptrollerate-General series of historical novels, he also writes on history, culture and the failures of international intervention in south-eastern Europe, and translates Albanian poetry. A practising life and writing coach, he divides his time between the Balkans and Cornwall. He is neither an adventurer nor a gentleman.

Visit www.robertwilton.com for free stuff, information, and a conversation about the curiosities of history.

Printed in Great Britain
by Amazon